Gorgeous

Rotten

Scoundrel

Nina G. Jones

For those who have been with me since Strapped, here is a love letter for you all.

CHAPTER ONE

"I've been traded to Houston," Brock confessed as I prepared his breakfast. The egg I was breaking into the glass bowl cracked awkwardly and some shell fragments fell into the mix.

"Damn it. I hate it when this happens!" Brock knew I didn't really follow sports and so even though it was likely plastered all over the news, this would be a surprise to me. I continued cooking, silently searching for the proper way to respond to his announcement.

I was upset, but I didn't want to show it. For one thing, Brock and I had grown really close over the two years I had been his personal chef. On top of that, he paid me so well that I had gotten far too comfortable. So comfortable, in fact, that I centered my life around serving him. Sure, there were other clients, but not enough to maintain the lifestyle I had come to enjoy. Not only did he pay me well, but my schedule was so flexible that while I was at his beck and call, I still had to time to take care of my own business. Most importantly, he let me take all the time I needed to visit with my grandmother, who lived alone. In time I could find more clients, but Brock and I had such a good thing going. And even if he invited me to follow him, I couldn't go to Houston. I am a New Yorker for life, and my grandmother needed me here. I was all she had left.

I never imagined he would be traded. He was one of the stars of the Knicks, but I should have known that no matter how valued you think you are, you are never immune from being traded.

"Are you mad at me?" *See?* I told you Brock and I had a good relationship. I mean, normally what NBA star would even give a shit about what his chef thinks about his trade? In fact, I think there was a period of time where a more intimate relationship could have developed, but I was too busy being faithful to my ex-boyfriend -- who was too busy hitting any available piece of ass this side of the equator. Brock was there for me when the shit hit the fan with the cheating bastard, but that's when he was with some playboy model turned wannabe singer. Later, when we both were single, we were both scarred and in anti-relationship mode and I began to see him as something of a big brother. In all honesty, I liked that we were friends. It meant I could trust him, because he wouldn't be motivated to hide anything from me the way that people do when they are in a relationship. Isn't that strange, how people become closer, while at the same time growing further apart?

"No. I'm not mad, Brock. Why would I be mad? I am just shocked. I never thought you would leave New York."

"Trust me, neither did I. This new coach is a dick. He thinks I have a big ego. I miss Coach Broadus, he got me."

"God, that sucks. So when do you leave, next season?"

Brock laughed a little under his breath. "Two weeks."

"What?"

"Yeah, this is how it works sometimes."

I slid his goat cheese and sun-dried tomato omelet onto a plate and he reached out for it. "Wait," I commanded.

"I am going to scarf this down in three minutes, Sade," he protested as I garnished the omelet. For the record, he pronounced it like "laid," not like the "Indecent Proposal" singer. It was his thing, no one else shortened my already short name but Brock.

I sat down across from Brock, waiting for what he would say next. There was nothing I could contribute, I was powerless.

"You could come with me. Become my live-in chef."

"You know I can't leave my Nonna here alone. And I don't know if I am ready to start over in Houston." This trade

6

was making me begin to realize that I couldn't revolve my career around one person.

"I had a feeling you would say that. The offer will stand indefinitely. I am going to miss your food out there." I smiled. "You know, I credit you for getting me so lean these past couple of years."

"Ugh, why do you have to go!"

"It's part of the career I'm in. A lot of money, a lot of fame, but at the end of the day, we're shifted around like cattle."

He finished his omelet and brought his plate to the sink. Other clients would have left it for me to clean up, but he had been raised right.

"So, what's the plan? How much longer will you need me?"

"I start packing everything early next week, fly out next Friday. So, I was thinking you could prepare my meals for next week in advance and freeze them since all the pots and pans will be packed. I'll pay you for the rest of the month."

"Thanks Brock. Here, let me get that," I said, heading to the sink the clean his plate.

"You're the chef, not the maid."

What the fuck am I going to do? I have rent to pay, a car payment, bills, student loans.

"Okay, well, I'm going to grab ingredients for lunch and dinner. I'll be back later this afternoon."

"Sounds good. Think about it seriously though. Coming with me. I'll give you a raise," he pouted.

I nodded, but unless I became completely desperate Houston was out of the question.

In the lobby of the gleaming high rise I greeted Nando, the doorman. A short man with salt and pepper hair, Nando was always buzzing with positive energy.

"Hey Nando!"

"Need a cab, chef?"

"How'd you know?"

"Oh come on! You gotta give me more credit than that. It's Tuesday. Grandma's right? Wednesdays you go to the market and get Mr. Jameson's food." I was always impressed with his attention to detail and how he seemed to know the smallest details of the tenant's personal lives, like how someone's kid had been studying for a spelling bee, or another tenant was training for a triathlon. But I think he remembered me because whenever I had a late-night urge to bake, I always brought him a tin of cookies.

And no one forgets my cookies.

I always visited my grandma's little pillbox apartment on Tuesdays, using the time between breakfast and lunch to prep some of her meals for the week. My grandma raised me since I was seven, after my parents were murdered. Yeah, I know--that takes your breath away a little, doesn't it? It does that for everyone I tell. I usually skate around the subject because it makes people uncomfortable. What do you say to someone whose parents were murdered? It was so long ago; to offer your condolences seems a little late in the game. To pretend it is no big deal is equally awkward. Then there's that little glimmer in people's eyes. They want to know how it happened, but we all know asking is considered rude. Trust me, some people don't give a shit, they'll outright ask. But others, they ask with their eyes. People hate violence, they hate death, but they still want to know the details. The end result is not as important as how it happened.

So, I know you are wondering, and yes, I will tell you. Because I get it. When someone on Facebook writes R.I.P. to so and so, I Google the name, trying to find out who this person is and how they ended up as a tribute on someone's page. I won't force you to do that.

It's a lot like the story of Bruce Wayne, in fact as a child I was fascinated with Batman because I thought he was my kindred spirit. My parents were walking home from date night without me. No big deal. New York is pretty safe for a large city.

8

But they came upon a twitchy crackhead with a gun who wouldn't take no for an answer. My dad tried to be a hero and they were both shot. Just like that, I was an orphan. My grandmother took me in and has raised me since. She's my Alfred. Then, when she reached her 80s and slowed down significantly, it became my turn to do the same for her.

Honestly, I'm not broke. Well, I sort of am. My dad created a trust for me before he died. He was always a planner; it was horribly ironic that the one time he acted spontaneously and tried to thwart the mugger, it cost him his life. Unfortunately, I can't touch the money until I'm 30. That's two years away from now, and even further from the day that Brock told me he was leaving for Houston. So I have always lived in this limbo, sort of wanting to advance my career and work really hard, but knowing that if I wait it out, I'll get a pretty decent windfall. I figured I should just play things safe career-wise until I came upon the financial security of my inheritance.

While I was sitting in the cab, I ran through my contact list trying to think of who I could reach out to and let know that my schedule had opened up for more clients. It was important that I didn't sound desperate – that I spun it as an opportunity for them, not me.

Getting the gig with Brock was purely a lucky break. A couple of years earlier I was dragged to a party by my friend, Mindy, who was dating an sports agent. He was way too old for her, but disturbingly wealthy as he worked with many of the top names in the sports world. It was New Years Eve, and she promised it was going to be the party of a lifetime. She was right. The agent had a penthouse on the Upper East Side, with the kind of views of New York City that most people only get to see on postcards. Even people like me, who lived in New York my entire life, rarely saw the skyline from these angles. Being up there, surrounded by floor-to-ceiling windows with views past Manhattan out over the rivers and on to the ocean on every side, the random yellow and white squares of light that peppered the buildings around us, the sweeping curves of glowing suspension bridges, the little dots of movement on the streets below of cars driving to their own celebrations like hundreds of little glowing bugs: this was the best way to celebrate New Years in New York City. Not in some crowd of drunks, freezing your ass off, so that you could get a glimpse of some giant lightbulb slowly collapsing while swatting away an inebriated tourist who is trying to fulfill some scene he saw in a movie by stealing a kiss.

You could tell by their attire that the guests were either important or at least trying to project that impression. Dozens of black and gray suits, exquisitely but discreetly tailored, drifted from small social group to small social group. Thin, beautiful women shimmering in sequined everything threw back champagne liberally, no doubt internally calculating the calories of every bubble. The typical high-society party wardrobe was broken up by the usual silliness of New Years Eve: beaded necklaces, giant glittery headpieces and glasses that were cleverly designed to display the numerals of the year without blocking one's eyeballs. The sounds of carefree laughter and the collective humming of voices was broken up by the occasional drunken tooting of a party horn.

As soon as we arrived, Mindy made a beeline for Mitchell, her agent-boyfriend who was talking to Brock. Like I said, I don't follow sports, so I knew very little about him. I just saw this six-foot-eight, muscular, caramel-skinned guy with a radiant smile. Normally, basketball players are not my type. I usually go for the square-jawed, sleek-haired, athletic and muscular (but not too bulky) type. Think Ralph Lauren model (*I know, setting the bar really high there, Sadie*). But Brock didn't have that privileged air about him like so many of the other party guests. You could tell he came from humble beginnings, and while he loved the scene, he also probably spent just as much time with some of the people he grew up with. That attitude instantly made me feel comfortable with him. It didn't hurt that his face was astonishingly attractive, I couldn't help but notice that he wasn't awkwardly long and lanky like most ballers; instead, his limbs were well-proportioned and muscular.

After Mindy made the introductions, she quickly (and slyly) found a way to mention to Brock that I had just graduated from culinary school and was really into nutrition. What do you know, Brock was looking for a chef! So I met up with him later that week and he hired me right there on the spot. That's how I found myself in this tough situation, having put nearly all of my eggs into the Brock Jameson basket (*and now picking the broken bits of shell from his breakfast*). I hit a big break early on in my career, and sure, I got some other clients based on referrals from him, but feeding him and being his quasi-personal assistant became a full time job. I became far too content with that, and dropped my guard.

I had no choice but to hesitantly call Mindy, who I hadn't spoken to in a couple of months. She is a lot to handle, so I can only take her in doses. But she was always down for whatever. I could call her out of the blue and she'd make time for me even though she has always been insanely busy and career-focused. She knows lots of people with money and she works at a top talent agency. There had to be someone on her roster she could hook me up with.

"Sadie? Oh my god, how are you? It's been so long!" I imagined her sitting in the back of a Town Car being driven around Manhattan.

"Yeah, I know. I've been super busy with work and my grandmother."

"How is she?"

"She's okay. She doesn't want to leave her home, so I am doing the best I can to make her comfortable for as long as we can keep her in her apartment."

"That's great to hear. So what's new with you?"

"Not much, I was wondering if you wanted to catch up since it's been so long and my schedule has died down a bit." *A.K.A. I don't have a job.*

"Of course! Let me check my schedule. Hey, I'm free next Thursday. Does that work?"

I paused so that I didn't sound too available. "Yeah, that should work."

"Okay, can't wait to see you!"

The cab arrived at my grandma's apartment building, and as I let myself into the lobby, I felt hopeful that my meeting with Mindy would lead to some new opportunities.

CHAPTER TWO

"Well, I guess this is it," Brock said as I packed the last of his meals for the week in his fridge.

"Yup," I replied, shrugging.

"What are your plans now that your world won't revolve around me?" He said with his usual playful cockiness.

"I'm meeting Mindy for lunch today to discuss potential clients." She didn't know that, but that's what was going to happen.

"Good luck. And like I said, you can always come to Houston if you want. My door is always open," he said, extending his arms for a hug. "I think you'll be begging to join me in warm Texas come January."

"I know, thank you." I walked over to him and he engulfed me in his gigantic frame. "So, I gotta go meet Mindy. Don't forget me just because I'm not cooking for you any longer."

"You know I won't. I'm still not convinced I can't get you to come."

On my way out of the building, I stopped at a mirror in the quiet lobby, touched up my makeup, and pulled my long black hair out of its ponytail so that it fell into thick waves down my back. The restaurant we were meeting in was only a few blocks away, and so I headed over on foot, arriving slightly earlier than Mindy.

I heard Mindy before I saw her. She is one of those people who is always on her cell phone. She's not obnoxious enough to walk around with a Bluetooth like it's some hideous earring, but she might as well.

"Yes, if you can increase the royalties by two percent, then send over the contract. We'll have a deal. That's what he wants, and he's not taking a penny less. Listen Al, I have to go. You know what to do." She sighed and sat down across from me. "Sorry about that. Fucking cheap assholes." She slid her phone in her purse, which was a good sign; it meant I might have her attention for more than 30 seconds at a time. "You look amazing, woman!"

"Thank you. You do too." Mindy is a bottle blonde, but she actually looks better that way than as her original brunette. Her hair was slicked back into a ponytail that said: I care a lot about my appearance, but not as much as I care about my job. She hung her latest Chloé bag from the table on one of those portable purse hooks.

"So, tell me what's going on! By the way, I heard about Brock, tell me you are not moving to Houston to be his live-in chef!" She said, dramatically palming the table as if she would just die if I left. *I told you she was a lot to handle.*

"No, he asked me to, but I don't think it's smart. I can't follow one man around the country like that, no matter how good the money is."

"That's a wise decision. Those sports careers don't last forever, or he might get married and the new lady won't want a fine-looking thing like you prancing around the house."

"I hadn't even thought about that."

"That's what I'm here for," she said, tapping on her temple with her index finger. "So, is it a big hit? Do you have something else lined up?"

"Yeah, he paid well so that I could be at his beck and call."

"What are you going to do?"

"I don't know. I liked working for Brock, I just came and went as I pleased as long as I got his meals prepared and did whatever else he needed me to. He was pretty easy to please. I would love something like that. Restaurants are crazy, totally different atmosphere."

"I am so glad you said that!"

"Why?"

"Well, I think I have someone for you. It would only be for the summer, but it could buy you some time. You could also meet some other potential clients through this gig. I just didn't want to propose it if you didn't want to remain in the personal chef game."

"I'm intrigued! Who do you have in mind?"

"You know me, my wheels are always spinning!" She beamed with her unnaturally boundless energy, which seemed to come from some sort of never-ending supply source. *Was it nuclear?* "Where the hell is the waiter? Anyway, I have a client who is going to be in the Hamptons for the summer. He is a bachelor, needs to stay fit, yadda, yadda. He asked me a couple of weeks ago if I knew anyone who could kind of be a live-in chef slash assistant. I thought of you, but I knew you couldn't do both the Hamptons and Brock so I told him I'd look for someone. You don't mind being an assistant too, do you?"

"My position with Brock kind of morphed into that anyway. I guess it depends on who it is."

"Sadie, I am saving the best for last."

The waitress finally arrived at the table and I could tell that Mindy was annoyed. She always has several hundred to a thousand thoughts running through her mind at once and cannot tolerate those around her who do their jobs slowly.

"We'll just put our entire order in since it might take a while for you to come back again," she said, so nonchalantly that it was as if she had no idea she was being insulting. *That's Mindy!*

The server graciously nodded. I am sure she has dealt with Mindy types many times in this restaurant.

"I'll have a Caesar salad. No croutons, no parmesan, no dressing." I wondered why she would pay $20 for chicken on dry leaves.

"I'll have the salad as well, no modifications, and a cup of tomato bisque. Thank you." I hoped my politeness would assuage Mindy's harshness.

By the time the server left, I was bursting. "Well, tell me dammit!"

Mindy glanced around the room and leaned in. She said it in an almost-whisper: "Heath-fucking-Hillabrand." This is where she lost me. I responded with a blank expression. "Ugh, you need to get out more. Here." She pulled out her phone and rapidly bounced her thumbs off the screen. "Look at him," she said, shoving the screen in my face. On her phone was a black and white photo of a man with both a perfectly chiseled physique and jawline. He looked off into the distance gazing at some invisible sunset. *Damn, his everything is perfect.* Printed across the white briefs adorning his ample crotch were the words *Calvin Klein.*

"That guy? I've seen him on Times Square!"

"Yeah, he's one of the highest-paid male models right now. He does some TV hosting too, and woman, he is just as stunning in person. He's also kind of a socialite, or whatever you call a male socialite? Maybe it's socialisto or something. So, he's known to rent a house in the Hamptons every summer and throw great parties. He wants someone to not only cook for him, but help organize these parties. It sounds like he is taking it up a notch. Doesn't that sound like fun?"

"It actually does."

"Great! Because after I saw the headlines about Brock, I told him I had someone. I knew you wouldn't leave," she grinned mischievously.

I shook my head. Mindy always gets ahead of herself; luckily she was right this time.

"So what's next?"

"I am going to set up a meeting. You'll have to drive out to the house. Does early next week work for you?"

"My schedule is very open these days," I said dully.

"Perfect. I'll get back to you later with a time after I get in touch with him."

After the quick lunch with Ms. Important, the lost feeling I had about Brock leaving began to subside with news of this potential new client. It sounded like a nice change of pace: planning parties, organizing the caterers, rubbing shoulders with the Hampton elite. Mindy has always been so clutch. Sometimes I felt like I was drowning in her boundless energy, but it was times like this that I realized she is really a great person to have on my side. I met Mindy in high school. She came from a rich family and she was one of those people who bought her friends. She took me on vacations, bought me clothes (even when I insisted she didn't), so much so that I often felt like I was using her. But really I liked having her around. She was secure, she would always be there, and she could be a lot of fun. She just wanted to have the same in return.

I felt so great about the news that I decided to walk the 20 blocks to my Nonna's instead of taking a train. Maybe Brock leaving would be a good thing after all, just the kick in the butt I needed to step up my career-game.

CHAPTER THREE

I arrived at my grandma's rent-controlled apartment on the Upper West Side about 40 minutes after ending lunch with Mindy. Although she had slowed down in recent years, she loved her apartment and was fiercely determined to stay there. I was going to help her do that until it was no longer possible.

I usually helped prep her meals for the week, and we also paid for a part-time home attendant to visit for a few hours every day and make sure she had everything she needed. This was the only reason I knew she would be fine with me in the Hamptons for the summer. I should still have been able to come down a couple of times a month, but even if I could not, the nurse would make sure she was taken care of and had company. I would have never even entertained the idea otherwise.

"Oh, hi dear!" she said cheerfully as I entered the living room. She was sitting in her usual floral upholstered chair.

"Hi Nonna," I scooted down to kiss her on the cheek and took a seat on the floor beside her. Almost all of her furniture was covered in clear plastic, the kind that nearly rips off a layer of hamstring skin if you sit on it while wearing shorts on a hot day, so I avoided sitting on it as much as possible.

"How are you sweetie?"

"Good. I think I have a new opportunity for the summer."

"That is lovely."

"Yes, but I don't want to get too excited about it. It's not even close to being in the bag. Watcha watchin'?"

"Come again?"

"What-are-you-watching?"

"Oh, yes. *The Price is Right*." Her speech had become more labored in the past year. I could tell her mind was still sharp, but her mouth couldn't quite keep up. I would also have to speak loud and slow, the way you speak to someone who barely understands English, otherwise I would have to repeat myself indefinitely.

"Your favorite."

She smiled, revealing her pristine dentures.

"So I am going to make you some chili and some chicken soup. You can alternate throughout the week. How does that sound?"

"Whatever you like to make. Just make sure the chili is mild or my hemorrhoids will act up."

"Noted!"

As I was prepping the veggies for the chili, I got a text from Mindy.

Mindy:
He wants to see you sooner than I thought. Can you do tomorrow at 11?

Of course I was available, so I accepted the meeting. She replied that I would need to drive to his house and meet him there. He'd fill me in on everything, including the requirements, payment, and the length of my stay should he choose to hire me.

Mindy:
My advice is to wear something that highlights how attractive you are. Not slutty, but this is not a corporate thing, so you have some freedom.

I thought the suggestion bizarre, but I figured what Mindy was alluding to was this was not just a chef opportunity, but a party planner opportunity and I needed to look the part. Not a problem, I am a clothes horse and had plenty to choose from to show him that not only could I cook, but I could be hip too.

With no real chores for the rest of day, I stayed with my grandma until after dinner, far later than I usually did, until she was ready for bed. After saying our good nights, I headed home.

Home was on the border of Williamsburg and Bushwick in Brooklyn. Unlike my grandmother, I was not one of the lucky ones to have one of the few dwindling rent-controlled apartments in NYC and I wasn't an NBA superstar or Wall Street banker. Don't get me wrong, I wasn't Oliver Twist or anything, I lived comfortably. I wasn't going on any yacht trips to the French Riviera anytime soon, but I paid my bills, I had food, and some money left over for treats to myself. Really though, I loved living in Brooklyn. It always felt more like home to me than Manhattan. And since I was at Brock's and my Nonna's all the time, I got my fair share of life in the center of the city.

I lived in an old warehouse turned apartment building. My apartment was a studio, about six hundred square feet, which is a shoebox in most of the country but is pretty spacious for New York City. The building hadn't really been updated, and it was one of those work/live spaces, so it had that rustic (*read: old and weathered*) appeal. Despite not being rich, I had a taste for the finer things when it came to fashion and design. So, in my free time, I scoured eBay and Craigslist for furniture and decor. I was lucky to have a friend like Mindy who was often sent designer duds for free or received them in swag bags at events. She also revised her wardrobe nearly every season. So, between my thrifting and Mindy, my clothing collection was pretty impressive, even to the astute eye.

My apartment had gray-painted concrete floors, chipped throughout to reveal the cracked gray bare concrete. Why my landlord painted gray floors gray is beyond me. These weren't the luxurious, heated concrete floors you see in the magazines. No, they were cold as ice, even in the Summer. So I almost always wore house socks and covered my floors with an eclectic

21

collection of rugs. In fact, my entire apartment was a well-curated hodgepodge of items I had picked up over the years. It wasn't huge, and nothing was new, but it was my little personalized box of space in this enormous city.

There were no closets of course. The space was literally a box. So all of my clothes were hung on rolling garment racks placed against the wall or folded in various mid-century modern dressers I had snagged online. I stared out the original-to-the-building windows, which tilted open instead of sliding up and down (they sucked as insulators, but were still one of my favorite features of the apartment), and looked out through the dozens of rusty panels at my view of the city: industrial buildings, an elevated subway station, storage facilities, and squat red brick buildings. I sighed resolutely, and turned back to face the apartment to prepare for my unexpected interview.

CHAPTER FOUR

I woke up the morning I was to meet Heath with a sense of resolve. I was going to get this gig. *Party Planner to the Stars.* Mingling with wealthy partygoers all summer would be just what I needed to expand my business network. This was mine.

I used a barrel curling iron to press soft curls into my long black hair. For makeup, I went with a soft peach blush, nude lipstick, and some variations of olive green eyeshadow and hunter green eyeliner to bring out my honey-speckled eyes. I rocked some edgy, skinny faded black jeggings with a horizontal leather detail on the knees, pairing them with a cream silk blouse, leaving the top few buttons undone (just enough for sex appeal without being an invitation to motorboat). Black ankle boots with just enough of a heel for added height, but not too spiky as to elicit thoughts of how they might look in the air, topped off the look.

I hopped into my 1999 Toyota Camry, which was about as average of a vehicle as one could have. But it was all paid for and well-maintained, and it wasn't worth investing in a new car as much as I used public transportation. In fact, I only kept the car for transporting food to catering gigs. The weather was nice enough to drive with the windows down, and surprisingly, I enjoyed the drive, already making plans in my head about how I would return to the city every two weeks or so to check in on my Nonna. As the meeting fell on a Wednesday, traffic was minimal and I got to the East Hampton home in three and a half hours. Since we were meeting at his home, I stopped for a quick bite to eat and to kill time so as not to catch him off guard. At about

10:50, I pulled up to the road that the GPS indicated would lead me to his house.

When I turned up to his driveway, it did not look at all like the traditional Hamptons homes I expected from endless *Real Housewives* episodes and the occasional spread in *Vogue*. The driveway, which wound through tall stalks of bamboo, was paved with tiny pebbles Elegant, vaguely Japanese water fountains trickled into lily-dotted ponds and faux water pumps rhythmically poured water, allowing for a retreat-like feel. It had just the right amount of Asian-inspiration, providing a zen-like ambiance without feeling like I had entered an Epcot version of Japan. I pulled up to the garage and parked my car in front of one of its closed doors. There was not a peep of life outside of the home. The house was multi-tiered with a flatness about it that complimented the Asian modernist theme. If I had to guess, I would say they were cedar planks that lined the exterior walls of the house; a brownish-black dark steel framed the entire structure.

I tip-toed to the front door and took one last deep breath before ringing the doorbell. I stood there for maybe a minute or two, but there was no response. I pressed the doorbell again, this time harder, feeling I may have not done it properly the first time. Another thirty seconds. *This house is big, give him some time.* I rang again. Nada. I remembered that Mindy gave me Heath's cell number just in case I got lost, so I called him, feeling very uncomfortable and embarrassed that I might have driven out all this way to get stood up.

After four rings, the phone went to voicemail. His voice was deep, but playful.

This is Heath, leave a message!

I hung up, feeling a mixture of frustration and disappointment. The previously tranquil sounds of the water fixtures now served as mocking reminders of the silence around me. *One more ring and I'm gone.* I should have left right then. I took another deep breath to calm myself and pressed the doorbell. This time, the door whipped open. Heath stood there, squinting into the sunlight. His blond hair was disheveled. He was shirtless, in a pair of worn jeans with the top button undone and barely holding onto his hips. He brought his right arm overhead and leaned it against the doorframe; the tension this created made his abs flex. *Mindy was right, even half asleep, he is divine.*

He cleared his throat. "Oh yeah, the chef, right?"

I nodded. "Did I get the time wrong? Mindy said..."

"No, no...come in. I had too much fun last night." He stepped aside and extended his arm to welcome me in.

"Have a seat." He was barefoot and hadn't even attempted to find a piece of clothing to cover his bare torso. *I guess I missed the memo that this was a shirts-optional interview.* Heath strolled over to the fridge with the ease of someone who hadn't just woken up to an interview he had completely forgotten about. "Orange juice, coffee, vodka, all of the above?" He sounded a bit like a car salesman.

"No, thank you. I'm fine." Guys like Heath have always made me tense, at least upon first meeting them. I know his type. They walk around like they own the world, like they can have whatever they want, and it's because they do and they can. But I had my share of guys like him, and I vowed since the last one that never again would I fall for the bullshit. I don't just mean fall in love, I mean even as a friend, I wouldn't fall for the fake charm bullshit. I would be the thorn on his side. I would tell him exactly what I thought of him.

"Suit yourself." He poured himself a glass of juice before taking a seat across from me in a camel-colored leather Herman Miller Eames chair. *I want that chair.* He placed his cup on the ottoman (I prayed in my head that he would not spill OJ on that extremely expensive piece of furniture) and leaned forward, narrowing his eyes as if examining my face. I leaned back subtly, uncomfortable with the scrutiny.

"Where are you from?"

"New York."

"No, I mean ethnicity. You've got a look about you."

"A look about me?"

"I mean that in a very good way. Different. Intriguing."

"I'm Italian, Puerto Rican and Japanese, in varying percentages." *Does he realize he's breaking about ten different employment laws in this interview and it hasn't even been ten minutes?*

"That's an interesting mix."

"Yes. And you? What *are* you?"

"Oh, I'm just white. Some German, British, I think I'm one millionth Portuguese or some shit," he said, taking a swig of his juice. I nodded, waiting for the interview part of the interview. "So, yeah, I heard you are a good chef, that you used to cook for Brock Jameson? I need someone to help keep me lean. Traveling a lot has gotten me off course."

"You look great."

"I know, but I have to maintain." *I know. Typical cocky response to a compliment.* "You must know how to cook healthy. I always imagine chefs to look like Paula Deen, but it looks like you have a tight body under that blouse. I mean that in a professional manner, I have to see nice bodies all the time in my line of work." *Woah. If he was ugly, he would so not get away with this shit.*

"Thank you. I guess."

The clacking of heels from somewhere in the large house came closer and closer until a leggy, amber-haired, Slavic-looking chick appeared around the corner. She was wearing high-heeled mules and a button-down dress shirt – mostly unbuttoned. That's it--*That's where his top must have been all this time.* My presence seemed to be of no consequence as she headed to the kitchen and began to make herself some coffee.

I think my mouth must have been agape because Heath interjected. "That's Ilyana. She's a guest of mine. Say hi Illy." If

26

by *guest of mine* he means *the girl I humped last night and was probably humping when the doorbell rang*, then sure.

"Hi." Illy said dryly, with a sarcastic little wave. Her accent was indistinguishably Eastern European. Her left boob would come in and out of sight as the shirt moved with the wave.

I cannot believe I am seeing a stranger's tits at 11:30am on a Wednesday.

Heath turned back around to face me and he gave me the quick once over, clearly trying to peek into the opening of my blouse. *Pig.*

"I need a smoke. Let's go outside."

"Sure." *I hate smoking.* He lead me out the back of the house to a lush Japanese garden. It was hard not to swoon over it, it even had one of those little bridges over a little pond. "Your house is gorgeous by they way."

"Thanks, I just rent it for the summer." He pulled out a bowl of weed, lit it up, and took an inhale. "Want?"

He has to be fucking kidding me. "No." And then I finally blurted out something to him that was out of the bounds of proper job-interview conduct, but we were well past that point thanks to him. "You know, if you're so interested in preserving your looks, smoking would be one of the things to scratch off of the list."

He didn't say anything at first, not because he was speechless, but because he was holding in another lungful of weed. He puckered his full lips and slowly released the smoke to his right as to not get it in my face, all the while maintaining eye contact with me. *How polite.*

"You're right," he said, pointing his index finger at me with the same hand that held the bowl. "But, just a little here and there makes life so much better." He smiled the smile people pay millions to photograph. It's so beautiful that it's a weapon.

"Everything in moderation." I spat out the safest thing I could think to say. I began to wonder if this was some sort of joke on Mindy's part. I mean, this guy was such an arrogant bastard.

"*Not everything,*" he smirked. I pursed my lips and nodded uncomfortably, but he seemed immune to my discomfort. "So yeah, here's what I'm looking for. I would need you to start next week. Mindy said you were the best, and I only want the best this summer. I need a live-in chef, but I also want you to orchestrate the parties I will be having."

"What types of parties?" This was definitely not a joke, Heath Hillabrand is really this jerk in front of me and he's serious about hiring me.

"Well, the past couple of summers, I would go out to the clubs and have an after-party at my house. They got popular and things got out of control a couple of times. So I want to have better organization. I want catering, a bartender...I assume you would be able to arrange that, being a chef and all."

"Sure."

"I want security too. No more hangers-on coming into my home."

"I am sure I could help with that."

"Yeah, I'm sure Mindy knows some good companies that do that stuff. So basically you'd be a cross between a personal chef and event planner, a little bit of an assistant too. I'd rather have one person to go to about that stuff than hiring different contractors." He didn't seem so bad when he was just talking business.

"Makes sense."

"I should warn you, these parties get intense. You're not some religious type are you? You don't look it."

What the hell is that supposed to mean? "No, no religion here. I don't party much myself, but I guess that's good considering I'd be organizing everything, not partaking." My idea of a wild night was a bottle of wine and a great book. Occasionally Mindy would drag me out to a party, but I usually ducked out early and grabbed a cab just in time to watch a reality-TV marathon on Bravo, falling asleep on my couch.

"Oh you can partake. I'm not a hard-ass boss or anything. In fact, I bet you'd be a lot of fun."

"Trust me, I'm not."

"I have a way to get people out of their shells."

"Not this titanium and concrete bomb shelter of a shell I am encased in."

"You're funny. So you in?"

"What about other details, like how long will you need me? Compensation?"

"Oh yeah. Shit, I'm still half asleep! So you start next week and I would like you here until the end of September. Payment...what did Brock pay you?"

"Six thousand a month, but I also had the freedom to do gigs on the side. If I work for you this summer, I'll have to turn down a lot of work." I really, really needed the job, but I could tell he wanted to get this process over with and I could take advantage of that.

"Okay, well how about sixty five hundred per month and an additional one thousand per party?"

"Can I think about it?"

"Yeah, but I need to know by tomorrow."

I know people always say yes to you Heath, but I am going to make you wait.

Heath looked like a lightbulb went off in his head. "You want to see where you'll be staying?"

"Well--I might not--Sure."

We entered the house again. Illy was watching TV half-naked with a cup of coffee in hand. Heath guided me past her like the sight was nothing unusual. We walked upstairs and to the left end of the hallway, I spotted large double doors, which I assumed led to the master bedroom, but we stopped short of reaching them. He lead me into another room, which was enormous and had a loft inside of it that nearly doubled the living space. The bedroom was bare except for the furniture. It was clearly an unused guestroom, but my mind immediately wandered with thoughts of how I could make it my own.

"Nice right?"

"Yes, it's huge."

"Here's the bathroom," he pushed open a door to an Asian-inspired bath with muted gray and sandy tones. Pebbles and bamboo were strategically used as accents in just the right proportions, in keeping with the Asian theme without being too garish. I could see myself reading many books in the soaking tub this summer. "I'm just a few doors down. We'd be roomies," he said jokingly.

"I guess we would," I laughed uncomfortably.

By the way, I should remind you that he was STILL shirtless. His perfect body made my eyes shifty and my body language rigid. It forced me to maintain near constant eye contact with his baby blue eyes, which were very striking despite his lax demeanor.

"So that's everything. I just need you to accept so we can have a wild summer."

We both had no idea just how wild it was going to get.

CHAPTER FIVE

I called Mindy during my drive back home. Heath invited me to stay for lunch since I had driven so far, but I declined, telling him I needed to get back home. There was a lot to think about and I had to get out of that den of debauchery while his supermodel sex-kitten piece of ass was gallivanting around in next to nothing.

"How did it go?" were her first words when she answered my call.

"Bizarre. He's so full of himself and he had a naked model prancing around the house the entire time!" Mindy howled with laughter on the other line. "I'm glad you think this is so funny."

"I'm sorry," she said between breaths. "It's just that I know he can be a bit much, but I didn't want to turn you off to him. I thought he might surprise me and behave."

"A warning would have been nice."

"I didn't know he would have a naked chick there. I just thought he would be his usual careless self."

"Careless would be the understatement of the century. He offered me weed for fuck's sake."

"What!" Mindy howled again. I was *so* glad this whole scenario was such a source of enjoyment for her.

"Yes, he pulled out a bowl and lit up. Oh, and he didn't have a shirt on, and he answered the door half asleep after like ten fucking minutes of me waiting outside."

"Okay, okay..." she caught her breath. "Besides him being high and shirtless, did you get the job?"

"Besides those minor details, yes, he offered me the job. He would have offered a homeless person the job. I think he might have still been drunk from last night. I felt like I was just there so he could brag to me about his amazing, party-fueled life. He didn't ask me about my qualifications or anything. I'm not even sure I want it."

"So you did get it? Yay!"

"He offered it, with good pay too. Like I said, I haven't accepted."

"You have to take it! It's only a few months and you'll make so many connections. How bad could it be? Think about it, what seemed to be really inappropriate professional behavior could make for a really fun summer."

"I can't stand guys like him."

"You can't stand guys like him because you have a weakness for arrogant assholes and you always end up dating them. As long as you stay in the friend-zone guys like that are really fun to be around. They're really only jerks to the women they feel they have power over. Speaking of arrogant assholes, guess who I saw last night at Nobu?"

"Don't tell me." I knew who she was going to name. My ex had recently moved down the block from her and she had already spotted him several times.

"Kenneth, with some future Real Housewife on his arm. And you know what he had the nerve to do?"

"Don't wanna know..."

"When he came over to my table so say hi, he asked about you!"

"Did you tell him I moved? Far away? To another planet?"

Mindy laughed. "I told him you were doing well and I made it clear you are doing wonderfully without him. What a shit stain, huh? His date is two tables away and he's trying to dig intel about you from me. Some people never change. He is exactly the same Kenny we all knew from high school, all that's changed is the 'esquire' attached to him name."

Mindy's arrogant asshole theory was right, I had a track record of jerks. I don't know what it was, maybe naiveté and a lack of a father figure, but I would pick these guys who were *real priceless gems*. Always hot (probably my first issue there) and they knew it. They were usually cocky and super-extroverted, life-of-the-party types. I think my more introverted personality gravitated towards those people, because they easily drew me out of my shell. The thing is, hot, cocky, extroverted guys are also usually pussy magnets. And that usually means cheating, or forgetting to call for a few days and then suddenly reappearing when they were in your neighborhood, or professing their love for you one minute and going MIA the next.

But those people were short term relationships and that was all well and good. I never thought I was going to marry those guys, I figured I would kiss a few frogs and then land the prince. I thought that I had finally broken the cycle at one point, and that was who Mindy was really referring to: Kenneth Hull. I thought Kenneth, well I called him Kenny, was different. But I was a stupid, stupid little girl. See, he was all of the things I just described, but the difference was we were friends. I had known him since high school. Ironically, I had become friends with him when this other girl I knew begged me to speak with him on her behalf when they had broken up their *very serious* and *intense* two-week relationship (*high school bullshit*).

We ended up talking on the phone for hours and hit it off. The thing was, he was gorgeous, and popular, and wealthy. I was still working my way out of the awkward phase, and studious, and lived on a budget (the insurance money my parents had left behind, administered by my grandmother) so I didn't have all the pretty outfits and makeup. Don't get me wrong, I was comfortable, but in NYC, circles of friends can vary wildly when it comes to income levels. My competition was early bloomers with Bebe obsessions and Sephora credit cards.

Through all this, I was Kenny's shoulder to lean on as he hopped from one girl to the next, sometimes several at once. And

33

I was pretty much a ball of hormonally-charged teenage love. I obsessed over him, but never had the guts to tell him how I felt.

Then he went to UPenn and we drifted away for a bit, keeping in touch online and trying to catch up during the holidays. It was the summer after he graduated when he took a job at a huge law firm in NYC, that we became reacquainted. By this time, I had nice clothes, and my curves had filled out, and I walked with confidence. I had dated plenty of guys and was no longer afraid of penises and boys and whatnot.

One night, I came over to his place for dinner, and well, you know: *we bumped crotches.*

Then, all those feelings surged back up. I became that supercharged teenage version of myself again. I never had closure with Kenny and I felt vindicated that I landed the guy all the other girls tried to get. I was different, we were *friends*, and he had known me so long. I thought his past behavior was irrelevant, I thought I was somehow the exception.

We dated for two years, and when he proposed to me, I said yes. *I had won.*

I considered myself to be a somewhat decent judge of character, that I could spot a complete and total scumbag. Like when I casually dated my usual type of asshole, I knew deep inside he was a jerk and wasn't surprised when he turned out to be one. Maybe hurt, but not surprised. But with Kenny, I was blind, blinded by my love and arrogance to think that guys like him change for anyone. That I was special enough to make a miracle happen.

It all happened innocently enough. Kenny was in the shower, after a late night at the office. His work at the law firm was *very* demanding. I had left my phone charger at Brock's and just needed to make a quick call, so I grabbed Kenny's phone. And then I saw it: a message. Not a regular text message, it was some sort of app that he had forgotten to log out of.

I just wanted to say I miss your cock already. Can't wait to see you tomorrow. Supply closet, maybe? I'll wear that thong you love so much. XOXO <3

I can't tell you what a betrayal like that does to a person. When someone you had pined over since you were 14, had told yourself that no one else could *get you* like he did, takes your heart and puts it through a meat grinder. How could he be so heartless? How could he betray the person who had been there for him through all of his bullshit? I didn't obsess over the boys on Tiger Beat, I obsessed over Kenny and I GOT him. But I never really had him. Because guys like Kenny (and, let's be honest, guys like Heath) don't actually give of themselves, they take. They just float through life being given, not knowing what it's like to want something and not immediately receive it. They take everything for granted.

Even though I was past my teenage years, it was like I was there all over again, the heartache was so strong because I was still that girl when it came to Kenneth. Rescinding wedding invitations, the humiliation of explaining why I had broken off the engagement, the looks of pity: I would *never* subject myself to that again. *Never.*

I had learned my lesson late, but I had learned it. Stay away from those types. They will ruin you. Any sweetness I had left had bittered. Even nice guys like Brock I rolled my eyes at, because I could see glimmers of Kenny in him: his taste for trashy siliconed-infused Playboy types or his inability to be in a relationship for longer than two months. After a while I started to see that nearly every man has a little Kenny in him. And Heath, well he was a new breed. Even Kenny at least *pretended* to be civilized.

Mindy tried to reason with me: "Was Heath mean to you?"

"No, not mean. He was actually overly friendly and familiar."

"See? He'll be fun!"

35

"Ugh. I guess you're right. And it'll only be a few months. I forgot to mention, he made some comments about my looks too."

"He's a bit of a horn dog, I thought I had warned you about that. Sorry again."

"Nope, no horn dog warning. I went in completely blind. In fact I recall you encouraging me to dress attractively."

"I wanted you to get the job. Guys like Heath don't want to see your résumé, they want to see that you can fit in, and all he had to hear was that you used to work for Brock and see that you're a hottie. Like I said, stay in the friend zone and you two will have a fabulous summer."

"That won't be a problem," I said, with a sprinkling of disgust in my tone.

"Trust me, I work with him and he's cool. Despite acting so carefree, one doesn't get to where he is by being a total airhead. He's actually quite sharp, he's just..."

"Used to getting everything he wants."

"I guess that's one way to put it. Yeah, he is very focused on his career, but when it comes to everything else he is a little carefree."

"And since he's rich and famous and everyone wants a piece of him, he's used to people caring about what he thinks and not the other way around."

"Look at that! You should be a shrink, not a chef."

"I'll stick to the kitchen, thank you very much."

"So when do you start?"

"He wants me to start next week and he wants a response tomorrow."

"I'll definitely be seeing you up there at least a few times. I love summertime in the Hamptons."

"Well, let's hope I don't wring his neck before it's all over."

"Let's."

I got home at about five and scoured my fridge for something to eat. Funny thing was I had been so used to eating on the run, I barely had anything to eat in my own house. I moved to searching the cabinets and found the only thing acceptable to my refined and delicate palate: Velveeta Shells and Cheese.

As I waited for the water to boil, I ripped off my fashionable getup and threw on an old sweatshirt and plaid flannel pajama pants. One bowl of mac and cheese turned into another as I became seduced by a *Keeping with the Kardashians* marathon. I had these evenings often when Brock was on the road. They always reminded me of how alone I felt, but I had resigned to this lifestyle, at least for the foreseeable future. My previous relationships were such unmitigated disasters that I had committed to the safety of a tattered sweatshirt and flannel pants. So, whenever the loneliness crept up I looked for a distraction, usually in the form of some sort of terrible Lifetime movie (not the new ones, the ones from the '90s are the best), a reality show, or a book.

This time, though, would not be a couple of nights. It could be much longer. Brock wouldn't return and force me to turn my attention away from the empty feeling; in fact, the feeling could metastasize to the afternoons and mornings if I didn't find a new gig to help me forget.

I stared at the gooey school-bus yellow substance (let's not kid ourselves, it's not actually cheese) that had remained at the bottom of my bowl. It's only there because my pointy fork wouldn't allow me to cleanly scrape the deep curves of the Velveeta receptacle. This is who I was becoming: the girl who was contemplating licking the fake cheese from the bottom of a bowl because some guy she cooked for had skipped town.

And so I knew it. I had to take this job, not just for the practical reasons, but for survival. I couldn't stand being alone with my thoughts for too long and I had the sudden realization, looking at the goo, that that's what it was about Heath that I couldn't stand. We were different, but I could tell that he was like me too. He couldn't stand being alone. There always had be a distraction. He was nothing like me and just like me all at once. *I fucking handled Brock Jameson, all six-foot-eight of his powerhouse, alpha-male persona. Heath Hillabrand wouldn't have shit on me!*

I retrieved my phone from under the heaps of knit throws and crochet blankets on my couch and dialed Heath's phone number. After a few rings, his already all-too-familiar voicemail greeted me.

"Hi Heath, it's Sadie...the chef. I know you needed a prompt response, so I just wanted to let you know that I accept your offer."

CHAPTER SIX

It all happened so fast. I accepted the position and days later, I was again driving through the bamboo borders to the front of the zen-like oasis that was Heath's place. He was gone for the day and so he left me a code to disable the house alarm system. Even though I knew no one would be home, my stomach fluttered with nervousness. This new role had more responsibility than I was used to and I was pretty certain I would be entertaining some elite company. Part of me felt thrilled about that, but another part of me was dreading it. I was not one of these insanely wealthy people who could own a 10-million-dollar summer home. I was just me. I lived a pretty simple life. I was a servant of these types of people and while someone like Brock made it a point to never make me feel that way, I wasn't so sure that would be the case with this crowd.

The house was so quiet and new to me that I felt like an intruder when I first entered. The place was surprisingly neat considering it sheltered a hard partying, weed-smoking, model-fucking bachelor. Upon closer inspection, however, I noticed an empty bottle of Ciroq overturned on the coffee table, and a bong on the island in the kitchen. *Mind your business Sadie. Buuuuut it is sort of your business now that you live here.*

I made a point to look straight ahead and focus my eyes on the things in the box I was carrying. As I entered the room I realized I was far too shocked by our initial encounter to fully appreciate how nice my living arrangements were. The spacious room had bamboo floors, a walk-in closet almost as big as my living room at home, and a gorgeous spa bathroom. It was furnished just enough so that I could make the space my own: a king-sized wooden platform bed, full-length dressing mirror, a large white lacquer dresser drawer and a black lacquer desk. The bathroom was like stepping into a high-end spa, a modernist's interpretation of a jungle. A stone path led to a Japanese soaking tub, which was surrounded by plants and bamboo accents. The shower was big enough to do the electric slide in it. A frosted-glass door that led outside drew in a flood of light. I opened it to find a deck and--get this--AN OUTDOOR SHOWER. *Fuck yes!* This was actually turning out to be pretty sweet.

I did a little fist pump and cha-cha'ed out of the bathroom, chanting *yesyesyesyesyesyes* to myself (in the conga-line melody), feeling very pleased with the brilliant decision I had made.

"Nice!"

My heart dropped down to my ass. "Oh! I uh...hi!" *Fucking-A.*

"That was a nice dance you had going there, don't let me stop you."

Of course he would make me soak in my embarrassment.

"I thought you would be gone all day."

"Why, were you planning on having a party for one?"

"No!"

"I'm kidding."

I sighed to get rid of the heavy feeling of embarrassment in my stomach. He really caught me off guard and it had me all frazzled. "Yes, of course. Sorry, I'm a little embarrassed you saw that."

"Ah, who cares? I'm sure you'll be hearing me sing in the shower from all the way over here," he smirked. The humiliation had finally cooled enough for me to really look at him. The day was very warm already, and he wore a loose, light blue tank top with wide armholes that allowed peeks of his physique. He wore it with a pair of heather grey fleece lounge shorts with a pair of leather flip flops. "Anyway, my afternoon appointment was cancelled, so here I am. I was going to hit the pool. Wanna join?"

"No, thanks. I need to finish unpacking."

"Your stuff will be here. Loosen up a little. If you're going to stay here, you gotta loosen up."

"I didn't bring a swimsuit."

"You didn't being a swimsuit to the Hamptons?" he said, rubbing his brow in dismay. "I have a collection from girls who have left theirs behind. Don't worry, they've been washed," he winked. *Gross.*

"Well..."

"Yes. Come on. We need to talk anyway, about business." And so in a way, now it became a duty to join him. I shrugged and followed him to his bedroom where he directed me to his closet. "That one. Have your pick."

When the large drawer opened, swimsuits popped up like they had been held prisoner all winter and wanted to be liberated. Pastels, neons and dark hues tangled together like a nuclear bowl of spaghetti. Several strings I managed to untangle didn't lead to much else, which is what happens when you are rummaging through the swimsuits of swimsuit models. Finally I found one in the thicket that seemed appropriate enough to wear in his presence. It was a bit of a throwback, a green and white polka dot halter top with a hipster bottom.

When I met Heath down by the pool, he lowered his sunglasses and cocked his eyebrow ever so slightly, but I didn't know him well enough to interpret whether it was approval or distaste for my conservative choice. Heath was in a very Euro-looking pair of navy swim trunks, the kind the guys wear in South Beach, and he could pull it off. I couldn't help but allow my eyes to wander to his bulge. I had always heard models stuffed socks into their briefs for the "full" look, but I guess Heath was the real deal. Either that, or his artificial soon-to-be water-logged balls would start to droop down to his knees with one dip in the pool.

I sat awkwardly in the beach chair next to him, crossing my ankles and clasping my hands, waiting for him to say something. After all, he made me come out here.

"Sit back, relax," he said, almost exasperated. "Want something to drink?"

"Whatever you're having is fine."

He rose and walked over to the bar, opened a mini-fridge and pulled out a Miller Lite.

"Hot as hell today."

"Yeah, it's nice that summer came early for a change."

He rose the neck of his bottle towards mine and we exchanged a half-hearted toast.

"So, dinner tonight..." he started.

"Of course, I can run down to the store and--"

"Woah, woah...I wasn't trying to make you cook when you've barely settled in. I thought I could show you around." I wasn't sure how I felt about the idea of going out to dinner with Heath. I think laying around half-naked together was enough for one day.

"Sure, but I'm beat. I could cook, no problem."

"But you literally just said you were tired."

"Well, you know to get dressed up and stuff."

"Okay. Well, you are the boss when it comes to food."

"I thought we could talk about your likes and dislikes. So I know if anything is off limits. Of course, you hired me because I specialize in making healthy food, but tell me anything you like. You'd be surprised of the things I can make that taste just like your favorite guilty pleasures."

"Guilty pleasures..." He purred the words at me as he searched his thoughts for an answer. "Honestly, I like everything. The only thing I don't like is fishy fish. I can hang with sea bass, whitefish and the like. But no salmon please."

"You're easy to please."

"Depends on what we're talking about." He tilted his head at me, looking over his sunglasses.

I rolled my eyes. If he was going to pull this crap, I was going to be a bitch about it. He could fire me if he wanted.

He shrugged. "Next order of business. I want to have a party here next weekend."

"Okay."

"So this is where your other duties come in. I want catering, a bar, live music. I was thinking security to keep the wannabes out."

"Wannabes?"

"Yeah, some assholes from the club who invite themselves to my house. The parties get too big for me to monitor attendees."

"Of course. And this is for next week?"

"Yeah, I know you can make it happen," he said, in a way that made me believe he thought his charm was going to make me swoon. My mind raced, wondering how I could pull this all off within a week, but after all, I had accepted the job knowing how difficult he might be to handle.

"That's what I'm here for," I said with flattened enthusiasm. "I should get back in and start prepping. It's already five."

"Can't wait to see what you come up with!"

I reentered the main level and for the first time noticed a mammoth art piece on the dining room wall. It's a strikingly contemporary piece, crafted from splattered paint in contrasting neons and blacks, a recreation of the billboard of Heath in Times Square.

CHAPTER SEVEN

After dinner, Heath left the house to meet up with some friends. He invited me, but I was as tired as I claimed I felt earlier that day and told him I'd much prefer to spend the night inside. I used the alone time in the house to finish setting up my room. One difference I quickly noticed between Heath and Brock was Heath's eagerness to include me in social activities, making it crystal clear he was okay with--no--*encouraged* me to mix business and pleasure. While Brock and I were close, it was usually within the walls of his condo. He had his celebrity friends, his girl-toys, and his parties. None of which I was a part of. It felt like Brock did that on purpose, like our relationship was something he didn't want to taint with the outside world of celebrity debauchery.

Heath, on the other hand, seemed to want me to delve into the mud pit with him.

Dinner with Heath was actually okay. Besides the fact that he was getting non-stop phone calls from people who wanted to meet up with him that night (really fucking annoying), I made a variety of smaller dishes so he could tell me what flavors he preferred.

I have to admit that I really couldn't stop staring at his face. Now, I found him to be insufferable and so I didn't want him, but his face, it was remarkable. You just had to admire its mathematical perfection. His eyes are a hazy blue, his nose straight with a small bump of the bridge, just enough to make what could be a weak nose appear masculine; his jawline is strong but not overbearing. He had the perfect amount of sunkiss on his face to make his eyes and dirty blond hair pop. Then his smile, it's like someone hooked up a lightswitch to his face. In a purely objective way, his face was fun to look at. Just like a sunset. I like to stare at sunsets, but it doesn't mean I want to hump them.

After setting up my space, I became woozy and knew I had to call it quits. I had a very busy week ahead of me scrambling to plan this "emergency" party. I dozed off at about 10pm feeling like maybe I had been a little too harsh in judging Heath.

***

The sound of a woman's laughter crept into my room. I tossed and turned a few times, but it only became louder as she came closer. Then I heard Heath mumble something and a loud SHHHH as they passed my room. I felt in the dark for my cell phone. *2:41 in the fucking morning.*

It's not your house Sadie. But one would think that maybe, just maybe he would have kept quiet knowing he now had a *roomie* whom, I might add, HE insisted live with him. I rolled over, turning my back to the bedroom door, as if that would make any difference. More giggling. I'm no voice recognition expert, but I was pretty sure this time it was another girl. Then I became certain as I heard her footsteps run past my door and her voice calling out "Heath! Heath! Are you two starting without me?"

At that point I was up and pretty pissed. I am a big fan of sleeping and not a fan of dumb bitches screaming throughout a house in the middle of the night. I debated whether I should go ask them to pipe down (politely of course), but it was my first night with this new gig and I just wasn't comfortable enough to do so. I turned on the lamp on the nightstand and sat up sharply, frustrated by the lack of consideration. The cackling got even louder, and eventually I stopped hearing Heath's shushes.

And then--hold onto to your asscheeks--music started blaring! They were having an all-out party. Maybe Heath had genuinely forgotten about me. I mean, that would be the only rational explanation for such assholedom. Finally, I figured I should just venture out and see what the party was all about. I slowly opened the door and poked my head out of the doorway. Underneath the loud hip-hop music I heard their stupid bitch-ass giggling coming from down the hall. I straightened out my hair, threw on a cardigan and slowly followed the sounds of debauchery to Heath's bedroom door, which was not wide open, but far wider than slightly ajar. I deliberated for a few more seconds if I should walk in or knock, but to my surprise I caught a glimpse of Heath's activities through a crack in the space between the door frame and the door.

Heath was sitting on the edge of a chair while two naked girls, one brunette with a severe bob, and the other with long blond hair, were on their knees giving him a blow job! Yes, at the same time! All three were so engrossed in their sexual escapades that none seem to have felt my presence just beyond the half-opened door. I froze for a few moments, in total disbelief of what I was seeing. I mean, what the hell?

How vile. How inconsiderate. How disgusting. And yet, I couldn't move. This dark hallway shielded me from visibility just enough so that I felt safe from being discovered. I was filled with revulsion, but at the same time, a deep sense of curiosity. Heath had to have known I could stumble into this room at any moment. In fact, the loud music almost guaranteed that.

The blond girl stood up, walked to the bed, and bent over. While I could hear the rhythm of their voices, I could not make out what they were saying, but it didn't matter, because in seconds Heath was pounding her from behind. She yowled like a crow, her high-pitched, ear-raping voice carrying out over the heavy bass blaring from the surround sound. The brunette then slid in the bed in front of her, spread eagle, and bam! The blond started going down on her!

WTF. I clasped one of my hands over my mouth in disbelief. Within seconds after seeing this, I decided I needed to go back to my room, if I got busted it would be tremendously awkward and I think I would have killed Heath on top of it all. Just then, the brunette crunched up while the blond was still munching between her legs, and squinted.

Heath, I think someone is out there. I am almost certain I read that on her lips as she pointed to the door. I froze, afraid my movement would call more attention to me. Heath glanced over his shoulder, his taut butt flexing as he did so, and literally waved off her concern, getting back to the very important business at hand.

Oh shit! Finally, my body agreed to make a move. My first instinct was to run but my socks on this slippery wood floor could backfire very badly, so I tip toed away as quickly as I could and quietly slipped back into my room, leaving one lamp on so I wouldn't be sitting in complete darkness.

I didn't know what to do. It was way too late in the night to call anyone. *What have I gotten myself into?* He was exactly who I thought he was. The kind of guy who fucks a new girl every night, parties his ass off with no consideration for anyone but himself and yet he gets everything he wants. He gets to have it all just because he was born with a beautiful face. Suddenly, the music was turned down significantly, as if someone finally had the realization that it might make some sense to maybe not have the music on full tilt at three in the morning.

My initial shock began to wear off and quickly morphed into rage. And just as the head of my rage thermometer was about to burst, the wailing starts again. *Dear god, how long are these three going to be banging tonight?* My anger diffused into laughter. Only I would find myself in such a situation. I am such a dick magnet. And I don't mean that in the way a guy means pussy magnet, I mean assholes gravitate towards me. I am a black hole for dicks...wait, that was a terrible choice of words, but you get my drift.

Brock was different, but he had his ways too, which my distance from him was finally giving me the perspective to realize. He always went for the same type, the girl with the hair extensions, 20 pounds of makeup, a sequined mini dress two sizes too tight for her breast and ass implants and 6 inch stilettos. He used to joke that one day he would like to settle down with a girl like me, whatever that means (I assume a girl that doesn't have liters of silicone injected into her body so that he actually knows what type of gene pool he would be procreating with). Well hello! I AM a girl like me. The idea that these guys could go around fucking these Barbie types and put "girls like me" aside on some sort of shelf when they felt ready enraged me. And we all knew the truth: even when they plucked one of the "nice ones" off the shelf, that didn't mean they would truly give up the groupies.

Men. They all disappoint.

Don't get me wrong, I didn't want Brock, not even close. This was not a Kenny number two where I waited sheepishly for some man to tell me how much he needed me, but I couldn't deny there was maybe a little mutual attraction there early on. And quite frankly he was the only person in my life who I could even remotely compare to Heath. And sometimes I felt that even though I now saw Brock as platonic, in the back of his mind, he had put me on the metaphorical shelf.

Eventually at approximately 3:35AM the never-ending sex marathon appeared to stop. I imagined them lying in a sexy tangle of long, tanned limbs and scattered sheets on his bed. I could only hope I wouldn't have to see those skanks in the morning.

CHAPTER EIGHT

My alarm went off at 8:00 am, dropping like a sledge hammer onto my slumber. I didn't, of course, sleep well at all the night before. I threw on a pair of weathered pale blue skinny jeans and a loose-fitting sage-colored tank over a bralette. I twisted my hair up in a messy bun and hid the bags under my eyes with a pair of thick-rimmed Wayfarer glasses.

I dragged myself down to the kitchen and pulled out the ingredients for Heath's breakfast, not that that twat-burglar would even wake up for the next five hours, but hey, this is why they pay me the big bucks. The house was soon filling with the aroma of onions sizzling on the skillet. And then I saw his feet (which were annoyingly perfect) slowly creeping down the stairs. As each step exposed a little more leg, I was sincerely terrified that he was going to emerge completely naked, but alas, he had on a pair of boxers hanging low off of his hips. I stopped my eyes from lingering on those *fuck me* lines that must be some sort of evolutionary mechanism to trigger thoughts of erect penises. When he was finally in full view, his eyes were squinty and his bed head was in full effect, much like the day we first met. He maintained a smirk as he walked over to the counter scratching his head. *How the fuck can someone look so adorable upon just waking up?*

"Hey," he said groggily.

"I'm surprised you're up so early," I said stoically.

"Good food smells always wake me up," he said. *Nice try, but the compliments won't work.* "Hey, could you do me a solid and make a few extra servings? I have some guests over." *They eat? I thought they subsisted on a steady diet of enemas, cigarettes, and ass-pussy.*

"Sure." I didn't make eye contact with him.

"Something wrong?"

"Nope. Actually, there is..." I could not let this slide. He tramples people, I could just tell that as soon as I met him. Just as I was about to blurt out my grievance, I saw legs as long as stilts coming down the stairs. And that stupid giggling, they were STILL doing that shit. Unlike Illy, at least these girls buttoned the shirts they borrowed from Heath. He raised his finger up so that I would hold my thought.

The girls looked puzzled by my presence in the kitchen. "Karen, Sarai, this is Sadie. She's my chef-slash-assistant this summer. Sadie, Karen, Sarai."

"Hi," the brunette said. The blond waved. I nodded and smiled hesitantly, pretending to be occupied by the food in front of me.

"Ladies, last night was a blast, but I have some business to take care of. So I'll see you at the party next week?" I was impressed with how smoothly he kicked them out. *Damn he's good.*

"Okay Heath," said the blond who kissed him on the side of his head as he sat on a barstool. "Call me!" She waved her pinky and thumb up to her cheek. *Ugh.*

They went back upstairs to grab their stuff and within minutes they were gone.

"I thought they were eating?"

"Well, you said you wanted to talk, so I got rid of them." I liked that he respected me enough to do so, but the way he dismissed them was also so typical of his ilk.

"Oh."

"So shoot."

He couldn't really be this clueless. He's clever, he has a way with people. Yet, he wanted me to say it, to remind him how badass he is, getting two hot women in bed.

"Listen, I know it's your house. And I'm not trying to tell you what to do, but I couldn't sleep last night. You guys were blasting the music at like three in the morning."

He nodded, absorbing my complaint. He stood there for a few extra seconds, waiting for more. "That's it?"

"Well, yes I guess." I just couldn't bring myself to tell him I had seen his menage.

He laughed a little, minimizing my anger and making me feel petty. "Yeah, I thought it was obvious that I am a bit of a nighthawk. If the music bothers you, I promise I'll keep it low during the week. Also feel free to just tell me instead of dealing with it. I told you, I am open, you can relax."

A knot of discomfort built up inside of me. He knew full well that if I had left my room last night (which I did), I would have seen him in the middle of sex worthy of its own porn series.

"Like I said, it's your house. Honestly, I don't feel comfortable enough to make requests like that in the moment." I slid his breakfast on a plate and placed it in front of him.

"Aren't you going to eat too?"

"Well, I'm here to cook for you. I was just going to grab something when I go run some errands." I usually didn't eat with Brock because I didn't live with him. This experience was a little different in that I needed to eat in the same home as the person I was cooking for.

"Nonsense," he said, cutting his omelet in half.

"No! Don't do that." He'd end up being hungry again in an hour and asking me to cook for him again.

"I want you to eat with me. I don't like this serve and watch stuff."

"I usually don't watch. I just leave."

"But, we are here having a discussion and I don't want to eat while you just stand there."

"Okay," I said. "I'll make myself breakfast while we finish up," I quickly threw a couple of eggs into the already hot skillet and whipped them up.

"So where were we? Oh yeah late nights. Meh, I suspect pretty soon you'll be staying up just as late as me anyway." *What the hell was that supposed to mean?*

"I doubt that. I don't have that kind of stamina," I said, plating my scramble.

"I bet you do," he said devilishly. *This fucking guy.*

"You know, for someone who is so interested in preserving his looks, you party hard."

"I take lots of naps, get lots of massages, drink lots of water, and get lots of facials" he said without a hint of jest in his tone, then taking a bite of his feta, basil, onion and sun-dried tomato omelet. "Dayum woman! This is good."

"Thanks."

"You will have fun this summer." He jutted his fork out at me. "I don't permit party pooping in this house."

"I've sensed that, but I don't think we have the same idea of fun."

"Oh, do you go to the library and read books all day?" he asked in a pouty baby voice.

"Oh shut it." As much as he got under my skin, I already felt comfortable enough with him for playful, or not so playful, banter.

We sat in silence for a few moments, but after a bit he stared at me as if he was trying to read my thoughts.

"Yes? May I help you?"

"I think I figured it out."

"What?"

"Someone did you dirty, didn't they?"

"Excuse me?"

"Some guy. Fucked you over badly. Maybe more than one. You seem bitter."

The callousness. The unmitigated gall. "You think you have me figured out?" I asked, resisting the urge to stick my fork in my new boss's eyeball.

"Just an observation. From the look on your face, I think I'm right."

I bit the inside of my upper lip to stop it from quivering. It was day two and I had already had my share of this man. *Think of the money* I chanted in my head. It's only one summer. Heath Hillabrand is not the only person who can read people. I have him figured out too. *Touché motherfucker.*

"I'm going for a run."

"You barely ate."

"I don't really have an appetite any longer."

He smirked. He fucking smirked. No: "*I am so sorry, I crossed the line my dearest new employee.*" A smirk.

CHAPTER NINE

My first week in the Hillabrand household flew by. Planning the party got out of control just as fast. Every time I accomplished one task, Heath wanted to add something new: valet service, gorgeous half-naked servers, go-go dancers, and even an ice sculpture. To top it all off, he failed to mention he would be flying off to be on a shoot location for three days in the middle of the week. His being gone for most of the week meant minimal sex screams and awkward innuendo, but I wasn't spared every night. There was that girl who sounded like a squeak toy every time his headboard hit the wall at five in the fucking morning, and one girl who was so hammered, she wandered to the kitchen after sex with Heath and then crawled back into bed with me! I almost judo chopped her in the neck when she tried to spoon me. Needless to say, I was glad for his absence for at least part of the week as I was not sure I could've handled a lack of sleep on top of all of that stress. Despite him being away, we spoke on the phone several times a day to keep in touch regarding the details of the party and any other tasks he needed help with.

Friday night rolled by and I spent most of the day setting up for the party. At about five, I stole away to take a shower and get ready. I put my hair up into a large bun, and zipped myself into a strapless black midi pencil dress. The neckline peaked into two points at the top of each cup and dipped very low in the middle, giving the dress a sexy yet polished look. I wore a pair of stilettos with a black front, nude back and heel, and gold ankle straps. My feet would hurt like hell by the end of night, but there was no way I was going to wear this dress with flats. For makeup, I went with a smokey eye and a nude lipstick a few shades paler than my actual lip. *Yeah, I looked hot.* I wanted to remind Heath that despite his image of me as a pathetic, book-reading, party pooper, I was fucking sexy and I could party, I just chose not to do so with his obnoxious ass.

Before I turned the knob to the bedroom door, I took one last look at myself and inhaled deeply. My night was going to be crazy busy and this would be the final moment of stillness before the insanity. I stepped into the hallway just as Heath emerged from his bedroom. His hair was styled differently, shaved at the sides and long up top, but slicked back. The stubble on his tanned face contrasted with the neatness of his hair. A pair of faded gray slim jeans with just the right amount of tatter hung low on his hips, propped up by his perfectly sculpted ass. A tight white shirt with short sleeves and a henley neckline, the top three buttons undone, revealed his prominent clavicle. His footwear was surprisingly playful: red all-leather classic Adidas mid-tops.

"Wow," he said, seemingly caught off guard. "You look smokin' tonight. Seriously."

"Thank you." It surprised me how validated I felt by his compliment.

"Shall we?" He offered me his arm. The gentlemanly gesture was pleasant, but unexpected. I accepted it and we headed for the stairs together.

"You look great too, but you already know that. You get paid for it." Oh how it pained me to pet his enormous ego.

"Compliments still mean something. I bet pros still like to hear they're good in bed," he winked at me. *He sure has a way with words.*

While we were upstairs, early arrivers had already begun to trickle into the house and I was surprised to find an already active party. When we got to the base of the staircase Heath leaned into my ear. "You did a great job. Everything looks great. Have some fun tonight will you?" He kissed my temple in a brotherly way, or so I thought, and called out to a group of friends before I could even respond. My goal that night was not to have fun. I was working; the many moving parts of this evening had to run smoothly. A headset kept me in touch with the lead of each segment: catering, valet, and security had access to me through it. I felt *very* official.

I had prepared for a tsunami of issues, but to my surprise things ran quite smoothly. This was mostly due to security being at the front gate and stationed throughout the property. This meant only exclusive guests attended and kept stupid assholes acting up to a minimum. Catering did an impressive job, consistently dishing out hors d'oeuvres via some very leggy half-naked servers dressed in red latex mini dresses. *Don't judge. Not my call, okay?*

The party was mainly relegated to the vast main floor which was chicly decorated in mostly white and illuminated with a pale blue hue. One of the top DJs in the country, part of the younger generation of of a well-known old-money family who has summered for decades in the Hamptons, agreed to DJ the party at the last minute. He was a friend of Heath's, which was the only reason he accepted a gig on such late notice. Well, that, and the knowledge that the party would be wall-to-wall models and dick-thirsty model wannabes.

An hour and a half later and the house was full; the place was bumping. Ironically, I felt I could finally take a breath as all gears continued to run smoothly. I grabbed a glass of champagne from a passing latex-clad cocktail server and found myself awkwardly standing alone. I hadn't seen Heath since we parted ways a couple of hours earlier and I wondered what he was up to. I knew no one at this event and against every cell in my being, I felt myself gravitating towards his familiar presence. *Fight it. Fight it hard.*

Then, as if it happened because she really owed it to me, Mindy came barreling towards me from across the room.

"Sadie!"

"Hey! I wasn't sure you could make it."

"No way was I missing your first party. This thing is the talk of the Hamptons. You did a great job, these signature cocktails are the tits!" *She's already drunk.* "Where's Señor Hillabrand?"

"I don't know. I've been so busy."

"Oh, they'll be fine without you. You've done your job. Let's find him."

"No, let's not."

"Uh oh, what's wrong?"

"Nothing, he's just a lot."

"Come on. He's not *that* bad."

"You don't know the half of it. My first night was a nightmare of epic proportions. The only reason I am not losing my mind is because he was gone most of the week."

"What happened?"

"The story is far too long to tell now, and I don't think you would believe me if I told you."

"I'm a manager. I'd believe anything after some of the shit my clients have pulled."

"Maybe I'm just too green."

"Come on, have another drink." She swiped a cocktail and handed it to me. "You need to loosen up."

"Why does everyone keep saying that to me?"

"Come on." Mindy grabbed my hand and dragged me through the party. "I bet he's upstairs!"

"Oh, no. We're not going up there. That means he's fucking someone."

"Or that's where the real party is!"

I didn't have the energy to continue protesting. We made our way upstairs and she's right, laughter spilled out from the media room, indicating there was fun being had. It died down a little as Mindy busted the door open and some Hamptons snobs turned their noses up skeptically at us. Heath looked up, his face flushed from alcohol consumption. "Minds! Sadie! Where have you been all my life?" (Minds is not a typo, it pronounced like

60

the "Lind" in Lindor Truffles, or the "Synd" in syndication. And don't roll your eyes at my terrible rhyming skills.)

Mindy gave Heath a big hug and claimed her space with him, making some of the women in his perimeter take a few steps back. "Come here," Heath reached out his hand to me. I looked side to side, feeling all eyes on me, and hesitantly gave mine up to him. He pulled me in close so that Mindy, Heath and I formed a tight clique, forcing the hangers-on to disperse and speak with one another.

"Did Sadie do a fantastic job or what?"

"I know! I told you she was good."

"I know why Brock wanted you to follow him to Houston." His hand moved around my waist and rested on my hip, making me tense up.

"I am so glad she didn't leave New York permanently. I would've literally died." *Mindy, such an exaggerator.*

"Thanks guys."

"You know what though? I don't think your friend likes me." He winked at me as he said this.

"I'm sure that's not true," Mindy chimed, looking at me, knowing full well that it was.

I wasn't sure what to say. I kind of hated him, even though he had his moments. If I bullshitted, it would be obvious. Luckily Heath spoke before I could say anything.

"The thing is I like her. I think she's smart and underneath the stiff exterior I bet she's a shit load of fun."

"She so is! Just wait!" *Mindy, please shut the fuck up.*

"I like women who put their guard up. Makes me work."

"I should go check on the catering." *Shit he smells so good.*

"No!" Mindy cried.

"Hells no! I'm sure it's fine and I am determined for you to have fun tonight. I'm the boss and I am ordering you. Let's go."

Heath put his arms around both of our shoulders and lead us back to the party downstairs. The eyes of all his potential ass-pieces bored holes through my body as we left the media room. *Don't worry ladies, he is all yours tonight.* The third drink was handed to me by Heath, who pulled me up to him to dance. Mindy had already found a young hottie to cling to and so it was just him and me.

I tried to shake Heath off, but eventually I relented to his persistence.

"Come on, take some shots with me."

"I have to stay alert. I'm already three drinks in now."

"Don't worry about it. The party is handled. Let's get to know each other, roomie."

We headed to the bar and Heath grabbed an entire bottle of Petron, a lime, and a salt shaker.

"Come on."

"Where are we going?"

"Follow me."

We passed the pool and a security guard. We were now outside of the limits of the party. There was a small wooden fence that I had never crossed, assuming it was the border of his property.

"Are we trespassing?"

"No! This is part of the house."

He opened the wooden barrier and beyond the lush green foliage there was a small path which opened up to a rock garden. It was palely lit by a few lanterns and looked so peaceful and serene in this dark night.

"This is so gorgeous."

"I know. Sold me on the place when I looked around. Check this out." He grabbed a rake and raked the sand. I stood there not sure if I should act impressed by the very mundane display. "That seemed much cooler in my head," he confessed. I tried hard not to smile.

"So you want to do tequila shots here? Doesn't seem like the proper venue," I asked.

"Yeah, it was too loud to hear you speak in there half of the time."

"Okay, but just two. I don't want to get sick. And we use arms."

"Strictly professional," he winked. *Dammit, he's growing on me again, like mold.*

We used our own arms to host the salt lick and so the first shot was purely platonic. I get friendly when I drink and so each drink bore another chink in my armor.

"You hate me? Don't you?"

"Why do you say that?" I asked.

"See? You don't even deny it."

"I don't hate you."

"Tell me. You can be honest. I won't fire you. I promise."

"A drunken reassurance. How ironclad."

"I think I've been pretty good to you so far, so I'd like to know. Honestly, this doesn't happen to me. So it drives me nuts when it does." I hold in a laugh. *That is precisely why I can't stand you.*

"I don't hate you."

"But I get under your skin."

"Really? You really want me to go there?"

"Bring it."

"I don't hate you. I just know your type."

"My type?" he asked, in an over the top innocent manner.

"You're good looking, you get all the girls, the world is your oyster."

"And that's a problem because?"

"Because people get hurt by people like you. The rest of us. The plebes."

"You're no plebe."

"If you say so."

"So wait, you don't like me because I use my looks to get ahead?"

"I never said I didn't like you."

"Right."

"It's just that you probably never suffer consequences. Guys want to be you and girls want to fuck you and so you can just do whatever you please."

"You know what's funny about you? You walk around like you are some sort of plain-Jane who has never benefitted off of her looks."

"I haven't."

"Bullshit. You think Brock would have hired you if you looked like Julia Child? Or I would have for that matter? The only difference between you and I is that I acknowledge my advantage and you just sit on your high horse while you benefit from the same exact thing." The strange thing about our conversation was, even though we were being so direct, we weren't fighting, at least it didn't feel that way. It was one of the more open conversations I can remember ever having.

"I would like to think I was hired for my skills and credentials." I knew that was total bullshit in this case. "The difference between us is far greater than that. And trust me, I consider people's feelings. I don't go through life using people just because I can."

"So I was right? Someone burned you bad."

I rolled my eyes at him. "Let's take another shot." Anything to avoid my pathetic love life. "What the hell, let's do it the way champs do!" The alcohol was starting to really kick in. *Yeah, I'm drunk.*

"Atta girl!"

I offered up my collarbone to Heath. He smirked and looked like a devil in the moonlight. He raised his eyebrows. "Let the record show that you asked for this, but when I give shots, I give 100%. So don't slap me." He leaned in to my collarbone and softly, gently, suckled on it. The hairs stood up on my arms and neck; my nipples perked up. A faint sucking sound emerged from his lips as he pulled away. He rose up and bit his bottom lip, keeping eye contact with me as he poured the salt on the wet spot. He licked the salt, barely biting my neck, threw back the drink and shoved the lime in his mouth, shaking his head to get past the strong taste.

"Your turn."

"Is this a challenge?"

"It's whatever you want it to be," he said with a mischievous smirk.

"Okay," I said, feeling dangerously flirty. I opened up the remaining closed button on his henley collar.

"Let me make it easier for you," he said, pulling it off. *No don't do that.* He did that. "All yours."

I pursed my lips, looking for a suitable spot to rest them upon. *Damn his body is fly.* I gave him a squinty look of mischief. "Lie down."

"Woah. I knew you had it in you."

"Shhh..." I said, stumbling onto my feet from the bench on which we were seated. I kneeled down and tugged on his pants just a smidgen and found that sweet spot on his hip bone. *I was drunk, okay? He is one of the hottest men on the planet and I am a red-blooded American woman. Plus, those fuck me lines are like sex magnets. Cut me a break.* I licked my lips and ran the tip of my tongue along his hip. He started laughing like a boy and it endeared me to him.

"Ticklish?"

"Can't you tell?"

I pour the salt on the spot. "Ready?"

"I just lay here like an innocent victim. Do what you must," he pressed the back of his hand against his forehead like a damsel in distress.

"Here," I put the lime in his mouth. His eyes widened in disbelief.

I dipped back down to his hip, this time mouthing his pelvis a bit, threw back the shot, and used my teeth to pull the lime out of his mouth, lingering for an extra millisecond.

"You are damned sexy," Heath said sitting up.

"Oh cut it out boss man."

"Cut the humble act."

"No, it's not an act. I'm being realistic. You date models. I'm sure nothing impresses you."

"You are just as hot, and most runway models don't have a rack or an ass like that."

"Watch it, Mister," I said, playfully jabbing his bare chest with my index finger.

"Hey, you're the one sucking on my pelvic bone." We both laughed. *Okay, now I'm hammered.*

"Purely professional pelvic bone sucking. We should head back inside," I said in a labored manner. "Mindy is probably wondering where the hell I went."

"Okay, help me up. Will you?"

"Lazy bum," I said giving him both of my hands. I try once, but he doesn't give me any assistance. "Come on, what are you, like six feet, 180 pounds?"

"Actually six-three, 195."

"Help a girl out. These heels are tough enough with my weight on them in this sand and not an additional two hundred pounds."

"Okay, let's count to three."

"You are so difficult. One, two, three!"

I gave him a big tug, and he stood up with great force at the same moment. Before I knew it I was losing my footing, stepping back into the sand, with Heath's frame falling over me. The sand puffed up like clouds around us. I squinted as the grains rained back down.

There he was: shirtless, warm, his chest pressing against mine with each inhale. We both laughed, a hearty, drunken, laugh. And then, he looked at me, and the way the new moon rested just above his right shoulder in the navy night sky, the smile in his eyes, the mischief in his smirk--In that moment, the holes in my armor allowed for a structural failure. He leaned in, and he placed his lips on mine. They felt like soft pillows; they tasted so fresh. My mouth opened just slightly, and he tugged on my lip with the perfect combination of sexiness and playfulness.

And then our tongues danced.

CHAPTER TEN

Ooh, it felt so good: the warmth of his body against mine under the night breeze, the reckless abandon of kissing this gorgeous man in the sand.

What the hell am I doing?

"Wait. Stop!" I pushed him away, I didn't want to, but I knew I must. This was the booze, and the moonlight, and our laughter culminating into this romantic moment and it was a very bad idea. This was the same guy who was banging two models (at the same time I might add) a little over a week ago.

"What's wrong?" Heath asked, as if this was all normal, as if a guy taking shots off of and making out with his assistant was perfectly normal. *Nothing to see here folks, just move along.*

"This. This is wrong. You're my boss and I'm drunk and you're drunk. And...it's just a bad idea. Okay?"

Heath looked at me as if I was speaking a foreign language, and I guess to him I was. Logic, common sense, and self-control: those were all foreign concepts to him. Just as he was about to say something, my headset (which was barely on my head) lit up with commotion.

I need back up at the front door!

"Shit, something's up I think," I said to Heath.

"What?"

"I don't know. Security said they needed back up. I gotta go check it out."

"I'll come with."

Heath helped me up and we quickly brushed off as much sand as we could from our clothing and hair. We made our way to the front of the house and were immediately met with a scuffle. Large men in jackets labeled SECURITY held back a person I could barely see, just the occasional arm or leg flailing out from the huddle.

"What's going on out here?" Heath asked.

"Sir, we've got it under control, please go inside."

I didn't know what to do. Heath had mentioned people who were not invited often attempted to get into his parties, but this was far more resistance than I had expected.

"Should I call the police?" I called out.

"We'll escort him off the property. We've got it taken care of."

"Is that him?" The mystery man's voice called out; I finally got a glimpse of his face. He looked to be in his forties, with a close haircut to disguise his baldness.

"Clark?" Heath asked.

"You son of a bitch!"

"Oh shit," Heath said under his breath.

"What is it?" I asked.

"Nothing. Don't worry about it. You should head back in."

"You son of a bitch. Tara just left me! She told me everything, you scumbag!"

Of course. No party was worth getting this worked up. It's Heath's dick poking where it shouldn't. And to think, just moments before, I felt special, like I was the singular focus of his attention. I bet Tara did too. Heath probably did deserve a punch in the face, but once again, he was being spared consequences.

I looked over at Heath in disbelief and hoping he would tell me there was a misunderstanding. But instead, he simply shrugged at me. *At least he's honest.*

"Unbelievable," I said under my breath. "I have to go check on the catering."

As I walked through the foyer, I shook my head in disappointment. What the hell was I thinking, getting carried away with him like that? I could only hope Heath's loose lips would be in my favor tomorrow concerning any post-kiss awkwardness. A guy like him must see women daily who he's done far more with; he can't afford to get all tense around those situations.

"What the hell happened out there?" It was Mindy.

"Don't ask. I cannot wait for this night to be over," I said, rolling my eyes.

"What is all this?" She asked, brushing her hand against my hair and dress. "Is this sand?"

Just then, I saw it on the big screen TV, ESPN was playing and there were clips of Brock on the screen. The ticker at the bottom scrolled the words: *NBA Star Brock Jameson, possible torn ACL.*

"Turn that up!" I called out, running over to the screen. I snatched the remote away from one of the guests.

"Early reports are stating that Brock Jameson, NBA All-Star, injured his knee during practice. Sources are saying that doctors are running several tests to determine the severity of his injury and if he will need surgery."

"Oh my god, what's wrong with Brock?" Mindy said when she caught up with me.

"I don't know. It's his knee apparently." I glanced at my phone, it was far too late to call. "This can't be good."

"I'm sure he'll be okay."

I suddenly felt guilty about staying behind. He would probably have to be off of his feet. Normally, I would be the one to feed him and run errands during such a stressful time.

Mindy wrapped her arm around my shoulders and lead me away from the TV. "We'll get a hold of him first thing tomorrow. Okay?"

"Heath kissed me."

"What?"

"We fell in the sand and he kissed me. I stopped him. The fight out front was from some guy who I think is claiming Heath slept with his wife or girlfriend. My first night here, he had a threesome in the middle of the night while he had the music on full-blast."

"What!"

"He is a nightmare."

"I need details, sister!"

Then, in the distance I spotted the devil himself walking towards me. I tilted my chin in his direction so Mindy would know he was coming and shut her trap.

"Can we talk for a sec?" he asked.

"I'm busy."

"Come on."

"Is it about the party?"

"No."

"Then I'm busy."

"Then it is about the party."

I looked over at Mindy who awkwardly shrugged at me. Heath lead me through the crowd, and that's when I saw Illy. *Ill* is more like it. She wore a teeny-tiny white dress, the front crossed over and dipped all the way down to her belly button, her tiny, perky runway model boobs a sneeze away from complete exposure. She cocked an eyebrow when she spotted Heath's hand on the small of my back and headed towards us like we were at the end of a catwalk.

Ever the *socialisto* (stole that from Mindy), Heath greeted her like everything was all rainbows and unicorns.

"Heath," she said in her accent, "I have been looking all over for you!"

She kissed him on the lips. Right on the lips that were kissing me minutes ago.

"You remember Sadie, right? The interview the other day?"

"Not really. I thought the girl who visited you was homely." She looked me up and down. "Then again, maybe I do."

What a heinous bitch.

72

Heath laughed a little to himself. "That must have been someone else. Sadie is beautiful." *Nice try Prince Charming.*

Illy finally acknowledged me by shoving a drink in my direction. "Could you get me fresh one?"

"Get it yourself, bitch."

Okay, let me interject here. Was it unprofessional of me? Yes. Did she deserve it? Absolutely. I thought they only made women that horrendous in movies. Normally, I could have composed myself, but just finding out about Brock being hurt and being pretty sauced, well, my inhibitions were down.

"Okay!" Heath said, pushing me forward to continue towards our destination. "Ladies, let's be nice. Illy, I'll see you later?" He winked at her.

She hesitantly nodded at him. *Take that!*

"So what did you want to talk about?" I asked when we finally reached a quiet spot.

"I wanted to fill you in on the commotion outside."

"Oh you mean the guy whose girl you fucked?"

Heath sighed. "He's gone. It's all taken care of."

"Great? Can I get back to work?"

"What's your deal?"

"Excuse me?"

"Are you mad about the kiss?"

The truth is, I wasn't exactly sure why I was mad at the time. Now I do. I was mad because it was a defense mechanism. I knew anger was the only way I could stop myself from riding his boner to Uranus. Instead of answering I simply deflected with an eye-roll.

"If I recall correctly, you kissed me right back. You sucked on my pelvis for Christ's sake. What kind of kinky shit is that?"

"Don't put this on me! You keep pushing me to drink and to have fun and to loosen up. I cannot loosen up. We have a working relationship. There is no room for us to be loose with each other."

"We're both adults and I don't prescribe to arbitrary rules."

"You are something else. You know that? Arrogant, pompous...piggish!"

He leaned in closer and closer. *Oh no, it's happening again.*

"Piggish? I've been called a lot of things, but never piggish. Where do you come up with this shit?"

"Happy to be your first."

"You want me to kiss you."

"No."

"Then stop me."

He leaned in to kiss me, and I sort of, kind of, pushed back. But I'll admit, it was a weak attempt, because dammit he's so fucking hot and his kisses taste like sex. If there was a sex-flavored popsicle, it would be called the Heathsicle. *Maybe we could do this just this once and get it out of our systems,* I thought to myself, pulling him in by his shirt collar as we kissed.

He moved to my neck, kissing it so softly, and it made everything tingle. *I cannot believe I am making out with a supermodel.* He buried his face into the crook of my neck, kissing softly, but pausing in between, caressing my skin with his warm breaths.

Why is he doing this to me? It's like he knows I have a weak spot for narcissists.

He ran his right hand up my thigh, pushing my dress up. All I had underneath was a thong, a flimsy shield for a sex machine like Heath Hillabrand. He grabbed my ass firmly, pressing me up against him and when I felt his huge hardness through his jeans, the reality of the situation began to sink in, but not nearly as much as when his fingers slid into me.

Oh god, oh god, oh god. This is the point of no return, get your shit together. You cannot be this fucking weak, Sadie.

"Okay, we have to stop," I said, pushing him away from me, as a I panted for air. My skin was prickly all-over with sex tingles and my body so wanted to keep on, but that sliver of sober brain I had left would not let me move forward.

"You're killing me..." Heath said, stepping back. I don't think anyone had ever stopped him before.

"I am not one of these skanks you bed. You don't go around kissing that Illy bitch, wink to her and tell her you'll see her later, and then kiss me. That's not how I operate. This milk does not come for free!"

Heath laughed his careless laugh. "Who wants milk? What do you want from me?"

"I just want us to be normal. Obviously I am attracted to you, but I see how you are and I do not get with guys like you."

"Except in the garden, and just now."

"What do you want from me? Why are you so persistent?"

"I don't know, but I feel like I have to have you. It's hard work so I really wish I didn't. You're exhausting."

"Well it's not going to happen. I know all you are looking for is some tail. What baffles me more than anything is you seem legitimately surprised. How could I think you are more than just a man-whore after my first night here, when you brought those two girls back?"

He sighed, recalling that night. "I thought you were asleep"

"How could I have slept though all of that commotion? That's besides the point. Since I have arrived, you have treated me in a way that is not acceptable in an employee-employer relationship."

"Likewise. You didn't seem repulsed a minute ago."

"Maybe this arrangement is not going to work out. I should have found a way to make it to Houston."

"Are you quitting?"

"I don't know."

"God you are indecisive," he said, pulling a cigarette out of his pocket and placing it in his mouth, unlit.

I didn't know what to do at that moment. I was worried about Brock, and I felt guilty, like he needed me. However, the truth was, I was Brock's chef. Not his physical therapist. He had family to fall back onto and doctors to attend to him; why would he need me, too? This Heath situation was more confusing than I had anticipated. He was crude, horny, inappropriate, vile, loose, and yet, I knew it was there: the basest, purest attraction. It was bad news. If I stayed longer, well then I was going to become a sucker. The best cure is prevention, and I knew waking up in his bed was inevitable--it was only a matter of time.

"Heath, I really appreciate this opportunity. You have been generous, but I think we have crossed some lines here that cannot be erased. I understand I am part of that. So, I think it's best that after this party I wrap everything up and resign from this position."

Heath shook his head in disappointment. "If that's how you wanna do it, then so be it. You're not cut out for this life anyway." His little dig, his little comment about me not being cut out for "this life," was another way of him telling me that I was uptight. I really hated when people called me uptight. Just because I do what is right does not make me uptight. "Well, I'll let you *wrap up* then." He threw little air quotes around "wrap up," in a mockery of my voice and walked away, lighting a cigarette.

What a jerk.

CHAPTER ELEVEN

Once Heath turned the corner to walk away, I suddenly became very emotional. It might have been the booze, or the fact that I was jobless again (*what the hell was I thinking*). I believed we were past the point of reconciliation. Guys like Heath like to prove to themselves that they don't need women, and so, once I made it clear I didn't need him, I didn't expect him to turn around and beg me to stay.

He saw me as a frigid bitch, and he was surrounded by plenty of beautiful women who would happily keep him warm. I sadly walked back out to the party. The crowd was dying down as it was pretty late into the night. Mindy spotted me and made a beeline.

"Where the hell have you been? I was just about to head out."

"I just quit."

"What? You're kidding." I am sure she was not thrilled, being my referrer and all, but that hardly crossed my intoxicated thoughts.

"No. He is unbearable."

"What happened?"

"I don't want to talk about it. I have to get back to work. My fucking feet are killing me," I said, whipping off my shoes. Just then, I caught a glimpse of Heath heading out with a couple of bros and *Illy--Ill--Gross. I should just call her Gross.*

"Should I stay?"

"No, go home. You have a ride and all, right?"

"Yeah, I have to get back to the city, but I can move some appointments. You look upset."

"I just need to take care of all this."

"Okay, call me tomorrow?"

The next hour, I worked on closing up shop. The house was a bit of a disaster area, but a cleaning service was coming the next morning to fix it all. I sat upstairs in my bed, unable to sleep, wondering if he would come back at any minute and what he might say to me. But another hour passed, and sleep eventually overcame me.

I dreamt of him. How instead of stopping Heath in the hallway, I let him keep his fingers in me, massaging me as he pressed his nose against mine. He smiled, looking into my eyes, and I giggled back, both of us acknowledging the naughtiness of the situation. And then he pushed my dress up, all the way so that only my thong covered my lower body. He reached down and unbuttoned his pants, holding his firmness. I waited with bated breath, this would be it, we would pass the threshold into more than just boss and employee. He smirked, and then I felt his tip graze against me.

DO YOU LIKE PINA COLADAS? AND GETTING CAUGHT IN THE RAIN?

My head felt like it was in a vice when I awoke to Mindy's ringtone. I didn't know which way was up. I knocked the stupid thing over, and then it vibration-danced beneath my bed. I hung upside down, feeling for it in the darkness, answering it in the nick of time. The clock on the phone read 5:43.

"Hello?" I asked in a froggy, upside-down voice.

"Sadie? Were you asleep?" She sounded distressed.

"Yes...are you okay? Is something wrong?" I asked, trying to sound more alert, but I was only more confused.

"I had the driver turn my car around, I was halfway back to the city, but I just got a call. Heath has been in an accident. I think it's really bad."

"What?" The information and the quivering in her usually unsympathetic voice was sobering.

"I'm his emergency contact. He doesn't have family here. I don't know what to do. They said he was unconscious when he arrived"

"Oh my god."

"Can you go? It's going to take me a while to get there. Someone has to be there for him and I fucking hate all the twats he hangs out with. Those fucking sycophants!" She loudly cried the last sentence in her more familiar borderline-psychopathic way.

"Yes, yes, of course," I said, trying to lift my body back on the bed. When I realized that would require some level of strength, I slithered onto the floor like a wet noodle instead. "What hospital?"

"I'll text you all the details."

"Okay."

I didn't know Heath long, but I was filled with dread as I drove to the hospital. I felt this was my fault. Not that I want to sound all self-centered, but I was sure he left the house because I quit and he was pissed. Pissed or at least wanted to make me sweat it. And now, he's laid up in a hospital. For all I knew he could be dying.

I ran into the entry of the emergency room and straight to the reception nurse.

"Heath Hillabrand. I am his assistant. Is he okay?"

"Are you a family member or a medical contact?"

"Yes. Mindy-- Amanda Sloane." *I learned that trick in the movies.*

"Okay." She stared at her little screen as though she was reading a dissertation or something. "The physicians have completed working on him and he is stable. The doctor will be out in a moment to talk to you."

I paced for another ten minutes or so when finally, a doctor approached me.

"Are you Amanda?"

"Yes. Is he going to be okay?"

"He was very lucky. He was in a car accident, drove into a light pole. The police have already inquired about speaking with him. Apparently someone else was the driver and he may have been drunk. That is all I know. He sustained several fractures and a severe concussion, so he will be bedridden for the next few weeks then after that he'll need to take it easy for the remainder of the summer. He didn't sustain any internal injuries other than a concussion, so I believe he will make a full recovery."

"Oh thank god! Can I see him?"

"You can go in now, but he might not be awake for a while, he's under quite a bit of sedation. We'll have to keep him here under observation for the next 24 hours."

I watched him lay there unconscious, his face bruised and swollen, his limbs in casts. He he looked so helpless, not like that cocky, blonde Adonis I had come to resent over the past week and a half. Finally, after an hour and a half or so, he awoke.

"It's okay, Heath, I'm here," I said as his eyes wildly scanned his surroundings. "Can someone help!" I called out. "It's okay, you were in an accident, but you're going to be fine." He grabbed his head with his hand and winced in pain.

The nurse came in and checked his vitals. He retched a few times, I suppose a reaction from the meds or the concussion. The nurse informed him that the doctor would be coming in to speak with him about his injuries.

Heath looked over at me, and grabbed my hand. The vulnerability in that gesture touched my hardened heart. *Damn I am such a sucker for that.*

"I AM Amanda Sloane!" The familiar voice carried into the room from a distance. *Oop*s.

I pulled away from Heath to address the situation I created out there, but he tightened his grip.

In a throaty, weak voice, he said the first words he had uttered to me since he had awoken. "*Stay.*"

CHAPTER TWELVE

Heath would have to be in bed for six weeks, after that physical therapy for another month. That's if things went well. How could I leave someone at the lowest point of his life? That's just not me. He needed me more than ever.

The morning after the accident I called Brock, but he didn't answer. So, I shot him a text to which he responded within an hour.

Me:

Hey Brock. I heard about your knee. I know you must be really busy trying to figure it all out, but I wanted to let you know and you are in my thoughts. Sending positive vibes.

Brock:

Thanks Sadie. I'm hoping for the best here. Missing your food like u don't even kno. Offer still stands for u to come :)

Me:

Don't tempt me, but I am stuck here and you know it! Seriously though. I hope everything is ok.

Brock:

Me too. I've got a lot of specialist visits coming up. I'll keep you in the loop. Or I am sure ESPN will, those bastads.

Me:

LOL. It's hard out there for a pimp ;)

Brock:
U kno it. ;)

There wasn't much I could do to help Brock, who I know was trying to keep a brave face (he had always told me a serious injury was one of his greatest worries), but I could be there for Heath.

When Heath was released from the hospital, he spent his first week and a half locked up in his room in the dark, recovering from the concussion. He was also hopped up on painkillers and slept much of the day. After his head stopped throbbing, he was softer, at least for a few days. A couple of people visited the day after he returned home, but the visiting ceased without the parties and access to clubs Heath provided. No one wanted to be around a melancholic, broken supermodel. Heath seemed sad as he realized this would not be the wild, party-filled, fun summer he had imagined. I would not be organizing grand soirees. Instead, I would be feeding him and wheeling him around the garden for fresh air when the nurse wasn't around to do so. I became more of a health aide than a personal assistant. But that softness, it quickly turned to something hard. Maybe it was because he had very few visitors, maybe because it became very quiet and that was the thing he dreaded most: to sit alone with himself in his thoughts.

Towards the end of the second week, I called through his bedroom door since my hands were occupied by the breakfast tray. "Heath, I have your breakfast."

He didn't answer.

"Heath?"

Still there was silence.

I slowly opened the door and I could only assume he was the lump in the middle of his bed under the covers. I slowly walked over and, guessing he was still asleep, laid the tray on a table next to the bed. I planned on returning later to retrieve it.

About two hours later, the home health aide arrived. Her job was usually easy, as besides the two fractured legs, one fractured arm, a severely dislocated shoulder and overall soreness, Heath was a healthy guy. She would help clean him, administer any meds he might need, wheel him around when he felt like going outside and then she would go on her way.

I welcomed her into the house and made my way into the kitchen, not even a minute later hearing the commotion.

"I said get out! Don't come back! I am not some goddamn gimp!" The screaming was accompanied by a crashing sound.

As I hurried over to the stairs I caught sight of the nurse scurrying down as she slung her purse over her shoulder.

"What's wrong?"

"I will not tolerate this treatment!"

"Are you okay?"

"He is refusing treatment and then he threw his food across the room. I am sorry, but I am leaving."

"Oh my god. I am so sorry."

She left in a huff, giving me a look as though she thought I was some sort of accomplice to his callous behavior.

I crept up the stairs, my heart thudding because I expected I might be the next to experience his wrath.

The door was wide open as the nurse had flung it upon exiting. Heath was once again a lump in the middle of the bed. I quickly scanned the room and saw the breakfast I had so lovingly crafted that morning was in a pile of shattered porcelain on the floor.

"Heath?"

Again he remained silent.

"Heath? What's going on? The nurse just quit."

"What part of fuck off does no one understand?"

"Excuse me?"

"I don't want a fucking nurse and I don't want any fucking food. I just want to be left alone goddammit!"

83

"And how do you suppose you'll get better without a nurse or food?"

"I don't care. You didn't even want to be here anyway. Just get out, when I need something, I'll be sure to text."

"Why are you acting like this?"

His lump under the covers shifted, a visual method of conveying he was setting in even more and was done with our conversation.

"Fine then. I'm not cleaning up after your tantrum," I said indignantly.

"I didn't ask. Now leave."

What an asshole! Who the fuck does he think he is? I ran downstairs, grabbed my keys, and stormed to my car. I didn't know what I was going to do, but I had to get some space. He confounded me, but I felt drawn to him, like an elaborate puzzle that I just had to piece together. I drove to the nearest beach. The weather was perfect, very warm, with an ocean breeze that swept the perspiration from my skin. To be honest, I'm not sure if I was sweating because it was hot or because I was so frazzled by his tantrum. I found the quietest spot and plopped my tush in the sand, not having prepared by bringing a towel or blanket.

I was at a crossroads with Heath. I thought I hated him, and then we kissed, well, more than kissed. Then he had the accident, and he begged me to stay; he was so vulnerable at that moment. Then he was quiet for a couple of days, and maybe I mistook that for kindness or softness, but maybe he was bubbling. Maybe he was slowly seething and today he blew. I could leave, no one was holding me back, but I didn't want to. If I left now, I would have failed, and he would have done what he has likely always done: gotten what he wanted or dismissed people when things got tough.

And then I realized why he was so angry. This time he had no power, there was no easy answer. He was incapacitated all summer: no modeling gigs, no parties, no "friends" to drink with. For once, there was no easy win for him. Once I realized this, that this was just some giant pity-party he had created for himself, I grew full of resolve. I would do what I intended when I first arrived here: cook and kick ass! And I didn't have to cook for another couple of hours.

I stood up abruptly, swatted off the sand from my ass and stomped back to my car. *I am going to show him what's he's been lacking, someone who will stand up to him and not just bat their eyelashes in his presence.* This time, Heath wouldn't get rid of me so easily. He should have let me go when he had the chance.

CHAPTER THIRTEEN

I fearlessly marched back into the house that afternoon. What was he going to do? Get up and attack me? He could barely wipe his own ass at this point with his bum shoulder. I threw my things on the entry table and strode up the stairs to the threshold of his bedroom door. He was still that lump in the middle of his bed. It seemed he hadn't moved since I left. I glanced over at the untouched mess from earlier in the day. *Disgusting*, I mouthed to myself.

"Alright, that's it!" I shouted loudly, walking over to the windows and pulling open the curtains.

"What the fuck?" Heath asked, shielding his eyes with his available hand.

"Oh come on. Who are you, Nosferatu?"

"I thought I told you to leave."

"Yeah you did and I did and now I am back."

"Well leave again then!" He said pointing to the door, trying to mask a wince. *Serves him right for using that arm to throw plates of food like a two-year-old.*

"No! I am not going to sit here and be an enabler to your pathetic pity party and I certainly will not be your punching bag."

"It's not like I am sitting here covered in plaster! My face all busted up."

It's true: his face was bruised, his lip busted, there were cuts, but the doctor assured him that it would all heal, there was nothing to worry about. But I could sense his fear, that his biggest asset might be compromised. Honestly, his pristine skin might benefit from a few small cuts, it would make him look all rugged, and if he added a beard on top of it...*stop it.*

"Yeah you are, but you're lucky you're not dead. *Oh poor Heath, rich super model who survived a major car accident with no long term damage.* You should be thanking your lucky stars all you have is a few broken bones. And if you want to get back into civilization, moping around like this won't do anything for you."

"So you're a doctor now?"

"No, but you asked me--begged me--to stay. If you want me here, you better act like you do. I am all you have left right now. You scared the shit out of the nurse, and I don't see any of your party-friends showing up with casseroles. Do you?" Heath went silent. I might have seriously hurt his feelings with that last line, but besides a couple of brief phone calls, no one has showed up since that first day. Even his sweet Illy was a no-show, he mentioned she was at a gig overseas, but whatever. Mindy planned on coming back, and checked in frequently, but she was loaded with projects between NY and LA. Maybe if he didn't act like such a douche, he would have better friends. "Listen, I want to help you. So why do you have to be such a dick about everything?"

"Me a dick? You have been the frigid bitch since we met. All stuffy and miss goody two-shoes."

"And yet here I am." Heath scowled at me silently. Though he said nothing, I could tell he was resigned. "So here's what's going to happen. I am going to prepare a nice dinner, and then I am going to bring it up here and you and I are going to eat like two civilized fucking human beings on your beautiful balcony. And if you want to act like an adult and tell me what crawled up your ass this morning, I'll be here to listen. *Capisce?*"

His face softened from a scowl to shock. He sort of looked like a deer in headlights.

"I asked a question."

"*Capisce...*"

"Alright, I'll see you in an hour." I confidently strode back to the bedroom door and glanced at the mess again on the way out. "Oh, and next time you do that, I am picking it up and throwing it right back at you. I dare you to try me."

***

I ferociously chopped vegetables for the sauté, feeling victorious in my decision to tell off Heath. In fact, I caught myself smiling several times thinking of the shocked look on his face as I marched out of the bedroom. It was about an hour before I carried the tray of vegetables and steak upstairs to his bedroom (as a model who could not exercise, Heath was now on a strict diet of lean meats and veggies to maintain his taut physique).

I was shocked to find Heath sitting in his wheelchair bent over in front of the splattered breakfast, holding onto a broom with his two disabled limbs: one arm in a sling, the other in a cast. Needless to say it was both pitiful and pointless.

"What are you doing?" I asked, as I placed the dinner tray on a table. I hate to say it, but I felt sympathy for him.

"I've got it."

If you can imagine a penguin holding a broom, well then you understand how he looked.

"Heath, I wasn't expecting you to pick this up. I appreciate the gesture, but the food will get cold...and let's be honest, you're not gonna succeed within either one of our lifetimes."

"This sucks," Heath said with a sigh, finally relenting.

"I know. Now, let's just forget about everything and go enjoy some dinner on this gorgeous evening on your fantastic balcony, you lucky bastard. I'll get it later."

"I'd hardly describe myself as lucky."

"That's your problem. You lack perspective."

Heath had already done me the favor of getting into his wheelchair (miraculously I might add), so I wheeled him outside and served our dinner. He was disheveled, his tan had faded slightly, but he was still a treat for the eyes. Surprisingly, the stubble and bed-head served to make him more approachably good-looking versus the flawless statue of David look he typically walked around the earth with.

"How the hell did you get in the wheelchair?" I had to ask.

"You have no idea. It took me the better part of the hour."

"You could have hurt yourself."

He glanced down at himself, "Can it get much worse? What's left to break? My dick?"

We both laughed. "Now that would be the end of you!" It was surprisingly nice to have glimpse of the old jokester, even if for a few seconds. Once the laughter subsided, his face turned unusually serious.

"Sadie...I'm not good at this...but...I'm sorry...for the outburst."

I was taken aback by his apology. So far Heath had done a myriad of things to me, but apologizing was one I had yet to experience.

I nodded in acceptance. "What was that all about? This morning?"

"I don't handle shit like this well. I mean, can you blame me?"

"No, but you can't act out like that. It's just not acceptable."

"I know...I know...I guess. It's just that...never mind."

"I hate when people do that. Spit it out. You can talk to me."

"I don't have anyone. I mean really have anyone. I thought I did, but I knew I really didn't. And even when people don't have real friends, they have family, but I don't have that either."

"Where's your family?"

"I don't know. I was raised in foster care. I have a biological aunt somewhere, but I haven't seen here since I was

13. I have a foster brother, but he's in Wisconsin and he can't get out here often."

I felt a bit like an asshole. See, as soon as I met Heath, I pegged him. I saw who he was in the present and I carelessly made unfair assumptions about him. I assumed he had always had it easy. In my defense, he had an easy, carefree way about him. His manner made you believe he never knew what it was like to worry.

"Is that why you always have people around? You're afraid of being alone?"

His eyes narrowed in on mine, as if I discovered a secret no one was ever supposed to know. "Well, not afraid."

"Afraid," I confirmed.

"What makes you think that?" he asked, mystified with a touch of disdain.

"I just have a way. I can sense these things. I could tell that you focus on the number rather than the quality of people who surround you. And that makes sense, if your concern is having no one around." *Post-Kenneth Sadie had become hyper-aware of common traits among attention whores and whores in general.*

"Except for now."

"I'm *heyah*." The tail end of "here" flopped out of my mouth like drool. I had to be careful with my tenderness, I had to guard it. I tried to stop the word from coming out, but it had full momentum and so, I sounded fresh off the first stages of a stroke.

"You okay there?" He asked. "Too much to drink?"

"Oh shut it," I said, mildly embarrassed.

"Truth is, the people I could call I don't want around. Sure, they're fun to party with, but honestly, I can't stand most of them: they're superficial, all they care about is money and status. I don't want those people to see me like this and I don't want to just sit around with them." His assessment of his so-called friends nearly mirrored my early assessment of him and I wondered if there was more to him or if he had a huge blind spot when it came to self-awareness.

Heath slid his left arm out of his sling, wincing in pain. Again, my instincts kicked in. No matter our differences, I didn't want to see him in pain.

"Let me get that."

"No, it's okay."

"You asked me to take care of you. Let me. This is what you pay me for. We need to let that shoulder rest."

"Okay," he sighed.

I slid my chair over to him and cut a piece of steak. Heath did not look thrilled by the prospect of being fed, so I used the same tactic that people use with babies to make them eat.

"Choo!Choo! Here comes the food train!" Heath's facial expression went limp, but it was hiding a smile. "It's coming!" I said as the steak approached his lips. Then it just kind of smooshed into them as he held his deadpan expression. "Oh come on! Eat the damned steak!" Just as I said that, he chomped at it like a angry dog and I squealed.

"Keep feeding me like a toddler and I might just poo my pants to teach you a lesson."

And just like that, an invisible door had opened, a new level of comfort had been reached. Those moments happen all the time, when you realize a person is not just an acquaintance, but someone who you could spend hours with, someone with whom you could sit for long comfortable silences. One hardly remembers the exact moment that that happens, but I remember when it happened with him.

He went back to our previous conversation: "I know you're here and thank you. We kind of got off to an interesting start, but thank you for being here when everyone else seems to have forgotten."

"It's my job and I'm sure people care, people are busy, ya know?" I was fibbing to make him feel better, which is something I promised I wouldn't do, but there was a tenderness about him that elicited my sympathy.

"I know, but you quit before this happened. I know you stayed because you have a big heart." *Don't say it, don't say I have a big heart. It's the weapon that has been used against me the most. Suckers have big hearts. I am not a sucker.*

"I stayed because it was the right thing to do."

"I knew I liked you as soon as you walked in the door that morning of the interview," he smirked.

"Oh?" I said, looking down at my plate.

"I don't mean it in the way I said before. I know, I'm a jackass...I mean, you, there's something refreshing about you. And then I was sure of that once I hired you. You had standards, you told me what you really thought of me. It's weird, you think you don't want that, but when you are surrounded by people who only tell you what you want to hear, who give you what you want without hesitation or thought for your longterm well-being, you start to crave the opposite: Someone who doesn't fear being banished."

I finally felt as though he was really speaking to me without all the pretense. He was just guy talking to a girl.

I picked up my glass of wine.

"Let me have a sip."

"You're not supposed to, you're healing."

"Sadie, come on. I'm healing just fine. Throw this poor puppy a bone."

I shrugged and passed him the glass. He raised an eyebrow -- of course, he couldn't hold the thin glass up at an angle with his shoulder injury. I placed one hand underneath his chin and used the other to tilt the glass to his mouth.

Up until this moment, if I looked at his face for too long, I would get caught in a mini-trance. He was just so exquisite: every contour, the curve of his cheekbones, the flush in his cheeks, the perfect pout of his lips, his plentiful eyelashes. I would get sucked in like one would looking at an intricate work of art at a museum. This time, he shifted his eyes over and caught me. Our eyes locked, and my heart fluttered for a bit. I put the glass down. He licked a drop of wine from his lip and then tugged his lip with his teeth. *Yum.* When our eyes met, I felt tense, the way he had made me feel when I first met him, all over again.

"Heath. I want to tell you that I know what it's like. To an extent." I had to say it. Because it was true and because I needed to shift the mood.

"What do you mean?"

"To be alone. To not have people."

"Your family?"

"My mom and dad...I lost them when I was little." I took a deep breath. "They were murdered."

He paused. I could see that he was both shocked and moved by this unexpected information. I observed him as he searched his thoughts for what to say. I was used to dealing with the awkward reactions from people when I told them, so I waited for him to find some words to say back. Finally, with more sincerity than I'd ever heard in his voice, he said, "I'm so sorry that happened to you and your family."

"It's okay. It was a long time ago. I don't have siblings. My parents didn't either. All I have is my grandma, but she's getting very old. So at least I have her, but that's it. And friends, I have always had a hard time really connecting. They just know me on the surface, but I don't have girlfriends who I can talk to about everything. People just kind of float in and out of my life. That consistency doesn't exist for me."

"What about Minds?"

"She might be the closest friend I have, but we can go for months without talking to each other."

"Well, at least you don't pay her to be your friend like I do."

"Don't say that. She very protective over you. It's not about the money with her."

His expression softened in a way I had only seen when he begged me to stay that night at the hospital. He looked into my eyes and I felt weak. "I'm *heyah*," he said. It broke the heaviness and we both smiled, which then escalated into chuckles. I found myself leaning into him and his smell...it was the faintest hint of musk and something lighter, like a citrus, mixed with the natural scent of his skin. *It was like catnip to me.*

"Well, it looks like we have our own little orphan club."

"It's very exclusive," I said in a high-brow tone.

"Let's finish the bottle."

"*Heath...*" I said, in a motherly tone.

"I don't want to get hammered. I just want to have a nice dinner. I like talking to you when you're not being such an icy shrew."

"I wonder what in the world would cause me to be less than hospitable to you."

But I relented. It felt right that evening, for me to stop being so hard on him, and he finally started treating me like something other than just another sexual plaything. I assumed the change was only because he was stuck with me.

We shared the glass: a sip for him, a sip for me. The wine opened us up in ways I had never anticipated. It made me giggly and less stern, and it dissolved his douchiness.

"How's Brock doing?"

"We texted. He had surgery, and the docs are evaluating the options. Knowing him he won't say if it's bad and he's probably getting 30 different opinions. He's ever the optimist. I just sent him a care package. Homemade cookies and energy bars."

"Well, just show him a pic of this and that'll lift his spirits because at least he's not me." I rolled my eyes. I would not play into the pity pit in which he was wallowing. "That sucks. They were hoping for a championship season, but it's starting to look unlikely with him being in and out like that." Then it looked like a lightbulb went off in his head. "Did the two of you...?"

"What? No...not all bosses hit on their workers!"

"Just curious. I don't know how any virile young man wouldn't try."

"Well, good thing you're now covered in casts, keeps you from being so goddamned handsy. Besides, Brock is the perfect gentleman. He would never stoop to your caveman version of chivalry." Except for that one night he came home hammered when I was supposed to be housesitting. He kissed me, but he was sloppy drunk and I put him to bed. I had always assumed he didn't remember.

"You are a cruel woman."

"You wanted direct."

"I am starting to rethink that whole schpiel."

"I was just thinking. The nurse, we'll have to get you a new one."

"No, I just want you."

"But I'm not a nurse."

"She barely did anything. I don't like it. I don't like her cleaning me up, or feeding me. It makes me feel like I am not in control, to have a strange woman bathing me."

"I don't know."

"I'll pay you more."

"It's not that Heath. You don't have to pay me more." It was because I was afraid to become closer to him than I already had. "Plus, I am so not wiping your ass."

"Excuse me, no one wipes my ass but me. You are just nasty. That's my point, I just need your help on some small things. The nurse is annoying. Plus, she smells like moth balls."

I spit up my wine.

"I can take my own meds. But sometimes I just need help getting in and out of my chair and there's a machine that does most of the work. I want you to do it, Sadie. I just want it to be you. I feel comfortable with you, and you smell like flowers. You're the only person I trust right now to see me like this."

How could I say no to that? To the crass young man-whore who had melted in front of my very eyes? "Okay," I said, in soft defeat.

"Thank you." He rubbed the nub of his cast on my hand.

"Well, I better clean this up and get you into bed." I stood up quickly and my head spun a bit. Only then did I realize how much I drank. *Bad nurse.*

I cleaned up the mess from that morning and returned upstairs to help Heath into bed. Luckily, he had this machine with a sling that wrapped under his arms and raised and lowered him from a seated position. Once he was seated in the bed, though, I had to help adjust him and get him comfortably under the covers.

"You're a big boy," I said, lifting his legs up.

"You're an angel," he murmured, woozy from the booze.

I used all of my might to push him in further, and slipped on the rug, falling on his chest. Our faces were within inches of each other, and yes, there was that pause, that moment of: should we or shouldn't we? But unlike before, he didn't jump at me. He respected me now, and it only made me enjoy him more.

"Alright, goodnight."

"Goodnight," he smiled warmly.

I meandered back to my bedroom, still heady from the wine. This quiet evening was the most pleasant one I had in a long time and I felt a surprising sting of sadness going back to my room alone.

I lay in my bed, staring at the ceiling, unable to sleep. I missed him. Like Heath, I too didn't want to be alone. I couldn't remember the last time I felt that way. It wasn't just physical, it's that feeling you had as a kid when you met a friend you liked so much that even though you spent all day with them at school, as soon as you got home you would call them up. Or the way you might stay awake as long as you could at a sleepover because no matter how tired you were, sleep was not nearly as enjoyable as the conversation with your friends. I wasn't ready for our time together that night to end.

The wine in my veins made me shameless enough to follow through.

I tip-toed to his room and slowly opened the door. In my gut, I hoped he might be asleep and I would change my mind.

"Is everything okay?" he asked almost as soon as I stepped foot in the room.

"Yes, I couldn't sleep." *What the hell are you doing? Tell him you're here to check in on him as his new nurse--yeah, that's the ticket!*

"Oh, me neither. It hard with all this crap on me," he said in an amused whisper. He did bizarrely resemble a living, modern-day mummy. And from my limited knowledge in Egyptology, I believe only dead people were mummies. Which would make him a zombie mummy. A really friggin' hot one. But I digress.

"I don't want to be alone tonight."

"Okay."

His cast-encased arm was splayed out to his side, and his legs were propped up on several pillows. When I imagined getting into bed with a male model, this was certainly not the image I had pictured. I gently closed the door behind me and slid under the covers with him, resting my cheek on his chest. I felt his chin rest gently atop my head. Then as if his presence triggered something in me, maybe a feeling of security, I quickly dozed off.

CHAPTER FOURTEEN

Shitshitshit. Those were my first thoughts when I woke up that morning with my head still resting on Heath's bare chest. Yet another terrible idea of mine. Listen, I wasn't hammered or anything the night before, but there was enough alcohol flowing through me to give me misguided ballsiness. And that wine-induced bravado mixed with the laughs, and the good conversation, the intimacy of feeding someone a meal as they tell you their innermost fears, I hadn't had that type of connection in a long time. I didn't realize how much I missed it until I had it again.

I gently lifted my head and hand off of him. Maybe I could slip away and pray the Percocets had left him in a non-life-threatening coma. But you know me by now--that would never be the case, as that would mean things work out for me, and it seems they hardly ever do.

"Good morning, nurse," he said playfully, the rasp of sleep still in his voice.

"Morning." I tried to sound easy, but the words plopped out of my mouth like anchors. "I will make you breakfast now." *That sounded ridiculous.*

"Strange, I always thought English was your first language. *I will make you breakfast now,*" he recited in a Russian accent.

I shook my head, clearly frazzled, nervously searching the room for a cardigan to cover my bare shoulders and cleavage, which were freezing in my light camisole. But, of course, this wasn't my room, so why would my clothes be lying around in it?

"Jesus Sadie, relax. It's not like we bumped uglies or something." *How eloquent.*

He's right, but it almost feels like what we did was worse.

"I'm fine. I'm fine," I said, more to myself than him, like I was trying to talk myself off of a mental ledge of sorts. "Okay, I'll be back. I think we should get you downstairs? Don't you? You've been cooped up in this room too long. We should get you moving." *You're rambling.*

I scanned him over. His legs and arm jutted out from his torso, covered in hard protective man-made shells. Movement was hardly an option for him.

"Whatever you say, nurse."

Nurse. What the fuck did I agree to last night? *Stupidstupidstupid.*

***

Somehow, we ended up on the couch. Well, literally what happened was that he had one of those chair lifts installed the week before that took him up and down the steps at negative five mph.

By the time we were wrapping up breakfast, my embarrassment had subsided significantly. Cooking has always been a calming force for me. I realized bumbling around like a middle schooler after her first kiss wasn't helping either one of us. So I bucked up and tried to go back to business as usual.

"So what do you want to do today, Señor Hillabrand?"

"I really don't feel like going out like this, not yet."

"Okay. Okay. Makes sense. No pressure."

"Why don't we just binge-watch something? I mean, I can do that. You don't have to stay here with me all day."

"No, that's fine. I don't have any other plans. It's not like I'm a lady of the town."

"A lady of the town?"

"Yeah, I don't know what that was."

We settled on Breaking Bad, as it appears we were both the last people on earth who hadn't yet seen the show and felt it must be destiny for us to do so together. So we spent the rest of the afternoon on the couch, Heath laying his encased body on it, and me sitting at his feet. Several times during points of excitement during the show, I hi-fived his arm cast nub. We were becoming buddies. Maybe this nurse thing wouldn't be so bad after all. It was like being paid to be his friend.

Hours passed before we decided to break from the trance-like state of binge-watching Netflix.

"This is kind of shameful, the amount of television we have just consumed," I confessed.

"Hey, I have a legitimate excuse. You're the one who should be ashamed."

"So, dinner?"

"Not really hungry, this lack of movement has kept my appetite down."

"Okay. Maybe I could put you in the wheelchair and walk you around the property?"

"Only if you want."

"Sure. I've been sitting all day. This will get me some exercise."

So I went through the tedious process of helping him up from the couch and into his wheelchair (maybe I should have taken the extra pay). It was then I started to feel something. Now that he backed off, that he wasn't trying so hard to loosen me up, or get in my pants, it made me want to be with him more. Maybe I missed being told how desirable I was, or I enjoyed playing hard to get, but now that he had completely pulled back, all I wanted was for him to tell me how much he wanted me.

I pushed him along the driveway. It was early evening; the chirps of crickets and the sound of wheels on gravel filled the otherwise quiet summer air.

"Confession. I lied." Heath's words broke the stillness.

"What do you mean? What about?"

"There is something I need to do."

"What's that?"

"Well, the nurse never got around to helping me wash."

"Oh...*Oh!* Of course." *So nursing doesn't mean watching Netflix all day.* "I am so sorry. I am pretty new to this."

"No need to apologize. I'm just afraid you won't want to hang around me if I start to smell like ass."

"Okay, well let's head back in then. I might need you to walk me through what she did."

We went through the tedious process of getting him back upstairs and into his bed. He told me the nurse had these wipes and where they were.

"These seem cold. I bet you miss a warm shower."

"Woman, you have no idea."

"I'm going to warm these up for you."

"You are a saint."

I took as long as I could before returning upstairs. He would be naked, and I would be rubbing his body with warm, soapy cloths. Every crevice, every muscle, would be a fraction of a millimeter away from my hand. And it was becoming harder and harder for me to see him as a repulsive man-whore. Now that the sycophants had nearly vanished, it was just the two of us, and we had found ourselves on a deserted island of lonely abandoned souls (since it's his home, we could just call it Manwhore Island).

My hands shook nervously as I carried the cleansing cloths up the stairs, I turned to the threshold and there he was, sitting up, shirtless, his boyish smile and thick dirty-blond hair every-which way. I felt that jump your heart feels when you know you want someone and you know that inevitably you will end up having that person, no matter what the rational side of your brain does to protect you.

But I had pushed him away so hard and so strong, that I finally got what I wanted: respect. And now because of it, I wanted him more. I wanted him badly. And I wanted him to want me back again, but I feared it was too late.

CHAPTER FIFTEEN

I placed the warm cloth on the nightstand and dimmed the lights. I figured that would be easier on him, though I am sure male supermodels aren't shy about exposing their bodies.

"So, what do I do?" I asked.

"Well, to start, you can get my torso."

I grabbed a cloth and rubbed it along his torso. My breathing tightened as I felt a surge of nervous energy. I rubbed it along his neck, the curves of his jawline, the ridges of his abdomen. His flawless skin almost glowed in the soft lighting of the room.

"Can you sit up?" I asked.

He smirked, the first hint of flirtatious Heath I had seen in a while. I am sure he was enjoying this spectacle and was not the least bit embarrassed himself. I placed one hand on his shoulder and rubbed the cloth along his back with the other. It was my first contact on his bare skin, and the nerves on the ends of my fingertips sparked. I reached over to get the far side of his torso, and I was close enough to smell him. Not his cologne, or shampoo, but the scent of his skin, which cut through his usually soapy scent since he had not washed up in almost two days. I found myself biting my lip, his smell released something primal in me, I honestly wanted to bite his shoulder right there.

Sadie, this is not a porn. Nurses don't actually fuck their patients in real life.

I stood up before my thoughts could wander any further.

"You can sit back now," I said softly.

I knew what was next, and my stomach clenched in anticipation.

"Okay...your boxers?" I wondered if he could clean his own dick, but part of me wanted to see the goods.

"I'll need your help. I wound up my shoulder throwing the plate yesterday." *Serves him right.*

"Of course." I involuntarily sighed deeply. The sigh betrayed me by showing how hot and bothered this experience was making me.

I slowly grabbed the waistband of his boxers and slid them down. To my surprise, he was semi-erect.

"Sorry Sadie, I'm trying to be professional here, but you're too beautiful."

I nodded. There was nothing of his usual cheeky manner in his tone; he sounded genuine. But when I saw it, how it responded to my touch, I too responded down below, with a flood of arousal.

"It's okay."

My chest was thudding with excitement. I had to touch him down there, but he was aroused and I was aroused and how could I just pretend that what was happening, wasn't really happening?

"If you don't want to, I can do it. My shoulder hurts, but I can manage."

"No...I've got this." I looked up into his blues, and my fucking sweet baby Jesus did he look hot as hell. I told him I had it covered but I didn't move, I just stared at him, and he recognized the look in my eyes. This is a man who gets paid to induce feelings of lust, because everyone wants to fuck him or be him. He spotted the look in my eyes like an owl spotting its prey on a moonless night.

"If I could move my arm. I would run it through your hair. You are doing a great job. I just want you to feel comfortable."

"Thank you. I am. Comfortable."

"Can I?"

"Can you?"

"Touch you."

"But your shoulder."

"It would be worth it."

"I don't know..." The remaining physical distance was the only thing keeping me from throwing the cloth in the air and shoving him in my mouth. But, he was already pulling his arm out of the sling, grimacing all the way. He very slowly ran his fingers through the hair on the base of my scalp, and like a kitten, I closed my eyes and titled my head down, rubbing my cheek along his hand. I nearly purred.

"This is bad, Heath."

"Why?"

"Because I'm me and you're you." I clenched the washcloth in my hands with nervous anticipation.

When I opened my eyes I saw that he was now fully erect.

"Okay." Dammit, he said *okay.* If he had begged, if he had asked, if he had given me something to resist, I would have had something to push away from. Instead, he stepped aside, and I just caved.

I wrapped my fingers around him, and his eyes went wide. I don't think he thought it would be that easy.

I gripped his erection and massaged him, it was so firm, it would have been perfect for me to mount, but I wanted to do this for him. I wanted to make him feel good and forget about his broken body. I assumed it had been a while since he came, as even his "good" arm was very injured and I knew he wasn't getting any visitors.

He moaned throatily and threw his head back. His abs flexed and relaxed with his deep inhalations. I was so turned on, watching this man submit to such a small gesture.

Sure, it occurred to me that I was jerking off a guy who was in nearly a full body cast. It's not the kind of thing one fantasizes about, but I don't think I would have done it any other way. It was his weakness, his total vulnerability that had become such a turn-on. His breathing sped up and his cast nub made a thud as it pressed against the night stand. He was coming close to climax. I took my available hand and pulled down one of the straps of my tank, revealing a breast.

He moaned a little bit louder when he saw it. I leaned down, rubbing my nipple on his tip, and then he came, letting out a lingering groan, making a thudding sound as his leg casts hit each other.

I felt dirty yet powerful. For all the teasing sexual advances I endured, it was me who took control. I popped his cherry. I was the person who moved the chess piece into the spot her opponent never saw coming: *Checkmate muhtafucka.*

Only because at that moment, I enjoyed the mindfuck (and honestly didn't know what else to do), I didn't say another word. I simply resumed cleaning him off as if nothing had transpired while he watched, his mouth agape. Oh yeah, I liked him, I liked him a lot, but I couldn't let him see all that yet.

CHAPTER SIXTEEN

That night, I laid up in my bed with a irremovable smirk on my face. After I finished wiping him down, I pulled up his boxers, said goodnight, and walked out.

For once, he said not a damned thing. It was glorious.

The truth was I had no plans. I didn't know what to make of it just as much I assume Heath did. That's why I said nothing and walked out--on the exterior it seemed like some sort of long term calculation, but really I was buying time.

I cannot tell you the thrill it gave me at that moment, holding the cock of the man whose face adorns billboards 50 feet tall. He's the guy you dream of when you masturbate, not the guy you actually masturbate! Watching him succumb to my hand and his subsequent flustered reaction was such a turn-on. Heath liked to make me nervous, he liked to see me squirm under the weight of his sexual energy, but now I was the one making him shift in his seat anxiously and I understood why he liked it: *it was a lot of fucking fun (pun intended).* So yeah, that night I played with myself, reliving the moment in my head, remembering how his lips curved when he tilted his head back as he came. *Yum.*

That next morning, I had to put the mask on again. I had no idea what would transpire when I saw him, but I realized I would have to wing it. Heath's total and utter confusion was my best offense. I upped the ante further with some visual cues that would send some implicit signals: instead of my t-shirt or tank and jeans, I put on a pair of spandex bootie shorts with a lower than usual cut tank top (and no bra of course!). *I know, I know. I'm such a tease!*

Oh god did my heart pound so fast before I opened the door to his bedroom. He sat there, wide awake as if he had been doing that all night, waiting for me to come back through that door.

"Good morning! Ready for breakfast?" *Yup, let's totally ignore the fact my nipple was on your dickhole last night.*

"Yeah...?" He wanted me to acknowledge what happened, but he would have to move his piece first.

"Alright then, let's get you in your chair!" *Now I was just being obnoxious. I am never this cheerful. I am simply rubbing it in his face.*

"Why don't you save yourself the trouble? Bring it up here. Let's do the balcony again."

"Well okay then!" I said, like Mrs. Cleaver.

So there we were, a half an hour later or so, on his balcony, just like the night I slept in his bed with him.

"It's gorgeous today. We should get you outside again. Maybe another walk?"

Heath shifted as best he could in his wheelchair and sighed. "Alright, maybe I am imagining all this. Maybe it was a dream from the painkillers. The way you're acting is making me think I hallucinated. But I could have sworn my penis was in your hand last night."

I strategically shoved a spoon of yogurt in my mouth.

"I should clarify, not like '*oh here let me clean that for you.*' It was more along the lines of: you jerked me off, pulled out your tits, made me come. That happened right?"

"Yes," I said in monotone. *I am a regular fucking wordsmith.*

"Well, thank you?"

"You're welcome?"

"Sadie, throw me a bone here."

"What?"

"Okay you are officially there weirdest woman I have ever met. First you hate me, then you kiss me, then you want to be just friends or my nurse, then you sleep in my bed with me but don't do anything, and then you jerk me off while bathing me and then pretend like nothing happened. What in the actual fuck?"

I honestly didn't know how to reply. Then I blurted out. "Well when you say it like *that*..."

"There's no *like that*. I am telling you exactly what transpired."

"Well, like I said, to answer your question, you didn't dream it."

"Thanks for the confirmation...So...is this a thing?"

"A thing?"

"Was it a full moon last night or will there be more where that came from?"

"Do I look like Illy to you?"

"What the hell is that supposed to mean? Why are you being so defensive?"

"I am not being defensive. Can we just enjoy breakfast and not have to talk about everything? Can we just let things be?"

"Okay, okay," he said pensively. Then he started to laugh to himself.

"What's so funny?"

"Oh, it's just that I deal with this all the time. Girls who I hook up with who want answers, who want to talk about it when I'm already done with it. And here I am. I never thought I would be that person. You are turning me into a groupie because seriously I cannot fucking figure you out."

"Well, maybe you've met your match."

He snickered. "I enjoyed it very much. Just putting that out there, into the ether."

"I'm glad you did," I said, offering him a bite of his breakfast.

"Okay, so for the record, the ball is in your court. I'm not gonna nag you, I'm not gonna ask questions. I am just going to be here whenever you need me." He winked and smirked. *Now that's the Heath I know.* "Wait, I lied. There is one more thing I have to say. I appreciate the gesture yesterday, but it's not my style to receive without giving back. So if you truly are selfless, you'll give me a chance to reciprocate in some way. Otherwise, I'll feel terrible, and you wouldn't want that. Would you? Okay. Now I'm done."

"I'll keep that in mind."

As I was cleaning up lunch, I noticed Heath's phone buzzing. He was still out on the balcony, oblivious of the call. To my chagrin, it was Illy. I wanted to smack that bitch so badly. As far as I knew, this was the first time she was reaching out to Heath. How fucking *convenient* for her to check in, weeks after the accident. There was something else, of course. Over the past few weeks, Heath and I created our own special bubble. We were connecting in a way that I could only assume would not be possible with his normal crew of friends. I saw Illy's call as a massive intrusion. If I let her back in, I would lose the Heath I was beginning to connect with. Part of it was for Heath's wellbeing too (I swear it!), finally he found someone in me who forced him to be a better version of himself. Illy would just bring him down with her stupid, vapid ways.

So confession: I deleted it aaaaand I blocked her phone number. It's something Heath wouldn't notice unless he dug into his contacts list and it gave me an instant sense of relief. I didn't know what my plans were with him, but I did know I wanted to find out without *Gross* coming back into the picture.

CHAPTER SEVENTEEN

The next couple of days, after the happy-ending bath, were filled with doctor appointments and more Heath-and-Sadie time. He wanted to get out more and showed a greater interest in his recovery so we took long walks around the property. He was coming out of his funk and we settled nicely into our new relationship, not just as caretaker and "patient," but as something else: Friends? Roommates? I wasn't sure what to call it.

The one thing that was annoying (and I know what you are going to say: that I am an annoying bitch who doesn't know what she wants) was that Heath kept his word. He didn't go for any cheap feels (not that he was dexterous enough to do so) and he stayed away from his usually pervy innuendo. On one hand, I craved feeling desired by this gorgeous man, but on the other hand, it made me feel trusting enough in his presence to open up more. And so, I would often spend time chilling in bed with him at night. We would just talk, about nothing really, just while the hours away laughing and creating inside jokes.

I liked looking at him. He thought I was just watching him speak, but really I would just drink him up, and I hoped that might be enough. It's kind of like how you crave a giant, delicious piece of gooey chocolate cake, but then feel satisfied after a bite because it's so decadent. Except we all know the truth: only skinny bitches like Illy or people on television who never have time to eat are satisfied after one bite. No, what happens to actual humans is you fight the temptation, you hold out on touching the cake, until all you can think about is the fucking cake, and then you tell yourself "just one bite" and then you take one bite, and then you wake up four hours later: in a back alley, 1000 calories fatter, with a chocolate mustache and an empty plate resting on your breasts.

Heath is chocolate cake. Staring at him did not squelch my cravings, they made me want to devour him.

So a few nights after the whole hand-to-dick incident, Heath and I were sitting in his bed. It was about eight or so, and his shoulder was starting to feel decent enough that he could let it rest outside of his sling.

"So, what would you be doing right now if you were at home in the city?" He asked, fiddling the very end of a long black lock of hair with his thumb and forefinger.

"You don't want to know the answer to that."

"Yes I do."

"It involves licking the bottom of a bowl of Velveeta."

"Jesus, something tells me it's been a long time since you've been laid."

"What makes you say that?"

"For one, the answer to your question. Two, you are a little tense, pretty much always."

"Well, that's none of your business."

"Tell me...how long has it been? Three months?" I kept a straight face. "Oh my god. Six?" I pursed my lips and looked away, feeling a little embarrassed. "Dear lord. Longer than that?"

"I'm not talking about this. Okay? I was in a relationship for a while and I took some time off from dating."

"I knew it! It must have been bad just as I thought."

"A nightmare. Now can me move on?"

Heath shrugged and then perked up. "Wait a minute, the healthy chef eats Velveeta?"

"That's exactly what she does. And I don't need to feel shittier about that than I already do."

"Well aren't you glad that instead of doing that, you get to sit here in bed with a modern day King Tut?"

I laughed from my belly. "You might be more famous than King Tut. He didn't have a billboard in Times Square. You should do some avant-garde photo shoot in your casts like they do on America's Top Model."

"That show is so ridiculous." He feminized his voice: "Today you are going to dress up as garbage men, but you better sell the shit out of it. I want to see the stench of filth in your smizing eyes!"

"So you do watch it! I always wondered if models watched that!"

"I think you're my best friend."

"What?" Heath had a habit of steering conversations with the finesse of a one-eyed, 80-year old woman. He would sometimes blurt out words or phrases that were completely incongruent with what we were discussing or use pronouns to refer to things we spoke about hours ago.

"You heard what I said."

"Well, yeah. You just caught me off guard. Do you really think that?"

"Why, you don't?"

"I didn't say that. I just...that's very sweet of you. I like you a lot too." *Did I just say that out loud?*

"Why does this kind of feel like when you tell someone you love them and then they say 'thank you' back?"

I rolled over onto my stomach. "*Oh, what do you want me to say Heathy?*" I said in a baby-voice getting close up to his face. "*I think you're my best fwiend too!*"

"You are such an ass. And no one has ever called me Heathy. Ever," he said, playfully mushing my forehead with his less busted arm, which I swatted away. "Ahhhh!" he exclaimed.

"Oh no, did I hurt your arm?" I asked leaning in. His facial expression quickly changed to a smile as he pulled me in, and when our laughter settled, it started to happen: that stupid pull, that irresistible draw. Like when magnets pass that threshold from a mild attraction to forceful slamming. I looked into those endless eyes, and I knew I was fucked, but I was resisting with any sense I had left.

Then the stupid whore of a doorbell rang. It's funny that I would call it that, because the queen of stupid whores herself, Illy, was on the other side.

"May I help you?" I asked, peeking my face out, making sure to keep the door only slightly ajar.

"I vant to see Heath."

No *hi, how are you on this pleasant evening?* No *please.* No *thank you.*

"Sorry, he's sleeping right now. He's very tired recovering from the accident. Maybe you should visit at a more reasonable hour."

"I have been trying to call him, but he vill not answer."

"Well, then maybe he doesn't want to see you."

"He always vants to see me." *Well when you introduce yourself pussy first, what guy wouldn't?*

"I'll let him know you came and if he wants, he'll call."

"Maybe you should tell him now."

"No, like I said he's asleep and recovering. You can't just drop by like this."

"I did not know housekeeper made the rules." *Stupidbitchwhorecunt.* Visions of triple roundhouses to her face played in my head.

"I'm not the maid. If you'll excuse me..." I motioned to close the door, then she stuck her size 15 between the door and the frame.

"Fine. I'll be back. I hope you don't think he likes you. You're cute--for average citizen--but, his tastes run very high." You would think someone who makes a living off of her looks wouldn't be such an insecure asshat.

"Wow. You are such a grade-A bitch. Good luck seeing Heath. Now go look for someone's else dick to suck on while I ride his." *Slam!* God, she had that coming and it felt so satisfying to finally tell that snotty trashy hellbeast off.

She didn't even know it, but she lit the match and put it to the gasoline, which ended up setting off a chain of events.

Maybe if she hadn't said what she said, it wouldn't have stirred up my emotions, overcoming the last bit of rationality I had left when it came to Heath Hillabrand.

CHAPTER EIGHTEEN

I ran towards the stairs, but then stopped abruptly, made a 180 degree turn and shot to the liquor cabinet, taking down two swigs of tequila. Yup, tequila; just like that night in the sand garden, I needed some liquid cojones stat. The rush of warmth came over me and I instantly felt loose, then headed back up the stairs and busted through the bedroom door.

"Who was it?" Heath asked, bewildered by my rough entrance.

"Just the FedEx guy. I was expecting a package." *Oh god. That line sounded straight out of a terrible porno.*

"At this time? Why are you so out of breath?"

"Shut up."

"Huh? What?"

"Just shut up before I change my mind."

"Wha--okay." I whipped off my shirt so that all I had on was a bra and silk pajama short-shorts. "Woah."

"Let's do this. That is if you want to." There went my self doubt kicking in. *I should've had another swing of tequila. Why can't I just be that sexy vixen in all the books?*

"May I speak again?"

"Yes."

"Hell to the mother fucking yes."

"Okay," I said, taking a deep breath and removing my shorts so that all I had on was a bra and thong.

Heath kind of melted in his spot on the bed. Having this insanely hot man do that at the sight of my body shot me with a jolt of confidence.

"You are fucking awesome. In every way," Heath said, with a smile from ear to ear.

"Oh really?" I said, unclipping and removing my bra. Now, I'll admit, I am rather well-endowed thanks to my Italian grandma. *Gratzi Nonna!*

"Wow. Your tits are fan-fucking-tastic. You need to come over here, like yesterday."

"Okay, here I come," I said as seductively as I could muster.

I crawled in from the foot of the bed, instantly realizing this was going to be a failed attempt at sex appeal, knocking into his casts several times.

"Ahh," he sighed under his breath.

"Oh god, I am so sorry. Maybe I should come around sideways," I said fumbling over his giant encased legs as I doubled back.

I walked over to the side of the bed, using my fingertips to pick up his sling from the bed, and flung it. Heath smirked as his eyes followed its arc across the room, then they came back to me as he licked his lips. He reached his hand over to me and gently glided his fingertips along my waistline and down to my hips, I squirmed.

"You're ticklish too."

"Very."

"I would come to you, but," he tilted his chin down and raised his eyebrows to remind us of his mobility issues.

"That's okay. I can come on you--to you."

"Why don't you take those off first," he pointed to my thong with his nub.

"Certainly, Mr. Hillabrand."

"Ooh, I like that...Mr. Hillabrand. I never commanded the respect that I should have as your boss. I think it's high time."

I slid off my underwear so that now I was completely naked in front of him: exposed, bare, in the exact position I promised I would never allow myself to be when I first met him. But I should have known better, some people just have to fuck, it's in the stars or something. I reached my left hand into his boxers. He was already firm. I knew his sexual appetites were large and that my one handjob left him craving much more. I could certainly tell based on how hard he was.

I grabbed his firmness all the while thinking to myself *I cannot believe I am about to fuck a Calvin Klein model.* He grabbed a handful of ass.

"Are you going to make me wait any longer?"

I carefully mounted him. "Is this okay? Does it hurt?" I asked.

"Even if it did I wouldn't give a shit. I have been wanting to do this ever since I first saw you on the other side of my door."

"You mean when you had just finished fucking Illy?"

"Fuck Illy. Get down here." I leaned over and my breasts grazed his chest, hardening my nipples. We were nose to nose for a moment, our eyes locked, but it was different than it was the night of the party when we kissed. Now we knew each other. When I looked into his eyes, I didn't just see aesthetic perfection, I saw him, I saw the small creases that formed when he *smized. He IS a model, they have smizing down to a science.* It made me suddenly meek, because this wasn't a purely physical encounter, we were committed to each other, at least until he got better. We binge-watched TV, took long walks, ate our meals together, laid on his bed and discussed nothing at all for hours sometimes. And he saw this in my eyes, because he grinned that fucking grin, the one that makes my stomach turn because it's so damned cute and then we both laughed, nose to nose. I turned my chin down as I tried to hide my girlish smile. I'm not a sex kitten, I don't wear my sexuality on my sleeve. It's not that I don't think I'm attractive, but at heart, I am just a girl who likes to cook, I'm simple that way. But occasionally I meet a guy who makes me think pretty much exclusively with my pussy and then all I can think about is rubbing it all over him. He was that person times a thousand.

He lifted my chin up. I could see in his eyes he was wincing, but he wanted to do this. He wanted to make sure I looked into his eyes, and so I didn't kill the moment by asking if he was okay. He was a big boy (in more ways than one) and he knew what he was doing. He kissed me. This time it was slow, it lingered, it was sweet like honey. Instantly, it calmed me. I didn't feel that nervous pit of performance anxiety or fear that I would not live up to the many models he's fucked. That kiss told me he was exactly where he wanted to be.

Then I really leaned in. I wanted to consume him, I had the first bite and now it was game over, I wanted all of him. His right arm, trapped in its cast, rested to the side, but that only meant his left arm went double time, running his fingers through my long hair, grabbing a fist full and pulling it at the roots so he could access and suckle on my neck.

Omgthisisreallyhappeningdotcom. Then he pulled harder, while clenching his jaw, so I would elevate further and he softly kissed my breast at its peak. At this point my crotch was on fire, in the best possible way. Then he stopped, directing my head back down so my eyes would meet his.

"I owe you something."

"Wuh?" All my blood was in my clitoris at this point, so understanding sentences was very difficult.

"I'll need you to do me a favor though and sit on my face. Would you do me the honor?"

I nodded, wide-eyed, and slid myself over his perfect face, resting my hands on the headboard.

"Mmmm..." he said before kissing her softly, tauntingly. Then he guided his tongue through my lips, gliding the tip from the back end up to the clit. I moaned, losing myself in the moment. It had been a long time since I had been with a guy, about a year in fact. Between the eye candy, the excitement, the pent-up sexual frustration, and the physical stimulus, I was about to blow a gasket. His mouth and my pussy just had a party down there. I mean New Years Eve level party: the sucking, this kissing, the licking, all done in perfect ratios and tempos. This is when it helps to fuck a slut--they have had tons of practice to get it right, like the Carnegie Hall of cunnilingus.

Honestly, I came really quickly, almost embarrassingly so, like a boy who nuts in his pants while playing seven minutes in heaven. But really, that was just the appetizer (I love food metaphors, can you tell?), because I still wanted him inside of me. Seriously, it was like all "fire in the hole!" and the only way to put it out was with his cock. So I slid back down and kissed his lips, which were made even softer from kissing my other lips.

I grabbed his cock, rubbing it against my wet labia, readying it to slide inside of me. All I could think about was riding him and releasing all the tension I felt inside my body and thoughts. Then Heath's voice broke through: "Sadie...maybe we should--well, we should--wrap it up?"

"Huh?" The prospect of sex with him plummeted my IQ and innuendo did not seem to be working with me. It was like my attraction to him had lulled me into some sort of sex-induced mania.

"Ya know, we wouldn't want the child soldiers planting a flag on Mount Ovary if you get my drift?"

Wait--did he just say what I think he said? Mount Ovary? Lord help us. "Oh, of course! Yes! *Duh.*" I said, as if I had been thinking about that the entire time. *I had right? I wasn't just about to do him raw? That's what irresponsible and reckless people like Heath do.*

Except he was the one reminding ME.

"It's not you. I do this with all of--" He realized he was about to refer to all of the women he sleeps with and surprisingly, had the decency to stop himself.

"Do you...?"

"Yes, right there in the nightstand."

I whipped it open and fumbled with a long, purple, shiny trail of condoms, ripping one off at the perforation, and using my teeth to open the foil. I pulled it out just as Heath and I had a moment of eye contact. His eyes were turned down at the sides, asking a question without words.

"Oh...you need me?" I pointed at myself then at his dick standing at attention as if it was eagerly waiting for me to shroud it.

"Yeah, if you don't mind," he said shrugging his shoulders. "It's not like you haven't had your hands on him before," he said with a satisfied look on his face. *I am going to fuck that stupid grin off of your face in about two seconds.*

"Just so you know, I'm on the pill. Trust me, I have no interest in procreating with you," I said, as if trying to regain some sort of credibility in this situation.

Heath didn't say anything. He just watched me with an amused look on his face as I rolled out the condom meticulously, making sure there were no air bubbles, trying to prove what a steward of safe sex I was. But that didn't last very long, because his dick was so hard and thick and as pretty as the rest of him and I *needed* it in at least one of my orifices in the next ten seconds.

I was so ready, because I slid right onto his cock as we both let out a collective sigh. If the oral was New Year's, his dick was like Chinese New Year, dragons, parades, acrobats and all. He brushed my hair back, and smiled at me in such a genuine way. I thought back to his question earlier that evening, this was a gazillion times better than licking orangish-yellow imitation cheese off of the bottom of a bowl.

I wanted to ride him like a unbroken stallion, but he placed his hands on my hips and with a smirk said: "slower babe." *Oh that's right, about 40% of him is broken and did he just call me babe?* I'm glad he slowed me down because it allowed me to really appreciate the feeling of him inside of me. I leaned over him, my hair cascading on either side of his face, so close I heard his shallow breathing, felt his warm breath against my skin. He cupped one of my breasts in his hands and gently pursed his lips around my nipple, placing just the right amount of pressure with his gentle tugs.

That triggered the fireworks portion of the parade in my cooch.

"Fuck," I moaned as I felt the tension build around his throbbing hardness. His dick seemed to hit every possible erogenous zone inside of me.

Again he fisted my hair, tilting my head back, sucking and gently biting all along my neck. I moaned louder.

"Sadie, god your pussy is so sweet," he said, his breathy voice so much heavier than his normally light and carefree manner.

"Heath..." I begged.

"Come for me. Let my dick make you come." His mouth returned to my breast at the exact moment it all went off like a burst of lightening, and we came together with a chorus of *fucks, I'm comings!, Sadies, Heaths,* war cries, and *oh gods.*

CHAPTER NINETEEN

I rolled off of him, a panting, quivering mess. Oh my god that was everything and then some. Then out of the corner of my eye, I looked over at him, at his satisfied smirk and I wanted to stab myself in the eye.

What the fuck Sadie? Fuckfuckfuck. You just fucked your boss. Not a handjob, or a kiss, or a flirtation, you just fucked your temporarily handicapped boss ten ways from Sunday and six ways from Saturday! You just gave him what he always wanted. All it took was a couple of weeks and you were spreading your legs wider than Illy's cavernous, used-up vagina.

My body wanted me to lay there, hell maybe even roll over and snuggle with his arm cast, but I had to disappear. I had to salvage any dignity I had left, let him know the ball was still in my court.

Fuck Illy, he said. Trust me, that sent a jolt through me like you couldn't imagine. He didn't make an excuse or defend her, she wasn't even a thought. But I am sure if Illy was wrapped around his dick, he would have said the same about me. Suddenly, I found myself angry at him over this hypothetical conversation I had just created in my head. I imagined Illy's loud, callous, man-laugh filling the room and Heath turning over to look at me in slow motion, saying "*fuuuuck Saaaaadie muahahaha*" (don't ask me how I would be there to see it).

Before Heath could open his mouth, which knowing him, was an inevitability, I rolled over and dismounted off of the bed.

"Where are you going?" he asked. His confusion seemed so genuine, I almost felt sorry for him.

"To bed," I said, collecting fragments of my wardrobe from various parts of the room. I felt more naked than ever.

"You don't have to go."

"That's okay. Bye," I said as I slipped through the doorway, only opening the door to the precise amount needed to slide out.

As I marched over to my room, I caught myself smiling. *Stop that dammit.* Then the next second, I was balling up my hair at the scalp, wanting to pull it out of my head, then smiling to myself again. And then my heart sank recalling the moment I lost myself, like some sort of moron: I almost forgot to use protection with this skankwhore! Normally, I would already be calling the CDC for a spraydown ala Outbreak, but clearly he seems to be more mindful of this kind of stuff than even me. My stomach swirled with an uneasy feeling thinking about how he made me act so out of character. Heath Hillabrand is bad news...no, he's the *worst* news. But the way he kissed me, it was almost tender. The way he could make me feel like I was the sexiest woman alive, made him irresistible. This couldn't all be a coincidence, could it?

I had to stop myself. I was better than this, I was above my fucking boss's 50s workplace policies. I had worked under Brock for years and I never fucked him, and I know I could have. What was it about Heath that sucked me in like a black hole? *Lawd, help me.*

Then in the way that you only remember shit when you are laying in bed, it occurred to me that Mindy would be visiting tomorrow, late morning. I instantly panicked imagining myself opening the door only for her to see SEXWHORESEXWHORESEX stamped all over my face. Mindy was sharper than an old man's toenails and she was in the people business. Sometimes I swore she had ESP. But alas, she was coming and there was nothing I could do but pretend I didn't taste Heath's sweet lips, feel his warm chest against mine, enjoy his wet lips on my nipples...nope, we just played checkers or some shit.

***

The morning after, I didn't do my usual check in with Heath because I wanted to lengthen the amount of time before I saw him after the whole dick riding thing that took place between us the night before. I texted him so he wasn't just sitting there with his thumb up ~~my~~ his ass (mistake and it's staying there) to let him know that I would be arriving soon with his breakfast. I know, nothing says "business as usual" as texting someone whose room you just walked by and could have easily spoken with. Not awkward in the least bit.

Eventually, I came upstairs with the food tray and took one lung-busting breath before using my elbow to open his bedroom door.

"Good morning," he said, more chipper than ever.

"Morning," I said curtly. He had to understand that last night meant nothing. The ball was still in my court, I didn't need him, hell I didn't even want him, except when I did.

We silently went through the morning ritual of getting him in his chair, which was easier now that he was several weeks away from the accident and healing nicely.

I ate my food silently. The chirps of birds and our forks clanking against our plates were the only sounds on the patio. I was stewing in self-hatred. How could I have fucked this pompous ass? Sure, just like Mindy said, assholes make great friends, but that's only if you never crossed the line, and I didn't just cross the line, the line fingered me, then I gave it a handjob, then it fucked me and ate me out. *I am such an idiot.*

That's when I noticed him looking up coyly at me from his plate, hiding a grin. That sly look on his face was like an invisible force tugging on my panties.

"What is it?" I said firmly, taking a sip from my morning tea.

"Are we going to play this charade every time? I'll admit it's cute, but it's a bit of a mindfuck. Maybe that's what you're going for. I don't know." I hated how blunt he was. Couldn't he just deal with innuendo and mixed signals like the rest of us human beings?

"There's no charade," I said casually.

"It would be a lot easier on you if you just admitted to yourself that it's okay to want me. I get it, I'm awesome."

"As if."

"I'm not even sure what that means."

"Don't flatter yourself is what I am saying."

He laughed in disbelief. "Am I living in another dimension? You rode me last night. You came to me and told me to shut up and fucked me. There, I said it!"

"So, what do you want me to do? Write a dissertation on it?"

"I want you to stop being such a fucking coward." Woah, that veered sharply into WTF territory. Heath and his not-quite non-sequiturs.

"Don't call me that."

"You fucking take what you want from me when you want it and then run away when you're done and you are goddam lucky I can't chase you."

"You mean what you do to everyone else? Someone can't take what they dish. What, you expect me to fawn all over you? I know your game, and I am not going to play into it. I am not the one!"

"So, that's what you think of me, some kind of emotional puppetmaster?"

"Not quite, since that would take cunning. You are a pompous, egotistical, arrogant, rude, tactless, asshole."

"God you're a bitch. I don't have to take your attitude, I have been more than nice to you. You know what you are, you are an uptight...yeah I know you love that don't you? Uptight, stuck-up, prissy, prudish, snob. And your pussy is wound up so tight that whenever I get close to it, you don't even know what to do with yourself."

I froze for a moment. That barrage of words might have been the most he has ever strung together since we met. I had taken advantage of his laid-back manner. He was an asshole, but in a dismissive way, not an aggressive way. But now I did it. I triggered something in him that royally pissed him off. And that was the point, I think, to turn him against me, to make him hate me, so that he would push me away and fucking wouldn't be an option. My plan was working, but why did it ache when he said those words? And why in holy hell was my crotch lighting up?

"Fuck you. I don't owe you an explanation and I don't need to take this. Mindy's coming later and she doesn't know shit and she better not know. You're on your own until then." Clear. Now all I had to do was march back into the house and this argument would have bought me (hopefully) another day without wondering what his dick would taste like in my mouth. I stood up sharply and turned to walk away, but then I felt a firm grip on my wrist. I tried to pull away, but it was solid, which was surprising considering how inactive he had been from the shoulder injury.

He pulled me back hard so that I stumbled towards him, and as I got closer he quickly pulled my night shirt so that I landed on his lap and the monument he had erected for me in his boxers.

I let out a hiss of air through my teeth. Just feeling his hard cock on my backside made all of my manufactured rage convert into something else.

"Sadie, I'm sick of playing fucking games with you and I am sick of your bullshit." He ran his hand up my back, over my ribcage and onto my breast, letting out a breath as he squeezed it. "I fucking love your tits." I was frustrated by his inability to really ravage me like I knew he wanted to. When those casts came off, all hell was going to break loose if we kept up this pace.

I clenched the arms of the wheelchair, pressing my toes to the floor to keep it from wandering away. My heart was speeding at a rate that I was sure was reserved for meth-heads, and then he slid his fingers over my mouth. I grabbed his large hand by the thumb and ring finger and mouth-fucked his fingers, wetting them, knowing what he would do next.

He took his hand and pulled up my night shirt.

"You're not wearing panties. I fucking knew it." And now I knew it, Heath was smart, he was calculated: there was the playful Heath, the non-threatening Heath and he used that to make me feel secure, like I was in control, but now he knew I wanted him so badly that I was lying to myself, and this gave him that power that I was so scared to turn over to him. But, *ooh* did it feel so good.

He slid his forefinger and ring finger inside of me, rubbing his palm against my clit. I leaned back, feeling his heaving chest against my back. He was sweaty, the sun was already heating up the balcony on this summer morning. My nipples stung against the thin fabric of my nightie, and I was feeling him all over my body, even on places he wasn't touching, like little firecrakers on my nerve endings.

His thick cock throbbed against my tailbone and I rubbed my ass against it. I wanted him inside me again, I needed him inside me again. I pulled my nightshirt all the way past my hips, a visual invitation.

"Your ass is so juicy," he said, biting my neck. *Who is this guy that looks like this and talks like this? Where* do *they manufacture these?* "God you are so wet, you're soaking my shorts," he said, pleased with himself I'm sure. I kept grinding against him, *let's do this*, I thought. I stood up a little, hoping he would pull his shorts down, I knew he wanted to fuck me, his dick was nearly ready to burst.

"Nuh uh. I'm not playing your little bitchy games."

"Whuha?" I asked breathlessly. He lifted his hand up to the top of my nightie, which had a racer back tank, and gripped the two ends of the top towards the center of my breasts, so they both popped out and were propped up by the way the nightie now framed them. I could see our transparent reflection in the sliding doors in front of us, and we looked so beautifully strange and twisted: his gorgeous body still covered in casts, my soft curves against the harsh white, his face-- that fucking amazing face that I rode the night before.

I leaned my head back and rubbed my cheek against him as he sucked on my neck, my cheeks, the edges of my lips, tugging them, pulling them so that it almost hurt, but then releasing them so they popped back. Our lips grazed as my hips ground against him begging to fuck me; my moans grew louder.

"Stop."

He left the tank top, which stayed put, nicely displaying my breasts and flattened his hand against my hips. He sensed I was about to come and he was right, he had me so hot that I was about to come from rubbing on his lap. I stopped and so did the sounds of our moans, so that now there was just bated panting with the backdrop of birds chirping. My first instinct was to protest, but I was still angry at him and felt that I needed to maintain the silent treatment, because, you know, it was *so effective*. I just wanted him to straight fuck me without any sort of dialogue so I wouldn't have to truly think about the fact that I found myself riding his dick AGAIN.

"I'm not going to play your fucking games anymore. If you want me to fuck you, then ask me to do it and I will do it wholeheartedly."

I clenched my lips, and I swear in the distance I heard the teeny tiny high-pitched voice of my pussy screaming: *Do it bitch! Tell him to stick his delicious cock inside of you!* I bit my lip. I needed to be defiant, I mean he called me all those horrible things. And yeah, so did I to him, but I was right!

"I guess you don't want it then." His lips were so close, I could feel them tickling my neck as he said this. I was so engorged, so full of arousal that for the first time I think I understood what blue balls might feel like. It wasn't even a choice anymore, I needed to feel him inside of me.

"That's okay. We don't have to do anything you don't want, Sadie. He slid his hand over my breasts, hyper-faintly rubbing one of my nipples. My hips involuntarily gyrated. "No. Not until you tell me like an adult what you want to do here. No shame, no looking away and pretending it didn't happen."

And then the rat-bastard ran his hand down my stomach, then in between my thighs, and massaged me again while his tongue licked a trail from my shoulder to the nape of my neck.

"Fuck me. Just fuck me," I said; my queen had fallen just when I thought I had the winning move.

He balled up the nightie and I pulled out his dick, I couldn't get it in me fast enough. And this time we both lost our senses, even though he made me ask, he wanted it just as badly and as urgently as I did. When I slid onto him, I can't even tell you the surge that emanated from in between my legs to every extremity. I let out a quivering cry of pleasure, he had made me want it more than I ever thought I could. He wrapped his arm across my frontside, clenching my right breast, gaining leverage so that every time I lifted off of his cock, he pressed me back down, going in deep...so deep. My ears filled with the violent creaking of the metal wheelchair and his breathing and stifled moans into my neck. His other arm, still in a cast, wrapped around my waist, I clawed at it and his arm, almost suffocating under his grip and my desire. I was fighting him, fighting myself, fighting how badly I wanted him inside of me with each thrust. But he understood, and held firm, I think I was loud, really loud, because he covered my mouth.

"Goddam, Sadie. Everything about you, your taste, your smell...the feel of your wet pussy..." I think I cried out his name with some other nonsense. The thought crossed my mind the neighbors might think Heath was killing me. "I can't...I'm about to..." I knew he was trying to warn me, but knowing that I was so desirable to him that Mr. Sex couldn't keep his dick from exploding inside of me set me off. We didn't--*couldn't*--stop this time and even pretend to be responsible adults.

Then I exploded, tensing, clenching, grabbing at him frantically, his cast, his hands, as if the feeling was so good I needed to escape my own body, but had no where to go. He kept his hands on my mouth and fought me, pressing me against him, and I felt his tenseness disappear as he released a guttural groan into my neck.

Seriously, I was frightened. I didn't know what just happened, I had never been fucked like that. It was almost violent and it jarred something in me. All I wanted to do was stay guarded since I met him, but this was a total unraveling, I came undone on his lap and lost complete control.

CHAPTER TWENTY

As seemed to be the frequent case during those days I was cooped up and isolated with Heath, I lost track of time. I glanced over at the digital clock in his room and saw the time: 10:35am.

"*Shitshitshit!*" I exclaimed, panicked, yet glad have an excuse to escape the dense air around me. I couldn't even look him in the eyes right now. I tried to dismount Heath, but I stumbled, not realizing how weak in the knees I still was.

"What is it?"

"Remember, your manager is coming over! And you know she's always on time. I have to shower. And you...shit!"

"Take a breath. I have an arm now, I can handle the whole waterless bath, not that I needed your help before. I cannot fucking wait to get these casts removed."

"Just a few days," I said, out of breath as I scrambled to put everything back on the tray. "Wait, what?"

"Huh?"

"What did you say about not needing my help?" I knocked over an empty glass.

"You can get it later," he said.

"Are you implying that whole thing was some sort of ploy?"

"Just trying to get you to not go all dark on me."

"You don't drop a nugget like that and then tell me to leave. I should stab you with this fork!" And shit for a moment I forgot about how I quivered around his cock and yelled out, how he bit into my neck, how he swelled inside of me as he came...and I looked him in the eyes. And just for a fragment of a second, there was a knowing look, that there would be a pre-balcony fuck Heath and Sadie, and a post-balcony fuck Heath and Sadie. Then everything went back to its normal pace. I didn't feel like I had to assure him that Mindy shouldn't know, I think he knew whatever was happening between us, we should keep between ourselves.

"I was just messing with you. I wanted to get you to talk. Now go!"

I ran into the shower, letting the hot water rain onto my body, and now under the calm of the soothing spray, I relived it all in my head. I watched the droplets roll over the spots where he touched me, where I swear I could still feel his squeezes and his bites on my skin. And I'll be damned if I wasn't getting horny all over again. I pressed a hand against the shower wall, ducked my head, and just rested there for a moment to collect my thoughts. I felt like I was losing it, like some stupid fucking juvenile who couldn't stop herself from obsessing over a crush. I couldn't make logical decisions around this man. He had me under some type of *dicknosis*. Over and over, I had to remind myself to breathe, because every time I thought of him, I would involuntarily stop. And mother of all things big and small, he was temporarily handicapped! I think I might actually drop dead if he fucked me while all of his limbs were in working order. That would be very soon. His fractures were healing nicely and the doctor said he would be out of the chair and on crutches by the end of the week. But there was no more time for ruminating because Mindy would be here any minute.

Luckily we planned on hanging out at the pool so I didn't have to think much about my wardrobe. I threw on a coverup and ran back into Heath's room to snatch something from his bikini drawer.

"Oh hey." He seemed pleasantly surprised to see me back so quickly.

"Just need to grab one of these if you don't mind."
"Not at all."

"Are you good?"

"All cleaned up, I might need some help getting on some trunks. These elephant legs make it impossible."

"Of course," I said, rummaging through the drawer trying to make odds and ends of the mess of bikinis. I silently attempted to calculate what the number of bikinis translated into as far as sexual partners. *Thank god he's responsible when it comes to wrapping up his johnson. I totally just lost my shit on that balcony.*

"The green one," he said.

"The one I wore when I first got here?" I didn't expect such a conservative choice.

"No, it's in there. Emerald green. It would look nice on your olive skin." It sounded sweet, almost endearing, but when I pulled it out I understood the real reason. It was all strings and triangles, but dammit, the truth was I wanted him to see me prancing around the pool in this thing.

I hastily put it on in my room (even though he had seen me completely naked, I was no where near freely dressing around him) and I returned to Heath. He was waiting on his wheelchair with his shorts resting on his lap, a single rogue tendril resting on his forehead, like a kid waiting for his mom to dress him. *Fucking adora--STOP.*

I was in such a rush that I forgot to throw on my cover up. I pulled off his boxers, pretending I wasn't just begging for him to stick that very dick inside of me twenty minutes ago. He had a semi again (I honestly had not yet seen his penis in a flaccid state around me), and then it grew steadily.

"Wow, you wear that bikini well."

"Thank you," I said as if he has just complimented my choice of mutual fund.

"I thought you weren't going to do this again."

"I'm not!" I said, wrangling the shorts over his casts. How was I supposed to act? Was there a textbook for how to act after your boss fucks you scared? When he makes you question your sense of ethics? When you live with him, bathe him, take him for walks...oh AND he's a fucking model? Because if there is, I'll one-click a bitch.

He's used to people being all googly eyed, all "call me whenever you want baby," but every time we did something, I convinced myself it would be the last time, including this last time.

The doorbell rang as if Mindy really possessed some sort of manager sixth sense that I had always suspected. She was really saving my ass today.

"I'll be back," I said, running down to greet her.

"Sadie!" She embraced me. Something about that hug made me feel like a fraud.

"Thank god you're here." She literally squeezed the words out of me. I quickly covered up. "I needed some estrogen in this house."

"Are you two wringing each others' necks?" I resisted to urge to burst into a combination of tears and hysterical laughter. "Where is that handsome fella?"

"He's upstairs. I gotta bring him down."

"Minds!" Heath said jovially as she walked in the room. How can he do that, just act all fucking normal, like his world didn't just implode and then explode like some sort of genital big bang?

"You look like you've lost some weight my sweets," she said placing her cheek to his and smooching. Sometimes I envied how she could be so openly affectionate, even though I usually saw it as over the top and garish when she was.

"Haven't been able to exercise, obviously."

"But you'll be out of the casts soon?"

"Very."

"Yay, I am so happy for you!"

Heath had a content look on his face, and then I remembered what he said to me, that day I first realized that underneath the piggish behavior, there might be a real person

138

underneath: he didn't have anyone. Right now, Mindy and I were his people. He had all of his people in one room, and that realization kind of kicked me in the stomach.

"Let's go to the pool!" Mindy exclaimed. "God, work has been a fucking grizzly bear. I would like just one afternoon to soak in the sun and maybe get laid by a handsome, young, wealthy executive of some sort. Is that too much to ask?"

I quickly darted my eyes away. *Sex is no big deal to you, act casual, nothing to see here.* In an effort to divert my eyes from Mindy, they somehow landed on Heath's and he did that shy smirk thing he does occasionally and just like that, my green bikini bottoms were dampened.

It was another beautiful summer day. We listened to Mindy bitch about all of her goings-on at work as we sat by the pool. Heath was quieter than usual, and I couldn't tell if that was because Mindy exhausted him as much as she did me sometimes or if it was because he was thinking about the balcony. All I was sure of is I could not stop drifting away as mini flashbacks continually violated my thoughts.

"Isn't that so ridiculous?" Mindy asked. About what? I had no idea.

"Uh...yeah." I said, faintly laughing, hoping that whatever she was referring to had a modicum of humor to it. I vowed to continue listening to her speak this time and I didn't even realize that I had again drifted away until another voice interrupted.

"Why the stupid grin?" It was Heath, and my brain registered it about five seconds after he asked, so that when I finally slowly turned to acknowledge him both Mindy and Heath were intently staring at me, stifling their laughter.

"Someone's head is in the clouds!" Mindy said. "Did you meet someone out here?" She asked in a syrupy-sweet tone, batting her eyelashes. She clearly didn't believe her words because: 1) everyone thinks I am uptight man-hater and no fun

2) I would have told her by now 3) I am a serial monogamist and I rarely do "flings."

It was an ambush, and my eyes shot around a bit bewildered, as if I had woken up from one of those terrible mid-day naps where you're not sure if you've slept for one hour or one day. "Oh shut up!" I said defensively. "I don't even remember what I was thinking." I imagined re-fracturing Heath's leg with a swift kick. Then her stupid phone that she can never be without rang.

"Fuck me sideways," she said answering it. "Mindy Sloane...What? No!...Fuck that...Get him on the phone right now...I don't care where the fuck he is. I am poolside in the Hamptons and he doesn't seem to give a shit about that, does he?...Fine...Call me back ASAP." She shook her head in dismay. "Another fire I have to put out. Anyway, I was going to mention that you fuckers are almost out of tequila." *My bad.* "I wanted to make some margaritas, so I'll go grab it."

"I can go with." *Please dear god, don't leave me alone with Heath.*

"Sweets, the call is confidential. So I need to be alone anyway." I had never heard her refer to anyone as *Sweets* until today, must have been some term she picked up from a client since I last saw her. I expected she would now overuse it until she tired of it in a month or so.

As she threw on her cover up and tote and headed for the house, I shot up. "Alright, well I'll put together some snacks while you're gone."

"Great, I'll need something to soak up the booze."

I followed her into the house like a puppy and my heart sank like a stone as she walked out the door. I was alone with a predator on the loose. I relished the solitude of the kitchen, as Heath never seem interested in the process, just the final product. As I bent over to pull out something from the crisper, I heard the ominous squeaking of his wheelchair. *I should have ripped his shoulder back out of its socket when I had the chance.* My

140

heartbeat hitched for a beat and I continued in my quest of regressing to a fifth grader by pretending I didn't hear him behind me.

"Nice view," he said.

He had my number. He wasn't going to tip-toe around me like I had trained him to do, he knew now that he could be forward and there was a great likelihood that I might fuck him anyway. I had a sample, and I was hooked: Heath was my dick pusher.

I placed the veggies on the counter without saying a word. If I just ignored him, maybe he would disappear. Mindy's words echoed in my head: *As long as you stay in the friend-zone guys like that are really fun to be around. They're really only jerks to the women they feel they have power over.*

Stupidstupidstupid.

"We don't have to talk," he said. I could feel him behind me and my whole body became rigid. I felt his lips on the small of my back. *Mmmmm.*

"Mindy could be back any minute." I said flatly.

"She *does* speak," I could feel his smirk. I rolled my eyes, and I had a sense he could feel that too. "You know Minds, she'll be gone for a while."

"And what makes you think I want to do anything but prepare some snacks?"

"Because I saw your face at the pool and because you're quiet. You only talk to me when you think sex isn't in the cards for us. I guess you hate me that much, but I'm willing to be the fall guy here."

"How selfless."

"I'll admit, something about your self-loathing every time we fuck is kind of hot."

"The only guy in the world who's happy to admit when a woman hates herself for fucking him."

"Well, I know you hate it because you wanted it, because you liked it. I was there remember? I could hear you whimpering like a puppy. Or was it more howling like a banshee?" *Pig.* He slid his hand over the crotch of my swimsuit. *Busted.* "See? You're wet."

I wriggled my hips, but it seemed to only provide him with better friction as he cupped the space between my legs, providing enough pressure to make me super aroused without overstimulating. I released the knife I was holding as a possible option for dealing with Heath. He bit the meat where my back curves into my ass. "When I'm back on my feet again, you are going to have no idea what hit you."

"That won't happen. This will be the last time. I'm your best friend. Remember when you said that? Best friends don't do this."

"Debatable." He abruptly swatted my legs open, followed by the act of pulling the swimsuit down to my knees. "I know we've made a big deal about your tits, but your ass..." Then he bit one of the cheeks, hard, and I jumped. *This is so bad.* Then I felt the warmth of his mouth, his tongue slowly making its way into me. He was measured, there was no rush in his rhythm. I overhand gripped the edge of the countertop that dug into my waist. I needed to hold onto something, to transfer the force that was gripping me, but the hard, cold edges of the granite weren't good enough. I reached behind to grab a hold of him, then I turned, to see his messy hair appearing over the horizon of my backside. He was deep in, moaning, enjoying my taste. I grabbed his messy golden locks. He responded with longer, more passionate strokes of his tongue, only stopping to tell me how hard I made him.

He reached around my hips, pulling me closer as if he couldn't get enough of me, taste enough of me. And it was happening again, I was losing control, my hips rocking back into his face like I was fucking it doggy style. And my mouth opened, singing all kinds of involuntary sounds. A combination of curses, calls out to the lord, and wails, all capped off with a "you motherfucker," poured out of my mouth. I yanked his hair. And

142

then there I was coming. Hard. Slapping down on the counter with one hand, and pulling Heath's face deeper into me by his hair roots with the other, all the while rocking my body back and forth into his face.

"All right, well I have to go. Glad we could--Oh god." The sound of something solid crashed onto the floor. I looked up, still mid orgasm and saw the giant "O" formed by Mindy's mouth. *Looks like I finally found a way to shut her up.* I was still doing the stanky leg, my body wasn't ready to stop even though my mind wanted to. Heath popped his head out of my nether-regions. "Oh," was all I heard him say.

She quietly knelt, feeling the floor for her phone, stood up, made a robotic 180 degree turn and walked back out. "I'm gonna give you two a moment..." she barely uttered as the door closed behind her.

"Shitshitshit." I said pulling my bottom back up. Heath, was of course, laughing.

I fumbled around for a bit, looking for I don't know what.

"It's just Minds."

"No. Just shut up," I said putting my hand up. "No one was supposed to know and this isn't even a thing," I said wagging my finger between him and me. "I am going to talk to her, let her know that was a one time deal and that there's nothing going on here."

"Yup."

"Because you are my client and this is unacceptable."

"Uh huh."

My legs were still iffy from the encounter, so I walked towards the entrance like a newborn deer. I found Mindy sitting on the veranda, the bottle of tequila open in her hands.

"Was it that traumatic?" I asked.

"I thought I'd kill the next few minutes while you two finished up." I sat next to her and she handed me the bottle with out even looking over. I took it.

"For the record, that was a one-time thing. Never happening again."

She slowly rolled her neck to face me with an expression that read: *you are so full of shit.*

"What I just saw looked like two people who have been secretly fucking, trying to sneak in a quickie. I highly doubt you chose my impromptu store run to give it your first go."

"I meant in the general sense it was a one time thing, the tryst. It's over now."

"Okay," she said nodding, clearly not believing a word I said. "Looked like it was good," she said, snatching the tequila back.

"It was okay."

She laughed hard, swigging back a shot. "Holy shit, he fucked your brains out, didn't he?" I scrunched my lips. "Sadie, he's gorgeous, he's fun, he's a playboy. I bet he's a great lay. This is exactly the guy who you want to fuck around with for the summer. Not everything has to be so clearly defined."

That's not how my brain worked. I needed clear guidelines around my relationships. And I knew that's all it would be to Heath: I would be the girl to hold him over until he was literally back on his two feet, then it would be back to model threesomes. I don't know how I could handle that, being another checkmark on his list of conquests.

"You don't like him, do you? I know you have a penchant for the emotionally unavailable, but he is like an alien as far as human relationship emotions go."

"No! He's fucking annoying and a jackass. I think it's the proximity. It's just the two of us. And yes, he's undeniably gorgeous, but I really didn't want to go down this path. I thought I could teach him a lesson."

"Oh fuck a lesson! Life's too short. Have you thought about the fact that maybe he's teaching you a lesson in having fun?"

"Bwahaha!" The laugh shot sharply out of my gut. "I am surrounded by enablers," I muttered.

"If you are looking to me for moral guidance, you have certainly come to the wrong place." She gave me the bottle. "All I can say is keep it straight fucking, don't fall in love. And you'll be golden, pony boy."

"Not a problem in the least bit."

"Alright, time to pull off the bandaid and go back inside," she declared.

As soon as I stood up, Mindy let out a wail of laughter.

"What?"

"There's a bite mark on your ass!"

CHAPTER TWENTY-ONE

Heath was by the pool again, I should have known not to expect an awkward reaction from him. That would require some sort of shame.

"Have you recovered?" he asked Mindy, with a smart-ass smirk on that son-of-a-bitch face of his.

"Just finished scheduling an appointment with my therapist," she said, dipping her feet in the pool. "Well I'm glad someone got some today, it doesn't seem like any gorgeous, enigmatic billionaires are dropping by any time soon."

"Don't look at me, your arrival left me with the most painful case of blue balls known to man."

"How appropriate," I quipped.

"Well, good," Mandy interjected. "You'll have to suffer along with me for as long as I am here. Misery loves company."

"Although I will admit, I think what you're lacking, Minds, are these sweet wheels," Heath gestured to his wheelchair, which glimmered in the afternoon sun. "Sadie can't get enough of me on this thing." I visualized pushing him into the pool. *Bet it would be tough to hold that content, shit-eating grin while screaming like a little girl, wouldn't it?* His blunt remark left me speechless for a moment because it was sort of true, but so damned cocky at the same time and warranted some sort of comeback. However, my mind drew a blank. Before I could set him straight, Mindy spoke.

"What's that saying? The squeaky wheel gets the taco?"

"Oh dear god," I huffed reflexively, under my breath, but loud enough for them to hear.

"No I think it's the squeaky wheel gets the lube, isn't it?" Heath added. "No...no wait...it's the squeaky wheel gets to put his face in Sadie's ass." Mindy's eyes almost popped out of her skull as they erupted into laughter.

"You are both terrible, vile people," I said in feigned disgust, crossing my arms and turning away to walk into the house.

Both Mindy and Heath continued laughing themselves to tears, humored by my mortification.

"You have to appreciate the food metaphor!" Mindy called out to me.

"Mind…stop…don't laugh," I heard Heath say in between his chuckles. *Could he be trying to be a gentleman?* "Seriously, Sadie makes the best tacos and I'm afraid she won't look at them the same again." Their laughter resumed.

"The both of you are cut from the same asshole cloth," I said with my back facing to them as I continued on my path, my lips curved into a tight grin.

"You love us!" Mindy called out as I sought some refuge in the kitchen to finish making snacks, but now the kitchen was tainted with our sex, and my one sanctuary now had his name written all over it.

***

Mindy decided to stay for the entire weekend, which was great news. I pretty much stalked her, knowing that her presence would keep me abstinent, not that I had any intention of sleeping with Heath again.

Then Monday rolled around and I took him to have his casts removed. Heath was overjoyed, but he wasn't over the hump yet. He had to wear moonboots (so I called them) and use crutches. He would be going to physical therapy every day to speed up his recovery. The one thing that struck me now that he was back on his feet was his height. I googled his stats (don't make that face): he was 6'3," just as he had claimed, which apparently was on the upper end of male model heights. Mindy was right, he had lost some weight, he would be the only person in the Milky Way to sit on his ass for six weeks and not get fat.

Instead, his muscles had lost some of their bulk, but he was still very much a specimen of physical perfection. He just leaned towards "I was born this hot" rather than "I go to the gym every day to look this hot."

The first thing he said on our drive home: "I desperately want a shower. A long, hot, steamy shower." He stretched out those last words seductively as he closed his eyes and ran his fingers through his hair.

"You sure that's safe? You're supposed to take it easy."

"I'll sit, I don't give a damn. I just need that. You have no idea."

Mindy being around helped kill some of the momentum and allowed me to recalibrate a bit. But now that she was gone, and he mentioned being in a steamy shower, my lady parts started to betray me again with a tingle. Our last encounter felt so incomplete. I was left wanting to feel his dick inside of me, to ride him again, but then Mindy popped in and it all ended before any of that could happen.

That's what do-overs are for? Right? I cursed under my breath at the thought.

"What was that?" Heath asked.

"Nothing."

I waited for him to make a lewd comment, to tease me, to generally try to make me miserable and hate myself, but he didn't and it made me more frustrated by his constant redirection.

"I'm going to get back to my old self fast, they say four weeks, I give it two."

"Of course, superman."

When we got back to the house, Heath, just as he promised, headed straight for the stairs in the direction of his shower.

"Let's get you on the lift."

"No."

"You just got your casts taken off, you're supposed to take it easy between therapy sessions."

"I am not getting on that stupid geriatric lift again. Ever."

"But it's *so* fast," I said sarcastically. He sneered at me. "If you fall, you'll kill us both."

"Well I guess we'll have to make sure I don't fall then."

"Stubborn jackass," I muttered under my breath. He looked at me out of the corner of his eyes and repressed a satisfied smile.

We labored up the staircase. With each step I grew progressively angrier at him, he was just so eager to get back to his old ways that he had me doing this shit.

"This is so stupid," I said, about halfway up.

"Do you have to fight me on everything?"

"Only because everything you do is stupid."

"Wow, you're moody today."

"I wonder why. It wouldn't have anything to do with this giant man putting all his weight on me."

"You could use the workout." *Yes, he went there.*

"It's funny you mention that, chicken legs."

"At least I have an excuse."

"I am so done with you today once I get you up the stairs. In fact, I plan to throw you back down. And my husky build will give me the perfect leverage to do so."

He let out a quick burst of laughter from his gut, betraying his asshole act.

Eventually, we made it to his bedroom and he plopped his ass on the bed, ripping at the velcro on this moonboots and kicking them off.

"You know I was just kidding, right? Your body is perfect. I needed to get you angry so your superhuman man-strength would come through. You almost turn green whenever I piss you off. Been exposed to any gamma rays recently?"

"No it's okay, I'm not 5'11, 110 pounds like your usual pick of the litter," I said, picking up clothes he had left strewn on the floor. *Slob.*

"Oh cut it out, that's what I'm mostly around, but that's not my preference. Besides you are grossly exaggerating, most girls with those stats are like 16 years old, and I know you think very lowly of me, but I don't mess with that."

"So what is your ideal?" I asked nonchalantly. I knew I shouldn't follow him down this path, but he sparked my curiosity.

"My type?" He leaned back against his palms, and thought for a second. "Slender but curvy. I love shapely legs and a tight ass. Perky, round tits. Natural ones." I looked over from the corner of my eye and he was eyeing me. I wasn't sure if he was just describing me to make me uncomfortable, or that I genuinely happened to be his type. "Brunette, height doesn't matter as long as it's not freakish in either direction. I like exotic types. Almond shaped eyes." His voice slowed with each criterion, as if his mind was drifting into a daydream or all his blood was transferring from his brain to his penis (the latter was more likely). Then he went silent. That's when I realized he had stealthily stood up and walked the three or four paces to stand behind me while I was bent over picking up a t-shirt from the floor.

"You aren't supposed to be on your feet without the crutches!" I scolded, as if that was the only thing wrong with this situation.

"Come shower with me." He ran his hand under my mini floral sundress. I shuddered as I stood up and felt his hardened cock on my back. He slid his hand over to my hip crease and then his other hand did the same on the other side, pressing me against him. *Oh god, he has two hands now. Someone save me.* "Come shower with me," he begged in my ear as he grazed it with his teeth. His voice changed, and something about the way he could do that, could go from silly and juvenile to throaty and sexy, lit me ablaze.

"No," I said, pushing my ass further towards his groin. He lost his balance for a second since his legs were weak, but he pushed back into me. One of his hands slid up from under my dress, flipping up the small ruffles at the hem, and slid up to my breast. Right then, I convinced myself I needed a do-over, I needed to know what it would feel like to have him eye-to-eye, both hands on me.

He removed the hand from my thigh and brushed my hair away from my neck, teasing, kissing, biting softly. "I can feel how wet you are. Why do you feel the need to fight me?"

"You know why," I said, giving him my neck. "Because you're a cock."

"I'll give you my cock."

"Case in point," I said as he ran his lips down my neck. I could hear him inhaling deeply, taking in my scent. "I know who you are. I had you pegged from the second we met. I am not one of your little whores."

He slipped a finger inside of me. "You're not?"

"Fuck you."

"Absolutely."

"You're such an asshole."

"I know and that's why you want me to fuck you."

I spun around. "You're just a pretty face Heath. It would serve you to shut the fuck up."

He sneered and shoved his face into mine, our lips never lost contact as he plopped back onto the bed. I clawed at his shirt whipping it off over his head as he pulled down the top of my dress.

"Keep it on," he said. I realized we weren't going to make it to the shower. He grabbed my ass and hoisted me on top of him, grunting like an animal as I rubbed myself on his cock. We were kissing hard, like we wanted to injure each other. He squeezed my ass painfully, but all it did was make me press against his body harder. It's like I wanted to get back at him for something by fucking him, although that made no logical sense. I wrapped my legs around his waist and in one explosive move I

152

was under him. I was surprised at how agile he was considering he was not even close to his old self.

"I'm going to fuck the smartass out of you." He looked genuinely frustrated as his brow formed a glisten of sweat. He nearly tore his belt buckle open, and ferociously unbuttoned his jeans .

"Good luck," I said as he pulled my thong so hard to the side, I heard a tear.

"You know what to do."

"Whuh?"

"Tell me you want it. I'm not going to give it to you otherwise." He had his thick, long dick in his hands, and he was sliding the smooth tip along my wet lips.

"No, you arrogant prick."

"He pushed it in a little past the lips, right the to point of entry. I was so ready, I thought he might accidentally slip in. The thought crossed my mind again to be try and be responsible, but at this point that ship had sailed. I wanted to feel *him* inside of me again, no barriers.

I grabbed his ass, tried to push him in but he resisted. "You're not going to walk away from this like and pretend it's all my fault. Tell me you want it."

"Yes! Yes, just fuck me for god's sake!"

And he plunged in deep, hard, I cried out, digging my nails into shoulders.

"Fucking son of a bitch," he called out when he sunk into me.

He bit my bottom lip and tugged on it. Again, we were all hands and hair, groans and curses, pain and pleasure. He bit the pale flesh of my breasts, filled his hands with one, sucked and tugged on the nipple with his teeth using the perfect amount of pressure. "Your pussy is so wet," he groaned in my ear. "God, your pussy feels so good," he said burying his face in my neck in defeat.

153

"Fuck me," I demanded. I wanted him hard, I wanted him so hard that he might hurt me. That way, I wouldn't want to do this again. "Your dick, it..."

"Tell me."

"It feels so good in my pussy. Harder."

The thrusting was violent, I thought I might see bruises tomorrow, but it was what I needed. I needed him hard and fast so that I would forget I was sleeping with someone I promised myself I wouldn't.

Then he pulled some acrobatic shit.

He wrapped his arm around my torso, the other supported my thigh, as my legs were already wrapped around his waist, and lifted up onto his knees. I was completely suspended, he was the only thing or person I was touching. My weight on him only plunged him deeper inside of me.

"God!" I called out.

"He can't save you now," he said, squeezing my thigh so hard I grunted from the thrill.

"Oh fuck Heath...oh god," I called out as I grabbed a fist full of hair and pulled his face out of my neck, sliding my tongue into his mouth. He kissed me ferociously, while nodding, as if telling me it was okay to let go. His hips thrust back and forth bouncing me up and down, I could hear our flesh flapping and the sounds of moisture whenever our skin met. His grunts got deeper, throatier. His cock swelled inside of me.

"I'm gonna come Sadie..."

"Come, come inside of me," I called out just before the waves of heat and tension rolled away from the epicenter of my pussy. *Who is this person?* It's like I was possessed by his demon cock. I buried my head into his neck, and his delicious scent filled the air around me.

He let out a loud groan as he held me close, my soft breasts pressing against his slick, firm chest. He collapsed on top of me, panting, sweating. It felt nice, laying there with him so close, but I knew I couldn't lay there for much longer. That would make it a thing, which we were not. We could talk and be friends, or we could fuck, but we couldn't do both at the same time because that would make what we were doing a thing. And we were not a thing.

But he was large and he was on top of me, and part of me felt like he was doing this on purpose as part of some little mental game. So I came up on my elbows, signaling that he should release me before he fell into some sort of post-sex coma. He rested his chin on my chest. All that was left of the accident on his face was the tiniest cute scar above his lip, which I was sure would fade away within the coming months.

"Before you go. I need to know."

"Know what?"

"Who was it? What did he do?"

I knew exactly who he was referring to. I had him pegged from the start, but he pegged me too.

"Just tell me one thing. So I can understand: Who was the asshole who made you hate assholes like me?"

I thought at least it gave us something to discuss, and it was my key to freedom. Strangely, I also felt he had a right to know. The truth was, there were quite a few assholes, as I seemed to have an unhealthy addiction to the attractive, cocky type. But there was the one man who I thought was different. The other guys, I knew what I was dealing with, but the one who really fucked me up was the person I allowed myself to fully trust. I foolishly thought he would change for me, but instead, he broke me.

I sighed, trying to blurt it all out quickly in one breath, but it took at least two. The faster I got it out, the less it would hurt to tell, I hoped. "His name is Kenny--Kenneth. I had known him since high school. We were close friends, he was popular and a huge flirt. He didn't see anything in me other than friendship. That is until we got older and I wasn't a tomboy any longer. And finally, the guy I wrote about in my shitty diaries wanted me. I thought that because he had known me as a friend for so long it would be different. And I reeaaaally believed that for the nearly two years we were together," I said over a sarcastic laugh. "But I made the mistake of borrowing his phone and I learned of the women he had been seeing through almost the entire course of our relationship."

Heath's eyes grew wide and his jaw dropped.

"I appreciated the extra dose of humiliation when I thought back to all the company parties I went to with him, where everyone but me knew he was sleeping around. Oh, I forgot to mention, we were planning our wedding when I found out. So, like I said, I know the type and I know people never change." The tone of my last sentence indicated I was done speaking about it.

"Wow. I don't know whether to be insulted or honored that you would put me in the same category as that caliber of asshole," Heath sighed groggily.

"Take it how you will. That's just the truth. Now you answer me one question."

"What's that?"

"How the hell did you lift me up like that without sending yourself back into the hospital?"

He laughed under his breath. "My tibias were fractured, not my femurs. And if you were impressed by that, you have no idea."

I snickered as he leaned over to the side, releasing me so I could continue my little ritual of forgetting this ever happened.

CHAPTER TWENTY-TWO

A few days later, I returned from a quick visit to my Nonna. I hadn't seen her in person since I came up to the Hamptons, but I spoke to her for a few minutes almost daily. I planned on bi-weekly visits, but with Heath being all broken, I couldn't just leave him locked in the bedroom for a few days while I headed to NYC.

During my time away, I pretended to check in on Heath on a professional basis with courtesy texts. But really, I wondered if he was starting to call up all those people who had conveniently vanished now that I had left and he was alone in the house. I took solace in the fact that I knew him well enough to know he wasn't going out into the world in that way until he didn't need the moon boots and crutches to move around.

I thought a few days away from Heath would be like some form of detox, but I found myself missing my life in the Hamptons. I chalked it up to the house and the beautiful beaches, but I knew there was a lot more to it than that.

I dreamt about him every night.

I headed back early that morning, convincing myself it was so that I could get back in time to grocery shop and catch up on things, but really it was because I just wanted to get back to the place that now felt like home. I arrived at about 8:30am, my heart beating through my chest as I drove past the bamboo and water fixtures. The day of Heath's cast removal was the last time we did anything, mainly because I was gone, but I was still really proud of this non-accomplishment. When I was in NYC, I spoke to Mindy briefly and I lied like a terrible human being. I emphatically told her how I regretted hooking up with Heath so much, and how it wasn't even worth it. But I was beginning to wonder if it wasn't. I mean, who needs dignity, right?

I entered the house quietly, as we set up a downstairs bedroom for him in my absence so he could avoid the stairs and I thought he might still be asleep. As I tip-toed into the living room I heard the strum of an acoustic guitar and a voice singing outside somewhere behind the house. The voice was raspy and melodic. I assumed Heath must have a guest over. At least it was a dude this time.

I quietly followed the music past the pool and over to the rock garden. As I got closer, I recognized the song. I loved that song. I arrived to the entrance of the rock garden and peered over the fence, and to my surprise, it wasn't a guest at all.

He was sitting on a bench, the same bench where we started these shenanigans, his legs crossed out in front of him. He was barefoot--sans moon boots (*bad Heath*y)--and his eyes were closed as he belted the crescendo of the song, his body rhythmically rocking as he strummed the strings of the guitar. He sounded...beautiful. I was a little embarrassed watching him like this and considered leaving him to have the moment alone, but he spotted me, and without missing a beat in voice or instrument, gestured for me to come over by cocking his head.

I sat in the sand and raked my fingers through it as he finished the song. I have to admit, it was nice. Really nice.

"Was that King?"

"You like Weezer?" He seemed surprised.

"Yeah, I especially like that song. Your rendition didn't make my ears bleed." That was about the nicest thing I could muster.

"Thanks."

"I didn't know you played guitar."

"You've barely known me with two functioning hands. I'm using guitar playing to get my dexterity back," he said making spirit fingers. "The PT said it was a good idea." *Shit, from what I could tell the other day, his dexterity was just fine and dandy.*

"How's Nonna?"

He remembered I called her that. "She's doing well. Still sharp, but her hearing is going slowly."

"So she wouldn't mind my singing then," he said with a smirk. He leaned towards the guitar, into the path of a ray of sunshine, and the way the sun reflected off his golden locks and his freshly sunkissed skin took my breath away.

"Well, I am going to run errands. Do you need a ride to the PT?"

"I extended a car service figuring you would be back later today."

"I would've done it for you if I wasn't going to come back in time," I said. I hated when he did things I was supposed to do. It threw me off and also gave me the underlying assumption that he didn't think I was on top of things. This feeling was now amplified by the fact that he had stuffed one of his body parts inside of one of my body parts and I didn't want him to think I was taking advantage of the situation.

"Don't worry about it."

I was trying to be adversarial, but he wasn't having it, he was enjoying the freedom of his functioning limbs and his guitar. "You need to put on your moonboots!" I scolded.

"Two weeks and I'll be running marathons," he shouted as I walked back to the house.

CHAPTER TWENTY-THREE

Heath surprised me with the news that his best friend was flying in from Milwaukee. That's right, Heath is a good ol' fashioned cornfed Midwesterner. I didn't know much about this person, I only knew about the poshy socialites Heath gallivanted with when I met him, but apparently Josh was the biological son of the last foster mother he lived with. He stayed with that family until he was seventeen, when he was discovered (it was his foster mother who insisted he send in pics to agencies). She had since passed away and Josh was the only trace of his childhood that he cared to remember and the closest person he had to family.

He rarely saw Josh, who worked at a plastics molding injection company, but Josh took his few days vacation to see his "bro" as they called each other. This was good, I told myself. It would give us time to go back to the pre-sex days and then we could just, ya know, kind of stay there.

Even though Josh was in no way related to Heath, in my mind's eye I expected them to look a lot alike, but he was nothing like Heath: prematurely balding, a small belly affixed to a body with skinny limbs, and maybe about five-foot-eight or nine. He was also ever the gentleman. He shook my hand, didn't give me the eye-fuck the way Heath did when we first met, and didn't walk around like he was the heir to Earth's throne. My plan was to leave them alone, but they invited me to spend the evening outside with them under some tiki torches with some beer so I obliged.

Apparently Josh played the guitar too, in fact he was the one who taught Heath. Much of the night was not spent talking, but singing along to random songs they tried to piece together from memory.

"Any requests, toots?" I don't even have to tell you who asked that question.

I rolled my eyes. "Hmmm. I'm going to make you work. How about Yesterday from the Beatles?"

"She's tryin' to get us all teary eyed!" Josh joked.

"Okay, okay, I got this," Heath said. It's actually a very simple melody."

"But you gotta put your soul in it. No fucking around Heath," Josh chided.

"Okay, okay," Heath said, putting a finger up to his lips to shush us all. Josh chose to sit this one out. As Heath tucked his chin down, closed his eyes, and started playing the familiar chords; my heart sank involuntarily. I instantly regretted the decision to request the song. Heath couldn't have possibly known, but my dad used to play Yesterday for me while my mother sang along. It's one of the only memories I have of them. And Heath didn't know it, because I told him his voice was just okay, but his voice wasn't just okay, it was really lovely and he sang with his heart, not just reciting the words like he was some empty vessel. Occasionally, between looking down at the guitar and rocking his head back as he hit some of the more difficult notes, he even looked me when he sang the words.

And then, shit, it started to happen, the lump in my throat and the moisture in my eyes met their saturation point. I hoped the night sky would hide it, but I knew from the way the glow of the tiki torches casted on Heath's flawless face, that they would only make my tears glisten. When he sang the last note, I felt like the silence that followed shone a spotlight on my emotions. Even Josh was quiet, because that song does that to people when it's sung beautifully. Josh reached over for a beer from the cooler behind him which gave us a few seconds of privacy.

"Are you okay?" Heath mouthed. I didn't want him to see me like this. I nodded and walked into the house, discreetly using the sleeve of my cardigan to wipe the tears away. I couldn't say anything because if I did, more tears would flow than just the two or three resting on my cheeks.

I grabbed a water from the fridge and fuck, I heard Heath come in through the sliding doors.

"You okay Sadie?"

"Yup. Fine," but my throat was clogged with emotion, my nose stuffy. It was obvious I had been crying.

"What's going on?" I couldn't take it: His concern, his kindness. I couldn't open up that side of myself to him. It wasn't safe for me to do so. I had already given him too much. "Sadie, you can talk to me." If there was anyone I knew who might understand, who might know what that absence is like, it would be him.

"I'm fine. Just go. Leave me alone please." *I'm such a bitch.*

He looked down and nodded and I think I truly saw what hurt feelings looked like on Heath's face. I never really thought he cared about anyone or anything other than himself. "Okay...Okay," he said under his breath. "We'll be outside whenever you're ready."

"Thank you," I said, quietly. When he left, I clenched the edge of the counter, my heart ached and not just from the emotions of a song I hold so closely to my heart, but because of Heath's reaction to my tears. *We have to tread lightly.* I reminded myself.

***

I lay in bed, trying to think of anything but Heath's face when he sang so passionately, but any stray thought wouldn't last for more than a few seconds. After the crying incident, I hung out with the fellas for another hour or so, and acted all fine and dandy, as if Heath didn't see my tears. Eventually, I retreated to bed. I was tired from the early wakeup and I wanted to let them have some bro-bonding time.

But my heart ached, it ached and I couldn't exactly identify why. I think it was because I was angry with myself.

After Kenneth, I nearly swore off all men, and dated Velveeta exclusively. I vowed only to consider the squarest, nicest guys. A guy that would really appreciate what he had. But I was never interested in that type. Shit, even Brock was a little too dull for my tastes. I tried to armchair diagnose myself as I lay there: it must be abandonment issues because of my parents. But, there had to be some guy out there who was attractive, interesting, funny, exciting, and loyal? Is that really too much to ask? My heart jumped in panic. Maybe they were already all taken. Maybe the last one was married off over a year ago and now the world was full of dull, flavorless squares, and hot guys who pushed your buttons.

I must have worn myself out with all this deep thinking, because I dozed off and I dozed off hard. I didn't hear my bedroom door open, or the sound of crutches against the floor. What woke me up was the feeling of warmth against my back, a tender hand on my hip and of Heath's lips grazing my ear as he whispered: "*I want you.*" For a fraction of a second, I thought it was another one of my dreams, the ones I had been having all week when I was in NYC. In my hazy half-awake, half-asleep state, the sound of his voice, his smell, his touch, it all had a dream-like quality, but it wasn't a dream. This felt so much better than a dream. Sometimes I would touch myself in this state of being, just before falling asleep or when turning over in bed, when a sudden urge overtook me that was not of the conscious mind. Everything felt so light, so otherworldly, every touch hypersensitive as the sleep hormones cloaked a soft haze over the intensity of my own touch. And now Heath was here, next to me, during this very rare twilight of the mind, and it felt even better than when I touched myself. My heart still ached, and I wanted to make the ache stop, and I knew he could do that. I didn't say anything and I didn't go through my normal ethical debate; if I did, it would fully wake me up and I would lose the feeling of limbo. *Just this last time. This is too rare to pass up.*

I slowly arched my hips to him, to let him know I consented, but that was all he would get from me. I wouldn't say a word, I wasn't going to think. I just wanted to be one body intertwined with another.

"I want you baby," he said again. And this time, it didn't feel angry or defiant, it was something else, I didn't let my thoughts wander to what that would be.

His hardness rubbed against my back as he glided his hands over my cotton slip, playing with my nipples through the fabric that provided a soft barrier for his firm touch. His face hovered over mine as he propped on his elbow, his hand slipped underneath me, cupping my cheek. Using a slight turn of the wrists, he pushed my face towards his so that the corner of my mouth reached his and he tugged on my lips, and then he peppered my neck and shoulders with lush kisses

"Your skin is so soft. Your smell...nothing smells better than you. Nothing tastes better than you." He snaked his hips back and forth against my behind. I felt for the hem of my nightie and pulled it up to my waist so that the only barrier between him and me were his boxers. I reached to feel for his smooth, hard phallus...I just wanted him in me, the feeling of his cock inside me as I tightened around would be the only thing to make the ache stop. He took my hand and guided it to my clit. "Touch yourself and I'll take care of the rest, baby." *He called me baby again.*

And I did what he told me to, under the lavender hue of my dream-like state, I rubbed my clit as he pushed himself inside of me slowly, so that I could appreciate every inch of his generous firmness. My nipples hardened to the point where just the soft cotton rubbing against them was its own form of foreplay. He tilted my face up further so that it would be close to his, kissing and sucking, some of which I knew would leave marks, but I didn't care. I felt like he wanted to swallow me the way I wanted to swallow him and it made me feel less alone. The ache had disappeared, now all I could feel was him inside of me and I wanted more of him inside of me, but there was never enough. There never would be enough because every time I got another bit of him, I wanted even more.

With every thrust into me I pushed my hips back towards him so that we would collide together. My thighs quivered each time, and he squeezed them vigorously, causing a sharp jolt of pain. The pain was good, it made me believe he might ache the way I had been aching.

His moans might have been the most beautiful song I had heard that day. And I felt myself coming both from inside where his cock rubbed against me, and on the outside, where I touched myself. The dreamy state made me feel as though he and I were floating away and I uttered the only thing I would say to him that night during our intertwining: "Hold onto me, don't let go."

"I've got you," he said to me. He gripped my face tighter, his other hand traveled up my thigh and wrapped around me, keeping me close so that I felt grounded to him. I could feel my insides clenching around him, and my clit electrifying, and I sharply tilted my head back and arched my spine. Heath knew what that meant, and he covered my mouth to muffle the groans and the cries. My entire body felt like it had exploded into a million little stars. And as those millions of little particles of stardust floated back down to earth, I recognized Heath's moans becoming more labored and the way he pressed his lips against the nape of my neck. I wanted to be there for him too and I reached for his head behind me grasping for tendrils of his golden silk and crossed my other arm to meet his hand which was still gripping me tightly. And he shuddered when he came, his body quaking against mine, stifling his groans of ecstasy into my neck.

This was okay, because it wasn't real. I could tell myself it was a dream happening in some other dimension, a place where reverie, fantasy, and deep desires floated out of reach to live in the stars somewhere. This didn't really happen, not this tenderness, not this closeness. Those people weren't Heath and Sadie, they where phantoms.

"You should go back to your bed," I said, with my back still turned to him. Now I was awake and this was real. We were Heath and Sadie. And we were not a thing.

I felt his breath hitch and the subtle caress of his head nodding. He slipped out as quietly as he could.

And the ache set in again.

CHAPTER TWENTY-FOUR

I woke up at the ass crack of dawn the next morning. Even though I knew he would likely go out with Josh for lunch, I did my duty of setting up a nice breakfast buffet that would serve as enough food for dinner too if they so pleased. I left everything nicely presented: some omelets on the warmer, and fruits displayed in a circular formation. I timed the coffee machine for the time I knew Heath woke up every morning, and then I made my escape. I needed air: air that didn't have his delicious scent wafting in it. I needed a view that didn't consist of his impeccable features. I needed room: a room I could enter that didn't give me flashbacks of our intense fuck sessions; by now, we had nearly done something in every room of that house. Only my bathroom was safe, but that's the place I used to touch myself when I thought of him, so even that room stifled me.

I left a handwritten note on the table. He was still my boss after all, I couldn't just vanish:

Heath,

Left to go run errands. Made plenty of food for you and Josh. Hope you both have a great day. Call me if you need anything.

- Sadie

I hoped that would prevent one of his check-in texts and buy me time until mid-evening.

I had no solid plans, I knew no one other than Illy besides Heath around these parts, and I would rather stick a flaming screwdriver in my eye than reach out to that wench. So, I found the local library, borrowed a couple of books, and headed to the beach, wearing the same emerald string bikini I wore when he ravaged me from behind in the kitchen. I was becoming pathetic: I wore it because the fabric against my flesh brought me back to the feelings of that day. Here I was, exiling myself from the home that kept us so close, feigning some great escape, but even after doing all this, I had to bring one little piece of him with me.

I enjoyed myself as best I could, engrossing my thoughts into the book in front of me when I heard a voice: "That's a great book."

I looked up, my eyes took a second to adjust to the blinding sun, and when they did, I saw a dark-haired guy standing over me.

"Oh, I hope so, just started." Really, I had started about an hour and a half ago but struggled to get past the first three pages. I kept reading paragraphs over and over again because my mind was elsewhere.

"Well, keep plugging along, it's a page turner."
"Thanks."

He turned to walk away, but then stopped mid-stride and turned bashfully. "Are you alone? A couple of my buddies and their girlfriends are over there if you want to join us."

Now, his features had begun to register and he was really good looking. Think dark shiny hair, brown eyes, great jawline, about 5'10" or so. He was polite, and based on his earlier comment, I assumed well-read as well. I should jump on this guy and dry hump his leg, but all I felt was *meh*.

Meh? Meh! This was not me, it was like Heath was ruining my pussy for all other men.

My first instinct was to say no, as was the case with my general distrust of humans with penises, but then I thought

170

aloud: "Sure." Why the hell not? I wasn't married. Hell, I wasn't in a relationship of any sort. Why not take up this very pleasant-looking man up on his offer to entertain me? The group of people ended up being nice enough and a nice reminder that the world didn't consist of only Heath, though he stayed ever present in the back of my mind. I couldn't help but glance at the phone every hour, wondering why he hadn't reached out, and if he wanted to, but had chosen to go silent after I kicked him out of the bed last night.

"I should go," I said at about seven. The sun was a couple of hours from completely setting, but swirls of orange and pink seeped into the clear blue sky.

I grabbed my tote and towel, lurching my way up from the sand, when Mark, the guy who invited me over, offered me his hand and I accepted.

"It was really nice meeting you. Can I walk you to your car?"

"Uh...okay." I wasn't used to this chivalry.

I'm not going to lie, I felt a little awkward. I knew where this was headed, and despite the hours I had spent with Mark and his friends, my mind was still battling with every neuron to be present. "I'd like to hang out with you again. If that's okay."

"Sure." He was nice and he *was* good-looking. I had to prove to myself that I wasn't somehow stupidly saving myself for Heath so we exchanged numbers. "See you soon," I said, eager to return home.

***

I was surprised to see Josh loading the back of a Town Car as I arrived.

"Hey," I said as I stepped out of my car. "Are you leaving already? I thought you were here for one more day."

"No, I leave tomorrow night. Heath wanted to go to a hotel, I guess he's a fan of it and wanted to show me around."

This was not in the plans. Heath and I had become a well-oiled machine. He should have asked me to book the hotel and he would have let me know he wouldn't be around this evening. Something was up.

I entered the house, dropping my tote on the entry table. Heath was walking into the living room on his crutches.

"Hey..." I said in a questioning tone.

"Hey," he said without stopping.

"You didn't tell me you were going somewhere."

He stopped his stride. "Yup. I am. I didn't know I needed to tell you where I was going." He started up again.

"Well it's just that--"

"Just that what?"

"I, uh...usually you tell me your plans."

"Well I just did. So are we good? Can you hold the fort down for one day?" He asked sarcastically. *Asshole.*

"Yeah. Will you need me to pick you up from the hotel? I assume Josh is leaving from there."

"I'll get a car service."

Within seconds and I heard the car door slam, and the car driving away on gravel.

Was he hurt? That wasn't possible. That would require human emotions. That would mean that he cared about something beyond sex. And yet, he had never acted like this before. We threw our punches and we threw them freely, unabashedly so, but I don't think I'd had ever seen him like this. I couldn't be imagining that this was personal.

I realized after a few minutes that I hadn't moved from the spot where I stood since he left and I shook my head to clear my thoughts. Then I did what I felt I had to do, because what I wanted to do was call Heath and make him explain what was on his mind. I needed to focus that energy somewhere. Heath was used to women begging for him. I would not be that woman. I shot a text:

Sadie:

Hi Mark? What are you doing tomorrow?

CHAPTER TWENTY-FIVE

Mark took me to Beau Marchais the next evening, and it was clear this was a date. The place had the nice white tablecloths, a French-inspired menu, and mood lighting. It was just the right amount of stuffy, without being over the top. *Good taste.*

Mark was ever the gentleman, exiting the car to open the door for me, and pulling out my chair for me to have a seat. I wore a red sundress with cap sleeves that stopped right at my kneecaps. Perfectly ladylike, belying my behavior during the greater part of this summer.

The conversation was pleasant. Mark was a hedge fund manager, *blah blah blah*. It was all very appropriate, and nice, and he seemed like a gem of a guy. And yet, while he was all the things I should have been able to check off my list and scream: bingo! Something was off. Something was missing. That was my problem and I knew it: I never gave the right guys enough time to grow on me. So while he wouldn't be getting a kiss tonight, I thought we could see each other a few more times and let things move really slowly, unlike the way things had moved with Heath.

He drove me back to the house and walked me to the front door of Heath's place. I had a feeling he expected something, but I didn't want to lead him on. I wanted to make sure I felt something before I kissed him.

"I had a great time tonight Sadie. I have to tell you again, you look beautiful."

"Thank you. And thank you so much for dinner. You have to let me get the tab next time." He smiled, I think because I had just confirmed we would be seeing each other again. His teeth were really, really sparkly under the floodlight. Almost artificially so.

"Never." *Ever the gentleman.*

"Well, goodnight." And before he could lean in for a kiss: "Listen, Mark, I want to take things slowly."

"Of course. No rush, let's just get to know each other."

"Okay, well I'll see you soon then?" And we hugged stiffly as we tried to figure out how we fit against each other's bodies. On the way back to his cherry-colored classic convertible, he looked back at me, his strong jawline prominently jutting at this angle, and smiled.

I felt perfectly pleasant, proper, and ladylike. This is how one is *supposed* to feel after a date. I glanced down at my phone, it was a little after nine, not too shabby, a perfectly ladylike time to return home after a first date. Furthermore, there were no bodily fluids exchanged, and so, I was feeling quite proud of myself.

I glided into the entryway, which had a direct view into the kitchen and was surprised to see Heath was already home, rummaging through some leftovers using *only* one crutch and no moon boots. *Stubborn bastard.*

"Hi, I didn't expect you to be home yet," I said, matter-of-factly.

He was mid bite and stopped. "Yeah, I just dropped off Josh."

"It was nice having him around."

"Yup."

"How was your stay at the hotel?"

"It was *a lot* of fun," he said raising his eyebrows. He was trying to taunt me. Images of him noshing on model's pussies flashed in my head. Orgies, dildos, swings, whips, lube...My mind was going to the furthest reaches of sexual experiences. It would make sense, Heath would want to show off all the ass he could get to his "bro." And he would go to a hotel, so I would be none the wiser. He could keep me compartmentalized in this home while he went around fucking anything with two tits and a head of hair. "How was your evening?" He asked very formally.

"It was very nice. I met a guy on the beach yesterday. A hedge fund manager. He took me to Beau Marchais tonight," I said casually, but with a little extra perk to my voice as I kicked off my shoes. Heath's jaw tightened.

"You mean when you were running errands?"

"I did that too." The bastard knew he could have called me if he needed me for work reasons.

"Well, I am going to head to my fort and hit the hay early. I'm really worn out from last night. Exhausting. It was *craaazy*." *You son of a...*

"Me too, I spent a lot of time partying with Mark and his friends yesterday afternoon." Really we just sat by a radio and chatted, but tomato, to-mah-to.

He hobbled on one crutch and no moon boots to his lair. I opened my mouth to nag him about his lack of compliance to doctor's orders, but this time I stopped myself.

I spent the rest of the evening laying in bed, staring at the ceiling. I knew what he was doing: he wanted to me to plead with him, to ask him what was wrong, and I was not going to play that game. So instead I grabbed the book I started yesterday (I was still stuck on page three) and read the same paragraph over and over again until I fell asleep.

***

For the next two weeks, Heath and I were like ships passing in the night. I went about my new social life, going on a few dates with Mark, and Heath went about his doing god knows what. Everything between Heath and I was business, no late-night talks on his bed, no guitar playing under the glow of tiki-torches, no sneaking into each other's rooms or breakfast on the balcony. And strangest thing of all, no...*arguing?* It wasn't that there wasn't tension, in fact that tension was thick. I felt it on my skin, in my gut; the air grew viscous and harder to breathe when we were in the same room. But instead of acknowledging it, either by being grownups and discussing it, or by releasing tension via bickering (followed most likely by fucking), we let it simmer. It was a slow simmer, just at the boiling point, and it built steadily, teetering on the edge of erupting. I didn't know how long we could last this way, but by being robotic, by acting like two droids and only interacting when we absolutely needed to, and doing so in short, efficient bursts, we were able to keep the tension at a low simmer.

That is until he asked me to the White Party. I don't know what prompted him, maybe he wanted a "date," or a prop, but just as I was heading up the stairs after plating his dinner and leaving him to eat alone, I heard him ask: "Do you want to go to a party tonight? It's one of those famous White Parties." His tone didn't have the usual level of excitement it had when he talked about parties, or anything else for that matter. It was flat, just the slightest hint of a question mark punctuated it.

I felt like someone released a gasket in my chest because I was happy that he wanted me to come; and yet I was scared of what could happen, even though I was extremely curious. In two days, he would be leaving for Paris to work his first modeling gig since his accident. I know he was really excited about the job, especially because just after the accident he genuinely felt that his career might be over. I was so happy for him and I wanted to share in his happiness with him, but we weren't really talking. Not the way we used to. The gig would only be a few days, but I thought about him leaving all the time. The thought of him leaving the country, with so much unresolved tension between us, weighed on me. It felt symbolic in some way, him leaving while he and I were in this standoff. It just didn't feel right. Yet I was far too stubborn to say anything to him, so I was glad he broke the stalemate by inviting me.

During the two weeks he and I had distanced ourselves from each other, just I had predicted, he was slowly going back to his old ways. After the hotel thing, he stayed home a few nights in a row, but the friends of convenience began to trickle back in again. It was just dinner a few times, but he was well-known in the area and couldn't go out without being spotted. I am sure dinners grew to something else as he would often come back late (yes, I listened for him).

I won't be needing your services tonight. That was his way of telling me not to make dinner. But I knew what he was really trying to say was: *I'll be out getting my dick sucked in the bathroom of SL East. Enjoy your night alone, loser.* I would simply nod, sometimes not bothering to look up, but would grind my teeth so hard that I thought I might not have any enamel left by September. And now, after weeks of pretending I was a human light fixture, he was inviting me to this pish-posh White Party.

"Sure." I am an expert at stoic, even though I felt like someone was playing ping pong in my chest using my heart as the ball.

The only white dress I had was something seemingly designed to elicit contrasting thoughts of purity and filth. A tight, short, cotton/linen blend, the top fit like a bustier and pushed my tits up to my eyebrows. The white color and tiny band of ruffles along the hemline gave the dress just the right touch of innocence to contrast with its sexiness. I had a pair of tall white stilettos, with heels that should require a weapons permit. Shit, even my toes had cleavage that night. I let out my black elbow-length hair and pressed in barrel curls, then shook them vigorously for that freshly-fucked look. I topped off the outfit with red lipstick and cat eyes. I would break him. I would get some sort of a human expression out of him.

"Ready?" I asked as I walked down the stairs. He looked up from his phone and kind of shifted a bit, but then stood firm. He quickly looked away, probably to stop himself from ogling.

"Yeah." His throat sounded dry. He stood up from the stool he was sitting on and I noticed him shift his pants. *Does he have a hard on?*

Damn did he look good. He had on a fitted white long-sleeved designer t-shirt, white flat front pants that hit right at the ankle, and canvas low-cut sneakers with a faint hint of grey. On any other occasion, so much white in one outfit would be out of place, but buying into the concept, he looked great: the white made his tan and crystal blue eyes pop.

The ride over in the back of the limo was quiet.

"So did you invite me for quiet contemplation?" I asked.

"No...I just thought you might want to go out. You've been staying at home a lot."

"Sometimes I go out with Mark when you're out. I don't stay home every night."

He looked at me out of the corner of his eye. "Well, whatever, I thought you would want to come. This is one of those parties people come here for."

"Well, thank you."

"Anytime."

He was right about this being a big deal. For one, Heath rented a limo (or someone paid him to come and rented it for him, as was often the case). The beach club shimmered with laid-back elegance through the gathering dusk. White washed wood planks formed the exterior, and white awnings with yellow borders gently danced in the summer breeze above all the windows. The soft yellow glow of lights illuminated the outside of the club. Just behind it, its backyard, the Atlantic Ocean, murmured against a pristine white sand beach. There was a queue out the door of one of the entrances and the street was lined with expensive cars dropping people off. Heath lead me right past the enormous man managing the entrance, greeting him with a nod, to the many eyerolls of wannabe-patrons who were stuck on the seemingly frozen line.

The club's main restaurant had a long bar at one end. The rest of the open-air indoor space had sunken lounge areas bordered with built-in seating covered in white cushions. However, the big attraction was the expansive outdoor deck that led out to the beach. On the deck there was another bar and dozens of white metal tables and chairs. On the beach there was even more seating in the form of an enormous wooden square, again, covered in white cushions, and a few outdoor beds. Besides the rare pop of blue or yellow the club could not mask, everything was white and everyone was in white. Black lights scattered throughout broke up the near complete void of color.

"Hey!" Some guy I recognized from the party the night of Heath's accident clasped his hand, I think some sort of music producer. I remembered him because he had some of the brightest naturally-red hair I had ever seen. His cheeks were flushed from drinking, and his perfectly oval head looked like a giant cherry tomato. "What's up bradduh?" Great, a typical bro. He turned to me while still clenching Heath's hand, and leaned back, eying me up and down. Heath picked up the signal right away.

"This is my assistant, Sadie." *His assistant.* Yes, everyone make sure you know I am a tier below you trust fund babies, and bankers, and Hollywood types. I was a well-established chef first, assistant second. Heath is not stupid, he was trying to rile me up, I just knew it.

"Nice to meet you Sadeeeee," he almost hissed like a snake.

"You too," I said coldly stabbing him with invisible laser beams from my eyes. *I am not the one.*

Heath was now walking on his own, no need for crutches or moon boots. He still had to ease back into vigorous exercise, but his fitness and youth was in his favor. I had barely known him like this, and when I did, he was at his worst and that was exactly what I expected to see. People filtered towards us, offering drinks. Pretty women hovered around him and his buds.

He didn't quite ignore me, but everyone else was surrounding him and I didn't want to fight for his company. I realized this was a mistake. I knew no one here and this situation forced me to cling to him, and that was exactly what I did not want to do. Heath was at least nice to enough to grab me a cocktail before getting swarmed again. I slowly pulled myself away and stood, arms crossed, for some time, before I found a comfy seat on a couch. If he were to look over, I knew exactly what he would think: *uptight bitch.* I was completely okay with that.

I did spot the occasional celebrity, which was cool.

Some guy tried to talk to me and I politely gave him one word answers until he finally got the signal. I looked down at my phone, and saw a text from Mark.

Mark:
Want to go to a party tonight?

My stomach tightened. This was *the* party, and my eyes quickly scanned the room to see if he was around, but I didn't find him. I debated whether or not I should reply, and then that's when I saw it: I spotted Heath, he had drifted to a wall, he was laughing, some girl with far too much makeup on and far too huge of a boob job was leaning against him. I looked up at the exact moment she started nuzzling his neck. I turned away quickly because I thought I might break one of the beer bottles on the coffee table in front of me and cut a bitch. *Fuck him. Fuck him with a baseball bat.*

Sadie:
The white party?

Mark:
Yeah. You there?

Sadie:
Yup.

Mark:
I'm already on my way, see you in 5.

I saw Mark coming through the entrance just minutes later. He wore a white button down with his chest peeking through, and linen pants, looking straight out of Martha's Vineyard with his dark perfectly coifed hair.

"Sadie!" He gestured with his hand, calling out my name. I stood up to meet him. He went in for a half-mouth kiss. *Yes, I hadn't even kissed him yet.* He really was proving to be the perfect gentleman by not pushing the issue. He invited me to the bar with him to refresh my cocktail, and I felt Heath's glare in my periphery. It fueled me with a surge of power. *How dare he?* How dare he think that he could bring me out here for the purpose of rubbing in just how little he gave a shit?

Mark leaned against the bar, and as we chatted, I made sure my body language would rile Heath up, grabbing Mark's arm, cocking my head back in laughter, licking my lips. I couldn't see Heath, but I felt him. The simmer was reaching an all-out violent boil. His heat singed my back from across the club.

"Excuse me, can I talk to you for a minute, Sadie?"

Wow, that worked fast. Mark perked up, he knew about Heath (I kind of bitched about him and how intolerable he was), but they hadn't met.

"Heath! This is Mark. Mark, this is my boss, Heath. What's up?"

"I need to talk to you in private. It's a work matter."

I looked over to Mark who gave me a subtle cock of the eyebrow. I assumed he thought Heath had some stupid work-related demand. "Take all the time you need," Mark said.

"Thanks," Heath said with just the right amount of sarcasm to leave Mark uncertain as to whether or not he was being sarcastic, then he lead me to a hallway towards the restrooms.

"What's up?" I asked perkily as if I hadn't a clue.

"What the hell are you doing?"

"Excuse me?"

"You brought Mark here to fuck with my head."

"Excuse me? You have some absolute fucking nerve you know that? You dragged me here just so you could rub these skanks in my face and you are upset that I have a friend here?"

"I think a better description is I invited you to a nice party after you've been such a frigid bitch to me."

"I've been a frigid bitch? You've barely even talked to me these past couple of weeks."

"I thought that's what you wanted! You want to fuck me, but you can't stand me right? I was doing you a favor."

"Oh please. You're just a regular martyr, aren't you?"

"Enough of this dammit. Why do you have to be so difficult? I brought you over here because...because I don't want you to be with anyone else."

"You have got to be kidding me. What, do I look like some sort of possession? Where you get to claim me while you do whatever the fuck you want? *Sadie the hotel was extra amazing, I was so worn out,*" I said in a faux-Heath voice while gesturing an air blow-job, using my tongue to appear as though a dick were poking through my cheek. "You just had some random chick necking you not ten minutes ago! Do you think I'm blind or stupid, or both?"

"Wait a second. She came after me and I pushed her away."

"Okay, well then you're one for what, twenty now? I'm sure you have been having tons of fun since you got your footing back, literally and figuratively! You are exactly who I thought you were! You needed me when you had no one, and now that everyone is up your ass again because you aren't a burden any longer, you are back to being a fucking manslut and scene-hopper!"

"What are you talking about? I haven't been with anyone."

"Bullshit! Do you take me for some sort of fool?"

"No, no I don't! And I am not who you make me out to be! Do you know how frustrating it is to meet someone who thinks you are the scum of the earth? Who finds you repulsive as a human being?" Those words jolted me. "Not that it's any of your business, but I haven't been with anyone else since the accident. I fucking swear it."

"Why should I believe you? You have made it a point to rub everything in these past couple of weeks. I would be an idiot to believe you."

Heath had steadily moved in closer and closer as we argued. The music of the club drowned out a good part of our shouting, but people were starting to look.

"I know the way I act might not make sense, but it's because you...I don't know how to...you confuse the shit out of me. I don't want you to be with anyone else. I think about you all the time. Seriously." The pitch of his voice dropped. He leaned in close to me, resting his hand on the wall above my head. His eyes turned down at the sides, begging for my understanding, for me to believe how serious he really was.

"Well, then, show me, but I don't think you will ever be able to prove yourself." Yes, Heath sort of opened up his heart to me, and I pulled out the bitch card, but I just wasn't quite sold yet. Kenneth said all those things to me and more and look where that got me. That was when it boiled over. He jumped onto me, smashing his lips onto mine. My heart jumped up to my throat. According to my maths, at that moment, I gave approximately negative-two fucks about the fact that anyone was around. Heath poured himself over me with his tall build, sliding his hand from the back of my thigh up to my ass, pushing up my dress so that half of my left cheek popped out. He pulled me towards him without breaking our locked lips as he felt for the wall behind him; it seemed he was familiar with this place. I paid no attention to where he was leading me, stumbling in my skyscraper stilettos. I only cared about his taste, and the feeling of his silky locks, the long and thick girth pressing against my abdomen, and his smell...*his smell.*

It was the broomstick crashing onto the floor that led me to conclude we were in the janitor's closet. Heath reached behind me and locked the door without skipping a beat. This was not the location of most sexual fantasies, but neither one of us gave a single shit. It was just him and me and weeks of simmering frustration and tension.

"I am going to fuck you so hard, you won't be able to walk back to that son of a bitch," he growled, making me wetter than I thought possible.

"I'd like to see you try."

My dress fabric was stubborn, and he pulled it so hard I felt the threads rip. I'd have to deal with that later. He fumbled with my micro thong angrily for about half a second before ripping it off of me, there was no time for this, we had already waited too long. He drove me into the door like a linebacker and it shook under the force of our impact. A gust of air burst from my chest, a couple of cleaning supplies spilled off of a shelf, and mops and brooms wobbled from the sexual energy reverberating from our combined force. Together we wrestled his shirt off; I wanted to admire the ridges of of abdomen and feel his warm chest against me as he fucked me. For two weeks I had watched him walk around the house without a shirt on, or come back from a dip in the pool dripping wet, the water trickling down his insanely perfect body. It angered me, because I couldn't help but think lustful thoughts whenever I saw him, and I knew he was teasing me. He had been trying to break me too.

"I want your pussy so fucking bad." He was shaking with pent-up desire, gripping my ass like he wanted to tear me to shreds. He bit at my neck, sucked on it until it was painful. It was perfect.

"I want your cock. Give me your cock you fucking bastard." He had been such an insufferable dick these past couple of weeks and it pissed me off how badly I wanted him.

It was so hard, and thick, and engorged. "I'm going to tear your pussy up. You fucking drive me crazy. You make me feel like I am losing my mind." He stopped and gripped my hair. "Suck it first." He pushed my head down and I dropped to my knees. It was so thick with weeks of sexual frustration, I was sure it would hurt my jaw to take him in my mouth. But I gobbled that shit up. I wrapped my lips around it, gripping his taut ass as he fucked my face, charcoal-colored tears stained my cheeks as he choked me with his dick.

"Oh god Sadie, oh fuck!" He slammed his hand against the door. "...fucking bitch." I cupped his balls, ignoring the ache in my jaw just so I could enjoy the sight of him tilting his chin up to the ceiling with his eyes closed as I made him my *bitch*.

"Get the fuck up," he said, lifting me up so forcefully my feet left the ground for a second.

"Now you," I said, pushing his head down. He smirked devilishly as he dropped to his knees and lifted one of my legs over his shoulder. Oh my sweetness, he ate me like he literally wanted to consume me, sucking on my clit, then tongue fucking me as he rubbed it with the pad of his thumb. He knew exactly when to stop before I got too carried away.

Heath rose, and again, he pushed me into the door, and gripped underneath my knee, hoisting up my leg.

He grabbed his cock, I loved when he did that, and rubbed the smooth head along the juicy entrance of my pussy. I couldn't hold out any longer.

"Oh god. Oh god," he said in breathy anticipation.

"Just fuck me already. Don't make me wait." I was already so close, he had the power to take me there without even entering me.

"I don't...I don't want it to stop," he said. I wasn't sure if he meant the feeling of this moment or the non-thing we had going on.

"Please," I begged into the safe crook of his neck, biting and gripping him as close to me as my physical strength would allow. "Fuck me. Hard."

He slid into me and we both let out a groan from deep inside. It carried up through our stomachs, chests and escaped out of our bodies at the same moment. I felt the vibration as it roared through us.

"Ah!Ah!Ah!" As I cried out with each thrust that slammed me back into the door, he buried his forehead into my neck.

"Sadie...Sadie," Heath begged, he sounded intoxicated by our sex.

"Heath!" *I can't get enough.* "Harder. Fuck me harder! Deeper!"

He grunted, sweat dripping down his temple, his teeth exposed like an angry wolf. He stayed inside of me, never fully pulling out, each thrust attempting to get that much deeper. The constant friction of his dick was so filling, and rich, and brutal. It was everything.

"I'm coming! I'm coming!"

He drove so hard into me, the force of his hips lifted me off the ground. One shoe dangled off of my toe and the heel of the other had broken off, resting sideways on the foot that was still planted on the ground.

One of my hands reached for something, anything to grip. I tried to palm the door behind me scratching at it, thinking in my Heath-induced hysteria that I could grab the smooth, flat surface. I howled. I howled like a wounded animal. Whenever he fucked me hard and dirty, I felt like a sex-beast, filled with so much primal energy that I wanted to crawl out of my skin.

Heath gripped me so tight, I could barely get in a breath as he released into me, his pumps slowing with each thrust, his warm groans echoed from my neck, spreading throughout my body. Heath kept his face buried in my neck, and then he slid down to his knees, gripping my waist. He rested his forehead at the lowest part of my tummy.

"Sadie..."

I ran my fingers though his hair tenderly and then it hit me.

"Fuckfuckfuckfuck!" I snapped us into the reality of the present. Mark was out there waiting for me and I looked like I had just completed a triathlon while being shot at with rubber bullets. "Oh no..." I said, in a daze, picking up my devastated thong from the floor and dangling it in front of me. "Oh no!" I said picking up the shoe that had its heel hanging on by a small sliver of glue. "I need to get back out there." I straightened my hair, pulled my dress down, feeling the silver-dollar sized hole in the seam on my right hip. "*Oh no...*" I said in mourning. I really liked these items he just destroyed.

It was then I noticed Heath watching me with an amused look on his face as he zipped and buttoned up his pants.

"This isn't funny!" I shouted at him as I waved my broken shoe in his face, but it was. It was hilarious.

"Here, give me that," he said taking the now useless panties from my grip. "We'll leave something for the janitor to talk about tomorrow," and he tossed it atop one of the standing mops.

I was still out of breath and began taking measured ones to slow my heart rate. "Okay, I think I'm ready," I said. Heath looked right at me and laughed.

"No you're not." He walked up to me slowly and I grew stiff, I could never trust what this clown was up to. "Here," he said, reaching for the utility sink and dabbing a bit of water on a paper towel. He gently wiped my cheeks as my eyes wandered down to his tanned and ripped torso. "Your makeup is all over the place."

"How bad is it?"

"Oh...it's not so bad..." he said almost drunkenly. The sex had taken his edge off, thank god. I knew from the way his lips curved at one end he was lying.

"It's bad."

"Well, your red lipstick is all over the lower third of your face and your mascara...it looks like you were just at a funeral."

"Shit."

"Don't worry. *I've got you.*" Deep in my stomach, I ached, remembering the last time he said those words to me. He gently wiped my face, as I made puppy eyes and pouted my lips, feeling like something awesomely terrible had just happened. The face made him laugh, and then I laughed, and he pressed his forehead against mine as we smiled wistfully.

But there was no time to talk or figure things out, I had to get back out there.

I did a quick feminine clean up at the sink, shook my head to get my game-face on and then headed for the door.

"You might want to wipe your pretty face too. It looks like you've been sucking face with a rouge-wearing hussy."

Just as he smirked that fucking smirk, my panties fell off of the mop. *That smirk can make my panties drop from anything.* "You go out first, I'll give you a couple of minutes while I freshen up in here. I don't know about you, but I am over this party. Want to head back home soon?"

I nodded. I was over this shit the second I walked through the entrance.

I did one last smoothing of my hair, puffed up my chest and whipped the door open.

CHAPTER TWENTY-SIX

Heath was right about something for once: I was hobbling. That typically happens when one foot is five inches higher off the ground than the other. And wow, were the people who had been waiting for the restroom staring at me. I could only imagine what it looked like from the outside: The violent and rhythmic thudding off the door that could only mean one thing, the high-pitched moaning that likely carried over the music, the woman who appeared to have been beaten by a gang of bandits exiting from a closet. I tried to hold strong and keep my chin up, but the knowing smirks and whispers wore that out very quickly. I sped up my Quasimodo hobble through the hallway, eventually whipping off the other shoe and dealing with the sticky floors.

Mark was sitting alone at the bar, looking none-too-pleased. I noticed 3 empty glasses had accumulated around him, one of them was mine.

"Hey," I said, acting like I had only been gone for a minute.

"That boss of yours--" he said, turning to face me. His facial expression quickly changed when he saw mine and gave me the once over.

"Can we go outside for a sec to talk?" I had to tell him I was going home, and I had to tell him this wasn't going to happen. This had nothing to do with any future with Heath, but that closet encounter just reminded me I was definitely lying to myself about Mark. Mark and I were not happening no matter how many dates we went on.

"Yeah," he said with a sigh. I could tell he was even more agitated now. We stepped out to the sidewalk to the side of the entrance. People buzzed around us as they entered and exited the party.

"What the hell is going on?" He asked.

"Mark, I don't think...I'm going to go home."

His eyes narrowed, his lips pursed tightly as he got a better look at me. "What the hell happened to you? Is that a hickey on your neck? Where the hell are your shoes?" I looked down, and felt for my collarbone. *Busted.* "Were you just back there fucking your boss?" He shouted angrily.

"Mark, calm down and let me explain."

"Explain what? That you're a fucking cock tease? That you've been stringing me along with this little innocent act, waving your tits and ass in my face, when really you're a fucking slut?" And then that's what I realized what was off: his perfectly polished hair, his over-the-top chivalry, his "understanding," his perfect veneers. It was all a facade. I had been so focused on trying to see through Heath's that I missed the manufactured Nantucket-Ken doll in front of me.

"Excuse me? I don't know who the fuck you think you are, but you don't know a damn thing about me! I was very honest about the pace I wanted to take."

"Except with that asshole. You just spread your legs in an instant for a paycheck! Then you have the nerve to bitch to me about how he doesn't respect women!"

"Don't you dare talk to me like that. You have no idea what has been going on between us."

"You think you can just waste my time like this? I've been turning down skanks like you all week to take you out on nice dates, all for a fucking hug?" He said grabbing my elbow forcefully, his dark brow furrowing. No this *mofo* didn't.

"Let go of my arm." I squeezed my stiletto in my left hand, preparing myself to use it if he didn't release me.

"Get your fucking hands off of her."

Both Mark and I turned our heads at the same time to see Heath standing there, a look of intensity I had seen only reserved for our conflicted sex romps. Mark's grip tightened.

"I have had just about enough of your bullshit tonight," Mark said to Heath.

"I said let go of her arm right now."

"Heath, I've got this covered," I wanted to diffuse the situation. People were starting to gawk, photogs were eagerly snapping away at us.

"Whatcha gonna do, pretty boy?"

"Guys, that's enough!" I called out, but they were both testosterone and alcohol fueled and they were guarding what they each felt was theirs. Did I ever mention Heath hates being called a pretty boy? Switching schools often as a kid, that was the thing people picked on him about the most. I know, *poor Heathy, too pretty.* That's what I told him when he first told me.

Heath shoved Mark, which served to get him to let go of my arm. I dove in front of Heath to push him back, and that's when Mark pushed me hard to get to Heath, so hard I fell to the sidewalk with a thud.

"You son of a bitch!" Heath said, lunging at Mark and planting a punch squarely on his well-defined jaw, that I now believed was crafted that way solely to be the perfect target for a haymaker. The crowd gasped audibly and the sound of cameras erupted to a crescendo. Mark stumbled back a few steps, clutching his jaw, then fell on his ass. Heath vigorously shook his punching hand.

"Your arm!" That asshole just got out of a cast.

"It's fine," he said, massaging his palm. "Don't you fucking get up!" Heath screamed, pointing down at Mark who was visibly stunned.

It happened all so fast, I was still on the ground watching in disbelief. "Come here," he said, helping me up. "Let's get the fuck out of here before the cops come." We slid into the limo and sped away.

A number of thoughts ran through my head: I was a little angry with Heath for escalating things because I hated violence. Mark was a jerk, but seeing him on the floor like that with his lip bleeding disturbed me. I was surging with adrenaline. I was embarrassed: how could I have gotten Mark so wrong? But most of all, I was hot, because *goddam that was hot.*

"What the hell was that?" I asked, panting. "I could've handled him."

"Sadie, don't start with that women's lib shit right now." He was clearly still on fire from the entire thing. "A man never fucking lays his hands on a woman like that. He did that in the middle of the street. What do you think he would have done behind closed doors? He's never touched you before, has he?"

"No...never. That was the first time I had ever seen him like that. I can't believe it."

"I knew he was a douche the second I saw him. Prep school piece of shit."

"I just think we could have maybe ended things more diplomatically."

"Fuck diplomacy. Do you think guys like him learn from diplomacy?" It seems Heath was working from the same playbook I had been using on him.

"Oh my god!" I said, having a sudden moment of contemplation about the wild turns this night had taken. I buried my face in my hands and stifled a laugh.

"Let me see," he said, grabbing my arm.

"It's fine," I said, looking up at him. *Oops, our eyes just locked.*

This time it was me who jumped. Have you ever watched those NatGeo videos? The ones from the African bush, where the camera man sits in silence waiting for the lioness to pounce on the antelope? Yeah, that's basically what happened. He fell off the seat and landed on the floor of the limo, with me on top of him. I think for a moment he wondered if I was trying to fuck him or fuck him up.

Here we were for the second time in one night, each of us viciously trying to consume the other. I felt my dress rip AGAIN as he manhandled it over my hips and pulled down the cups of the bustier top so that my breasts were propped up, waiting to be sucked. I spun over to his dick, angrily ripping it out of his pants, swallowing it as he sucked on my lips, tugging on them and letting them bounce back. Then he started using his tongue. I squeezed his thighs as I took him all the way to the back of my throat.

I heard him let out a long sigh. Then I thrust my hips on his face to encourage him to keep going.

"Eager beaver," he said under his breath. My hips instinctively wound on his face as all hands were on deck with his cock, gripping it, licking it, massaging his balls. I couldn't hold out for long as I violently face fucked him. I came, stopping my oral endeavors to dig my nails into his hips and rock back and forth on that pretty face of his to an explosive climax, arching my back and tilting my head up, my hair tickling the small of my back as I called out all kinds of obscenities.

"My fucking turn you *tease*," he said, turning Mark's words against me. I rolled off of him, my hands and legs quivering as he sat up.

"I'm gonna fuck you doggie style. I have been dying to do that. Your ass is so perfect it makes me angry."

He pushed me in front of him so I rested my hands on the ledge where the window met the limo door. Then he slid inside of me, and I felt his warm sweaty skin stick to mine as he thrusted jaggedly, each pump going in with maximal force.

"Harder you bastard..." I reached around to grab his hip and pull him in harder towards me.

"Fuck you," he said, plunging in so deep that I involuntarily clenched every muscle in my body. "How do you like that, smartass?"

"Harder. More. You asshole...you cretin!" I was running out of things to call him, but I wanted to use every name in the book at him as he assaulted me with his dick.

He wrapped my hair around his hand and pulled back sharply so that my neck was fully extended. Another thrust. I wailed. "What was that?" He asked like a smartass, pressing his cheek against mine, his warm breath blowing on my cheek.

"More. You stupid son of a bitch."

Another painfully amazing thrust. "I'm going to drive so far into you, my cock's gonna choke you from behind."

"You fucking animal...you pretty animal."

His intensity broke with laughter as his pelvis slapped against my ass again. He readjusted my head with another yank, biting my neck hard enough that I thought he might break the skin. I cried out. Then he pushed my face against the cold glass of the limo window, and his thrusts grew more frequent. The glass fogged and cleared with each of my inhales and exhales. He kept my cheek pressed there, pounding and pounding. My hands flailed, looking for anything to take a hold of as he rammed his long cock deep into me.

Amidst our NatGeo sounds, I heard a click.

"Close the fucking door!" Heath shouted. *Oh shit, the limo driver. Was he deaf or just incompetent? Or maybe he wanted in on the action.*

I didn't care, I had used up all my embarrassment walking out of the janitor's closet not an hour ago.

"Oh god...I'm going to spill my cum inside of you. You're fucking mine, Sadie."

"Come inside of me. I want your cum in me..." I wanted all of him in that moment and I know he wanted to give it all to me.

He reached over and pulled me up close to him, cupping one of my breasts, thrusting up, and this new angle was fresh and caused me to call out even louder. And he did exactly what he promised, burying his face into my hair, his warm breath penetrating the thick locks and tingling my scalp.

We both collapsed on the floor of the limo, a tangled, broken, messy, filthy, sweaty pile of limbs.

CHAPTER TWENTY-SEVEN

I woke up to the aromatic smell of coffee. I always found that the most pleasant way to wake up. I'm not going to lie, I felt a bit like I had been plowed over by a truck, but in the most incredible way. Everything was sore, including my little lady friend (she had really taken a pounding the night before), but it was all a welcome physical reminder of the night before. I looked around to get my bearings, then I remembered everything: the angst of seeing him with the girl, the closet, the fight, the limo. The way we laughed about how the clueless driver opened the door, fearing that we were continuing the altercation from the club. How we ran into the house, collapsing on the big comfy sofa in his living room, and fell asleep in each other's arms.

This is not a thing. This is not a thing.

I think this just became a thing.

"Good morning," Heath said from behind the kitchen island. His smile radiated with something new.

"Morning," I said, shrugging with a smile that glowed from the very center of my heart. I looked down, trying to hide my grin.

"What are you thinking?" he asked, turning to stir something in a pan on the range. *He's cooking for me. Swoon.*

"About everything. About last night." He did the panty-dropping shy smirk. "Why, what are you thinking?"

"Just that you look cute. Like a beautiful mess." I could only imagine the toll last night took on my appearance. I motioned to straighten out my hair. "Leave it. It's adorable. I like seeing what I did to you." Then he winked at me, plating our eggs.

I bit my lip as my stomach flooded with delicious anxiety.

"Welcome to my life. Catch," he said, tossing his phone at me. "We made page six. Congrats."

"What?"

I unlocked his phone to find an internet article:

Formerly incapacitated lothario and supermodel, Heath Hillabrand was spotted sucking face with an unknown curvaceous brunette at the very popular White Party in the Hamptons. Spectators watched in disbelief as the festivities moved into a closet. Later that evening, Hillabrand was spotted engaging in a brawl defending the raven-haired beauty's honor.

"The video's on TMZ," Heath said.

"Nooo!" I watched in horror as the scene unfolded on his phone. "Do you think he'll sue?"

"I'd like to see him try. He was assaulting you."

"You do realize we are ridiculous human beings?"

"It was the best night of my life." His words stopped me in my tracks, and I felt the ache lurch back for a second, because I felt like this might end, and if it did, I feared that ache would stay for a very long time. "Come eat."

I joined him at the island, sitting on a barstool. He stayed on the other side, eating as he stood. There was a comfortable but electric silence between us.

"So he cooks."

"These eggs have taken me the the apex of my capabilities. What do you think, Miss Chef?"

"A little overcooked," I said winking at him. "Thank you for breakfast."

"So...you know I'm going to Paris tomorrow for my first gig since the accident."

"Yeah..."

"Why don't you come with?"

"Me...uh, really? Why? Do you need help?"

"Not as my assistant."

"Oh." *This is definitely a thing.*

"Don't overthink it. Just come. I was telling the truth last night. I swear to you."

I was tired of fighting, and last night he finally accomplished his goal of fucking the bitch out of me. At least regarding this.

"But, I was supposed to see Nonna."

"She's doing fine, right? It's just a couple of days. How often do you get to pick up and go to Paris? I'm sure she'd want you to go."

He was right, she would. She was always a romantic and she always wanted me to find love especially because that was my only chance of having a family outside of her. In fact, after my brutal breakup with Kenneth, it was my grandmother who begged me not to let that experience ruin my ability to trust and love.

"I've never been to Paris," I said, already envisioning the millions of things I would want to cram into such a short visit.

"All the more reason to go."

"Won't you be working the entire time?"

"I extended the trip a day, so we'll be sure to have time to do whatever we want."

"Okay, I'll go, but only if you take me to the Eiffel Tower," I said, winking at him. I tried to contain my excitement, but it was buzzing on my skin and in the air between us. Heath let out a lungful of air as if he had been holding his breath while he waited for an answer.

"Of course, Sadie. Good...good," he said, nodding measuredly, but I could hear the happy smiles trying to escape his throat.

***

I found myself scrambling around town that afternoon, getting some last minute things together for the trip. Yeah it was three days, but I have a tendency to pack for a week's worth of clothing for every day of travel.

On my way back to the house, I was surprised to hear my phone go off with a call from Brock. I hadn't really spoken to him since he left except for a few texts to wish him well when I found out about his injury.

"Hey!" I was happy to hear from him.

"Hey Sade. How's it going?"

"Well, it's been a crazy summer since you left, but all in all, not too shabby."

"You're working with Hillabrand right?" Apparently they were familiar with each other from the "scene."

"Yeah. How are you?"

"Well, it's not great. I'm going to be out next season."

"Oh my god. I am so sorry!"

"I'm dealing with it."

"Well, please let me know if there is anything I can do."

"Actually, that's why I'm callin'"

"What's up?"

"I fucking hate Houston. I want to go back to New York for my recovery and I want you back with me."

"Oh...when?"

"I'm coming back in two weeks and I'll be going between New York and Houston for the rest of the year. I'm just not happy there and I don't want to spend the most depressing year of my life there." If I took Brock up on his offer, that would mean an early departure from Heath. Hell, I wasn't even sure what our employment arrangement would be at the end of the summer. All that was aside from whatever this thing was that we had.

"I need to think about this."

"I'll pay you whatever you want."

"I don't understand...why? There are other chefs."

"They're not you. I miss you, Sade. A lot."

WHAT?!? This could not be happening right now. Brock had me around for years and now he was...What? Trying to tell me he missed me? And if he meant it in the way the tone of his voice indicated (not just that he missed my special roasted quail), him offering to pay me whatever I wanted felt very prostitute-ish.

"Well I miss *working* with you too. You're like a brother to me, but I'm not sure what I want to do." Whatever Brock thought might be between us, other than friendship, had vanished long ago. "This is all very sudden. You know I'll need some time to think about it."

"Of course. Just let me know when you've made your decision. I really want you to come back though."

"Alright. I'll talk to you soon."

I knew the smart thing to do was to sit with the news for the rest of the week so I could process these new developments. But the truth was as soon as I hung up, I already knew the answer in my gut. If Heath asked me to stay, I would not be returning to work with Brock.

***

The next morning was a mess, the car service was late and I scrambled to get ready for the last-minute trip, but we got in the car with just enough time to hopefully make our flight. We were halfway to the airport when I realized I had forgotten something.

"Shit, where is my phone? I thought I put it in here..." I scrambled trough my purse. "Oh shit! I left it on the kitchen counter after talking to Nonna. Dammit!" From my level of panic, you'd a thunk I just found out I was on the no-fly list.

"There's no time to go back. We'll only be gone for three days and everything is squared away with Nonna, right?" The way *Nonna* sweetly rolled off of his tongue made me want to purr at him like a pussycat.

"Yes. The nurse said she has a mild cough, she gets allergies. But we spoke and she said she feels fine."

"Everything will be fine," he said calmly.

It was small things like this that I could see blossoming in us. Heath was the yin to my yang. I got stressed easily, and he trusted that things would work themselves out. I was generally skeptical and distrustful of people, Heath had a gazillion associates. I could be cautious (some might call that uptight), Heath went with the flow.

"We can get you a throwaway or you can just borrow my phone while I'm at the shoot. I usually shut it off when I'm there anyway. I'll give you the number of the director for an emergency." He put his hand on my thigh, and the tension released from my body.

Dating Mark was a good thing after all. I was beginning to understand that you don't know anyone until you really know them. I had taken Mark at face value and assumed he was a gentleman, and I had written off Heath as soon as he answered the door. And yet yesterday, there was only one guy who proved he would never let anyone hurt me. Now don't get me wrong, I was still cautious, but I decided that Heath might just deserve a chance. *Baby steps.*

***

Paris, ah Paris! I should have known that I would be a goner. It is the city of romance, outdoor cafes, beautiful architecture, and art. First, we arrived at the Four Seasons. Heath had told me we would be staying at the Presidential Suite (which I was super excited about), but unbeknownst to me, he upgraded to the Penthouse.

It was *a-fucking-mazing*. The bathroom was covered in seamlessly-veined tile and was the size of my entire apartment in

NYC. In its center was a deep soaking tub with a chromatherapy feature and a tiled ledge crowded with subtly fragranced candles. Our private balcony had an outdoor dining area and a dreamlike view of Paris; I felt like I could reach out and touch the Eiffel Tower if I tried hard enough. The room had an airy Parisienne feel: mostly ivory upholstery and bedding with touches of light blue and green. The opulence was in the details, fine crystal candleholders, glints of gold in the furniture and fixtures, carefully tended arrangements of flowers, intricately carved French doors, and mirrored dressers. While the room was contemporary, there were light hints of French baroque inspiration here and there, serving as a constant reminder we were in fact, in Paris. My perverted side noted that both the headboard and the wall behind it were padded, as if they built this room with our rage-sex in mind.

We were both exhausted, and Heath had a predawn wakeup for the shoot the next day, so we agreed to an early bedtime. I took a very quick shower to wash the travel scum off of my body, but could barely keep my eyes open under the warm spray of the shower. Emerging from the bath with an enormous plush towel wrapped around my head, I found Heath already in bed. He was tucked under the covers, wearing just his boxers, reading one of the books about Paris thoughtfully left on the night stand. He had taken a quick shower before me, and his hair had already dried into soft, fluffy, golden waves. I hadn't thought about what it would be like for us to sleep together like this. We did it once, when he was still wrapped in casts, but that was pre-sexual relations Heath and Sadie and things had changed drastically since then. I watched him for a little while, pretending to towel-dry my hair, partly because I loved watching the way the center of his brow crinkled a little when he concentrated and partly because I was nervous.

"Well, are you coming to bed or what?"

I slid in next to him, unsure of how to navigate this, but he wrapped his arm around me without even lifting his eyes from the book, dug his nose into my hair and kissed my temple. *Tread lightly Sadie.*

"So many things to do. I've been all over the world, but so many times I just fly in and out of a country without even experiencing it."

"Well that's sad."

"Yeah, I am going to try and remedy that, starting with this trip."

"Thank you for inviting me."

"Thanks for coming. Can I ask you something? I've been thinking about it for a while now, and it's been nagging at me."

I shifted to look him in the eyes. "Sure."

"You know the night with Josh, when we were playing the music?" I knew what he was going to ask. "I know you got upset with me..."

"No...listen, I am sorry about the way I reacted. I wasn't mad at you. God I feel like such a bitch."

"Talk to me. What happened?"

"It was the song and it was my fault for asking."

"Yesterday?"

I nodded.

"My dad used to play the guitar too and he used to play that all the time. My mom would sing along. It's pretty much one of the only things I remember vividly."

"I see."

"And...I might regret saying at some point seeing you don't need any more boosts to your ego, but you sang it beautifully."

"I knew you liked my voice. Chicks dig the guitar too," he said with a conceited smirk.

"See! This is exactly what I meant!"

"I'm kidding!" I snickered at him. "I didn't mean to upset you."

"No it was nice. It was a pleasant sadness. I hadn't felt my father's presence in a long time." Instinctively, I nuzzled my head on his shoulder. The moment was pulling me in and I couldn't fight it. "Do you remember your parents?"

He closed the book, rested it on his lap, and sighed. "No...my dad was never around and then my mother went to jail when I was 5. Then she died of an overdose when I was about nine, but I hadn't seen her since before she went to jail. She's a blur."

"Oh my god, I am so sorry."

"It is what it is, right? I bounced around for a while, but then I got lucky with the last family."

I felt a pit of shame in my stomach for how I had judged him. I had made assumptions about how easy his life and circumstances were. I assumed his success was solely due to luck without ever considering his character or work ethic might have something to do with it. Heath wasn't Kenneth, or the other guys before him. He never had a fair trial, I just collected evidence to suit my hypothesis.

After some comfortable silence I quietly spoke. "Heath, while I may not have been a fan of your tactics, thank you for having my back with Mark."

There was no response. I looked over to find Heath asleep, a look of calm on his beautiful face.

CHAPTER TWENTY-EIGHT

The jet lag wiped me out. I didn't hear Heath preparing to leave and only stirred when I felt him brush his fingers against my cheek and tuck a lock of hair behind my ear.

When I finally woke up I found a note on top of the book he was looking through last night.

Sadie,

I'll be gone until about 8pm. You know that I've been to Paris quite a bit throughout my career, so I thought I would plan a special day for you with my insider connections. My cell phone is on the entry table, number of the shoot director is under Evelyn in case of emergency. I set the alarm on my phone so you had time to get ready. Don't curse me if it wakes you up unexpectedly.

My driver will be waiting outside for you at 10am and he's all yours until 7pm.

Here's your itinerary:

- Have a croissant. You MUST. You are in Paris!

- The driver will first take you to Colette. I know you love fashion. I have a friend there who is expecting you. Her number is in my phone under Celeste, just in case. (I hope you don't mind, I know how you feel about people.)-Joking! Something tells me I will feel a sudden twinge of mystery pain today at work when you read that line.

- Then you'll go to a spa. Not just any spa. Trust me, your mind will be blown. Celeste will fill you in.

- I suggest that after the spa, you check out the outdoor market nearby. I know you will love it. The driver or Celeste can direct you.

Save the Eiffel Tower for me.

Your Rotten Scoundrel (I think that's the one thing you haven't called me yet. So take that!),

Heathy

His sign-off made laugh to myself. He was right, and I was a little envious I hadn't thought of that one yet and he HATED when I called him Heathy. I was completely blown away by Heath's attention to detail. I was so used to cooking for him and helping him with his plans, that I never expected that he would be the one to map out such a thoughtful and personalized day for me. Just as I put the note down, the alarm on both his phone and the clock went off and I almost fell out of the bed. In true Heath style, he picked the most obnoxious alarms and put them on full volume. I tried my best to send him those telepathic pain signals he mentioned in the note.

Anticipating the need for comfort, I wore a flowing white maxi dress, belted at the waist with a thin red belt and a comfortable pair of flat sandals. I loosely braided my hair and selected an orchid from the vase on my nightstand, pinning it above my ear. I arrived in the lobby at 9:30am, with just enough time to grab a croissant at a cafe just down the street. When I returned to the hotel, there was a black Mercedes at the curb. A young man dressed in all black except for a white shirt addressed me.

"Mademoiselle Sadie Lee?" He had the most adorable French accent.

"Oui," I said, feeling like a massive dork.

"My name is George. Monsieur Heath has told me all the plans of your day. Allow me to take you to Colette."

Colette, was a...*department store*? I wasn't quite sure what to call it, it had a much hipper feel than a Bergdoff's or even a Barney's. In fact, from the exterior, it looked like a large art gallery. George opened the door for me and a slim blonde in a boat neck cream summer sweater, a leather mid-thigh length skirt, and a pair of black and cream flat oxfords smiled across the room at me. Her look was punctuated with a bright coral pouch and matching necklace. She epitomized the effortless style one thinks of when they think of Paris.

"Sadie?" she asked. I've got to admit, my name is pretty fucking adorable in a French accent.

"Yes. Celeste?"

"Yes!" she said, embracing me with a light kiss on each cheek. "You must be very special. Heath wanted me to take good care of you."

"Oh, well thank you so much for doing this." I blinked, and laughed. "What exactly are we doing?"

She laughed too, tossing her barely shoulder-length pin-straight blond hair over her shoulder. "That's right, it's a surprise! I am a stylist here. We met a few years ago when I was just an assistant, but I have since worked up to head stylist. We often work together when Heath comes to Paris. Usually when he does Vogue shoots, but sometimes others too." I couldn't help but wonder if she was a friend like Illy or a friend like Mindy. She was definitely cute, and I wasn't sure if Heath would think about how pairing me up with a former fuck buddy might make me feel. "This is my specialty, so he wanted me to dress you up! He says you love clothes, no?"

"I do!" But ever in a million years did I ever imagine getting a trip with a personal shopper who has dressed people for the likes of Vogue.

"Okay, let's go cherie. You will be fun to dress up. You have a beautiful color and hair."

"Thank you," I said bashfully.

Celeste made a beeline to a fashionably dressed man and they kissed and chatted in French as if she was filling him in on some quick details. She turned back to me, "I know the staff here very well as I bring clients here. They are going to set us up with a dressing room. Heath said to get whatever you want. He will pay. I will handle all the details."

"Wow," I said, glancing over at a pair of shoes which I mentally converted to six-hundred US dollars.

She asked about my style and what I like, but I told her to dress me however she wanted as long as it was something I could wear with Heath tomorrow while we enjoyed Paris together. After all, what's the point of a stylist if you are going to tell her how to dress you?

We walked swiftly through the store, stopping at rack after rack for Celeste to snap up one item after another, pressing each against me and muttering to herself before deciding to keep or return to the rack. Then we made our way to a dressing room, where I relived the shopping scene from Pretty Woman that I had watched hundreds of times as a kid. Heath had said I could get anything, but I didn't want to take advantage of his generosity. I could have walked off with most of the store. But I insisted that we select one outfit, which here was still enough to pay my rent for two or three months in Brooklyn. Celeste tried playfully to convince me otherwise, telling me Heath insisted, but eventually she conceded. We settled on a chic shift dress that flattered my collarbones (*"très érotique,"* Celeste murmured approvingly), the softest and richest leather ballet flats, a deceptively simple purse in oxblood-colored python (sooo sorry, snake!), and (of course) an enormous printed silk scarf that Celeste tossed elegantly over my shoulders, knotting it firmly in that way that French women seem to be born knowing how to do. I felt like I was straight out of a French street-fashion spread in a fashion magazine.

"Before we finish, you cannot visit Paris without getting some perfume!" Her tone was mischievous. "This is more for him than it is for you," she said, raising her eyebrows.

"Well, if you say it like that..."

Celeste led me to the perfume counter. She chatted with the young lady who selected three bottles from a virtual laboratory on the shelves behind her. We dabbed all three on my arm, using coffee beans to neutralize the scent in between attempts. They were all lovely, but it was the Délire de Roses that blended perfectly with my chemistry, and had just the right notes of roses and fruit. The fact that the 1.7 ounce bottle cost well over $300 made me hesitate and ask the shop girl to put the bottles back but Celeste jokingly wrestled the bottle out of my hand and told the girl to ring it up immediately.

"Next we will go to the Hammam. Have you been to one?"

"No idea what that is."

"It is a Turkish bathhouse next to the most beautiful mosque. It is nice to be with a friend because there are some customs you might not know. I hope you are not shy because almost everyone is topless. There are only women however."

I thought back on the note: *Not just any spa. Trust me, your mind will be blown.* Now I imagined a much more mischievous tone in his voice.

The mosque appeared like a Moroccan oasis on a Paris street. Entering the women-only bathhouse, we were required to strip down to underwear at the very least, but when my new French friend, Celeste (as well as nearly everyone else) whipped off her top, I thought: *What the heck, I am in fucking Paris. Time to let the boobies fly in honor of Heath.*

The interior of the building was exquisitely decorated with jewel-like tiles and meticulously detailed wall paintings in rich, deep hues. Sweeping arches flanked by plastered columns and indoor fountains exuded an exotic, timeless luxury. The royal colors that enveloped us had all the vividness of a van

Gogh or Matisse painting. It felt like I had visited two countries in one day, instantly transported from Paris to Morocco.

This was not the Western spa of my previous (admittedly limited) experience. No, not even close: There is no such thing as privacy; naked bodies were everywhere. The gommage ladies (I'll get to that in a bit) actually get angry if you do things out of order--no gentle redirection, and certainly no New Age sayings or glasses of cucumber water! I was relieved and happy to have Celeste around to help me, despite accusations of misanthropy from Heath.

First Celeste and I had a quick shower and then a sauna with a special *savon noir* rubbed on our skin. This gave us some time to chat.

"So, are you close with Heath?" I asked her.

"We don't see each other often, but I consider him like a brother," she said. "He is a funny person, Heath. Makes me laugh." I didn't get the vibe they had anything other than a platonic friendship, but I never knew with Heath.

"Yes, yes he is," I said, tongue-in-cheek. "He can be very silly." I playfully rolled my eyes.

"I knew him when he was a new model, and I was new too as a stylist. He became on demand very fast. Very popular. I used to work for a boss who was very rude. In the high-fashion world it happens very much when you are an assistant, but Heath was always very nice. Once my boss screamed at me in front of everyone and Heath spoke to him, then he came to me alone and told me that it would not happen again." A pattern was beginning to emerge, Heath may be a lot of things, but he didn't like men who bullied women. *Swoon.*

After the sauna, we threw buckets of water on each other to clean off the *savon*. Then we hit the shower and then we did the GOMMAGE of HORRORS.

Now maybe I am a huge American pussy. Well, now I know I am. Because I couldn't decide if this was a spa or some sort of Turkish torture chamber. While other women waited and

214

watched, I lay naked on a table while a much older woman rubbed me down with a glove that I can only assume was made of the stuff used to sand concrete floors. I had to bite the inside of my lip to stifle screams of terror, but by the end I was as pink as a newborn piglet. I am sure I left the gommage with at least one less layer of skin than I came in with. Like I said, maybe I am just made of marshmallows. It is entirely possible. After the gommage, there was another shower and a honeymoon period where another no-nonsense woman massaged me with argan and eucalyptus oils, which seemed to make all the epidermal trauma more than worth it. After all the brutality, I was as smooth as the day I was born.

Celeste and I sipped some peppermint tea at the Hammam before getting dressed. She walked me out into the Parisian afternoon to the final leg of my day out in Paris: a street market on the Rue Mouffetard. This part of the journey was for me to go on my own as Celeste had to meet a girlfriend. We hugged, I thanked her for her hospitality, and we parted ways.

This was exactly the quaint, charming outdoor market one imagines when fantasizing about Paris. The narrow cobblestone street was lined with stalls offering brightly colored fresh fruits and vegetables, which spilled over from their crates begging to be plucked from a crowd of their peers. Small bakeries, cafes, and specialty food shops were tucked underneath antique block-lettered signs and awnings. All the tempting sights and sounds were on full display, each stand or shop vying for your attention.

I was starving, so I popped into Au P'tit Grec for the most delectable crepe with a touch of Nutella (I feared I wouldn't fit into my dress tomorrow with all the baked goods I had been eating, but not enough to stop). Feeling reenergized, I decided that for dinner I would put together a spread of fresh fruit, cheese and bread. I spotted the reddest most plump cherries I had seen in a long time and scooped a heap into a bag. I hand-picked tiny green plums, fragrant apricots, and grapes of several different colors. Fussing over fruit like this reminded me of my grandmother, who almost always got her fruit from the small Korean and Chinese fruit stands in New York. She always insisted they were a better deal and far better quality than the supermarket. She would have loved to shop this market with me. I ducked into a small and deliciously stinky cheese shop, and I did my best to ask about their offerings, using broken French as they patiently assisted me by conversing very slowly in French or translating to English when it was clear that I was completely lost. Apparently just saying the word "fromage" over and over again in shop with 300 varieties of cheeses only gets you so far. A wine boutique was conveniently next door, and all I had to do was show the proprietor the food I had purchased for him to select what he assured me was exactly the right bottle of champagne. Finally, I stopped at a bakery for a baguette, feeling like a very French cliché with it tucked under my arm as I went to look for the car. During my time at the market, I snapped a few photos using Heath's phone and sent them to my phone so that they would be waiting for me upon my return to the states. I looked forward to sharing them with my grandmother during my next visit with her.

George drove me back to the room in time to freshen up and prepare a little balcony picnic before Heath's arrival. I was just starting to cut up the fruit when Heath entered the suite.

He looked so tired.

"Hey." He barely had the strength to push out a smile.
"Long day?"

"You have no idea. I'm so jet lagged and I haven't been off of my feet since 4am. How was your day?"

"Heath...it was amazing. Seriously, everything. Thank you so much. But I do have to say that I think they used a cheese grater on me at the hammam."

Heath keeled over and laughed. "I wondered how you would feel about that, but it's something you must do while you're here. Tell me you went topless. I was fantasizing about that all day." He touched my arm. "Ooh, you're *soooft*."

"That's why you sent me there, so you could imagine me topless with Celeste?" I snarked playfully.

"How'd you like her?"

"She was really nice. She told me how nice you have always been to her. It was shocking." I said, cocking an eyebrow.

"I paid her to tell you that," he winked.

"Of course. So...she's like a sister to you or something?"

"Are you trying to ask me if she and I have ever known each other biblically?" *Am I that transparent?*

"Your words."

"No, Sadie. We have not. Contrary to popular belief I don't just stick my dick in random orifices. Besides, she likes *poisson* if you know what I mean...huhuhuh!" He did that last part in a stereotypical Frenchmen's accent. "I bet she looooved your tatas!"

"She's a lesbian?"

"One hundred percent. Completely hates the dick. Kind of makes the idea of you two topless together about 300% hotter." *Well, there went my worries about them ever having hooked up.*

"Oh so when she said she was meeting her girlfriend..."

"They weren't going to paint each other's toenails...at least I hope!"

I swatted Heath's arm and he pulled me in, kissing me softly, but passionately. He paused and leaned back to look into my eyes, and he just stood there for a moment, taking me in with the warmest smile. It was almost too much, and I broke the intimacy by speaking.

"I was just making us a little picnic here out on the balcony. I thought you might be too tired to go out."

"It's like you read my mind." He plopped face-first onto the bed. "Can you peel me off? I have to wash off all this crap they put on my face and body."

I looked at his arms. "You're golden."

"Yeah, I tried to get as much crap off as I could on the set. It was an editorial spread where I was an ancient Greek statue."

"Bwahaha!" I barked out a laugh. Heath sneered at me playfully. "I knew it! Your life really is like America's Next Top Model. Let me finish cutting the cheese and I'll come get you when I'm done. That should give you some time to wash up if you want. Though, I kind of like the gold," I said as I walked out the room.

"You said cut the cheese!" he called out, his voice obstructed by his face being smooshed into the mattress.

I took a few minutes to meticulously arrange the fruit and cheese and create a beautiful spread for us against the backdrop of Paris at dusk.

"Heath dinner's rea--" He was completely unconscious on the very spot where he had thrown himself on the bed. *So fucking adorable.* I grabbed an extra blanket from a closet and covered him. Then I was going to turn and leave, but I couldn't stop myself. My heart was so full watching him sleep there. I reached down and gently ran my fingers through his soft, golden tendrils, then I kissed him on the cheek, turned off the light and let him get a good night's rest.

***

It was about 3am when I felt Heath's tall silhouette standing over me. He had fallen asleep smack dab in the middle of the bed and I didn't have the heart wake him, so I slept on the loveseat in the adjoining room.

"What are you doing out here?" He asked, rubbing his eyes, his thick hair every which way, his boxers sitting low on his hips.

"You passed out and I didn't want to move you. You were so tired."

"Just shove me the the side next time. You can even use your feet if you have to. I'm pretty much a corpse in my sleep." He reached out his hand for me and helped me up. "Come back to bed with me."

I followed him and watched his back as slivers of outside light flickered over his still-golden body. Was this really happening? There was something about him I don't think I allowed myself to see before, or maybe he never allowed himself to show it.

He spooned me, caressing my hair and sliding his fingertips over the outer part of my arm. Nothing had ever felt so right before. *Tread lightly.*

"You're so beautiful." Sometimes when he said it, I found it hard to believe. I thought of it more as a throwaway line guys say to women when they want to bed them. He was constantly surrounded by beautiful women, what would make me so special in his eyes? But during this trip, I felt it. I felt it in the way he rubbed my cheek when he didn't know I was awake, in the way he left me the note after taking time to plan the perfect day in Paris for me, the way he felt my absence in the middle of the night. And now, I began to feel a new ache, this time in my heart. It wasn't just the ache of longing, it was the ache of longing and fear of loss. What if this wasn't real? What if this weekend was just a fragment in time, where the stars aligned perfectly, just like his seemingly unfortunate accident forced us to spend more time alone together than we had ever planned? What if we went back to the US and this became a hazy memory, only as real and as tangible as the dreams I had had of him?

And just like that night he had slipped into my room and held me as I exploded into millions of stars, I knew there was only one way to make the ache go away. I turned to face him and kiss him on his soft lips. He moved on top of me, his hardness had developed long before the kiss and now he seductively snaked his hips against me. He moved softly, tenderly, but he was so hard. His firmness was reassuring, it meant he wanted me in this way, just as badly as he had wanted me in the closet, and in the limo, and on the balcony. All I wanted was for him to be close to me, but close wasn't enough, he had to be inside of me, and even then I knew that wouldn't be enough. Each slow, deep thrust was an attempt to be that much closer. But I couldn't get enough of him. I wrapped my legs around his hips, and we kissed so passionately, so longingly, that the ache rose to my chest and it began to form in the back of my throat.

I ran my fingers along the firm ridges of the muscles in his arms and back. I had never wanted anyone so badly in my entire life. My yearning for Kenneth wasn't even close to this. Over time I had come to realize my feelings for Kenneth were wrapped in fantasy, an idealization of a boy I had carried with me from my teenage years. My feelings were more about finally getting him, proving something to myself, than they were about the man himself. Kenneth was a challenge I thought I had won, and then the victory was snatched from my grasp. But with Heath, all I did was fight, resist with every ounce of emotional fortitude I could gather. I didn't want to care, I didn't want to feel anything about him, but there was something undeniable there, something true.

And if Kenneth turned me into the bitter man hater I had become, what would Heath do?

Heath could destroy me.

"Sadie, come for me gorgeous," he moaned in my ear. I recognized the tenor of that moan, it meant he was near too. I hadn't closed the shades the night before, and the twilight sky cut through the window sheers and illuminated the patches of gold still on his skin. In that moment, looking into his glowing eyes, feeling the ache fighting to escape from my body in the only way it could, I knew. I knew.

"Heath!" I called out, my insides clenching around his girth. I drug my fingers into the smooth skin of his back. His forehead pressed against mine and his warm breath blew on my lips as he moaned my name over and over again.

I hoped the darkness would hide the tears welling from my eyes, but he knew right away. He didn't beg to find out what was wrong, or make me talk. He was just there. *I've got you.* He brushed my hair away and kissed one of the tears on my cheekbone and gently wiped the other one away with his thumb.

I think he knew too.

CHAPTER TWENTY-NINE

"I can't sleep," Heath murmured into my hair.

"Me neither."

"This is nice, lying here without you kicking me out or running away like you just stole something."

"It is." He finally got me to admit it.

"I hope this because you want to be with me and not because this is your only option while sharing a room with me in a foreign country."

"It is."

"Good, because I wasn't looking forward to tying you up," he jested.

"God, I am so weird, aren't I? I gave you a hand job and proceeded to clean you up like nothing had just happened."

Heath silently laughed to himself. Although I couldn't see him, I could feel his cheeks rise against the back of my neck and feel the vibrations of his laughter against my scalp . "Yeah, I didn't think anyone could surprise me until you did that. That entire night I was completely confused, replaying what happened in my head. I was sure you were going to walk in at any minute and tell me you quit again, then you just strolled on in like nothing happened. You are such a mindfucker."

"You mindfucked me the first week in the house. You kept having these stupid parties and I was about two MC Hammer songs away from committing mass murder."

"I guess I can see why you had a certain impression of me."

"Ya think?"

"Here's my theory: I think we're alike in many ways." I huffed out a sarcastic laugh and turned to face him to gauge if he's serious or if he's bullshitting me. "No, really. We both fear getting attached. Except, I just go from person to person and you put up the Great Wall of China of relationships. For some reason though, I feel like myself around you more than I ever could with anyone else. Like the Heath everyone else knows is some sort of act or role I am trying to fill. I didn't realize it until you came along though. I feel like I have a home when you're around. I'm not always searching, wandering, trying to find a place where I belong. A binge-watch marathon with you is so much more fun than a night of clubbing."

"Heath..." I didn't know what I was going to say, but I felt like I needed to stop him, because the things he was saying could not be unsaid. But he knew what I was trying to do and in his usual fashion, he persisted.

"I know it's scary, investing your feelings into someone who could hurt you, but then what's the point? I take risks. I am a risk taker and I want to take a risk on us because there is a chance we could be something amazing. But if you walk away and don't even place a bet, that's a guaranteed loss."

"I don't know if I can take that again Heath. And you're a risky gamble. I've seen your behavior. That's what all this has been...my avoidance, it's that I am prepared to have nothing at all rather than lose something important to me. I can't take any more loss. I just can't."

"Listen, you know if there is anyone who understands loss, it's me. I maybe carefree, but I am not careless. I don't ever want to hurt you. I know I've been an immature jackass. It's just when we met, there was something about you and I went into overdrive. It's what's worked for me in the past. I don't know how else to explain it other than that you turned me into a 16-year-old all over again. You made me nervous."

"Nervous?" I laughed at the absurdity of the male model telling *me* that *I* made him nervous.

"Yeah and damn you for that, no one has ever made me nervous. You were just so indifferent and unimpressed, and that doesn't happen."

"You're *so* modest."

"Oh come on."

"No, no, you're right. I've seen how panties disintegrate in your presence. That's why I struggle with this. I worked with an NBA superstar for years before you. Women throw themselves at him too. I know what that does to guys. I know what happens in relationships."

"Please don't compare me to those NBA guys."

"You know what I mean."

"I wish you wouldn't use other people as a way to measure me."

"Fair request, I suppose."

"And yes, you made me nervous. You're fucking gorgeous, and I know you try to pretend you don't know it, but you do. You knew what you were doing when you got dressed up for the interview, and the party before the accident. But when it all settled, when we could just talk, you're funny and intelligent and talented too. I spoke to Mindy about you, you know?"

"That backstabbing bitch! She didn't tell me anything," I said with a smile.

"She thinks you should write your own books and have your own show. You have so much fucking potential and with Mindy, you have the connections."

"I know, I just felt like I needed more experience before I did that."

"Fuck it, fuck being cautious. You are great *now*. Sometimes you just have to jump in and then learn how to swim."

"Also known as drowning."

"You're a pain in the ass." He brushed my hair away from my face. I admired his golden sparkling skin, his smooth flaxen tendrils, his incredibly deep blue eyes, all of which reflected the small amount of street light that filtered through the windows.

"I know."

"Those nights when you and I would just talk, don't tell me you didn't feel what I felt."

I looked down. "I'm here, aren't I?"

"Come on, let's put all of our chips on the table. Go big or go home."

"O-m-g, did you just take this terrible gambling metaphor to the next level?"

"Yes I did. I am a regular fucking Walt Whitman, except I love pussy."

I gasped and then laughed into his chest. "You are so crude!" I said in a faux-prissy voice.

"You love it. '*Sometimes with one I love, I fill myself with rage.*'"

"Methinks you are smart under that pretty face of yours," I say, surprised by his Whitman quote.

"Methinks you are sweet underneath that magnificent scowl of yours."

***

We couldn't have asked for better weather during our last day in Paris. The sky was clear, but there was a gentle, warm breeze in the air; perfect for walking around and taking in sights without melting into a pool of sweat. I wore my plunder from Colette: a navy blue and white striped pointe sleeveless shift mini dress with blood-red flats and that gorgeous scarf over my shoulders, although try as I might I could not re-create Celeste's perfect knot. *I felt very Parisienne.* Heath looked flawless as usual, with a low v-neck heather-gray t-shirt (the type only a model could pull off), under a cream linen blazer, and a pair of slim jeans with a pair of navy slip-on Vans. His hair looked like he had raked his fingers through it, pushing it all back and relying on its thickness to stay in place versus layering on product.

"I kind of miss the gold skin," I said to him as he loaded his wallet into his back pocket.

"We should have a body-painting party. Just you and me."

"That sounds messy."

"And fun."

I give him a suspicious look as I could see the wheels turning in his head, but he quickly changed the subject.

"Alright, are you hungry? I am fucking starving, I haven't eaten since yesterday afternoon."

"You poor thing," I pouted at him, with half genuine sympathy, half sarcasm. "There's a ton of cheese and fruit left over."

"We'll snack on that later in bed," Heath winked at me. *That horny rascal.*

As we were about to exit the lobby Heath stopped. "Wait right here." I watched from a distance as he walked up to the concierge's counter and engaged her in conversation. I could tell by the way she played with her hair and leaned forward as she giggled that she was already bitten by the Hillabrand bug. I resisted the urge to follow him and see what they were talking about; I didn't want to appear jealous or nosey. After a few minutes, Heath returned with a smile on his face and slapped my ass. I jumped and quickly looked around to see if anyone noticed, but everyone was buzzing around in the lobby minding their own business.

"Heath!" I scolded.

"Couldn't help myself," he smirked.

We arrived at Cafe Constant, a well-known restaurant close to the Eiffel Tower. Just as the hostess informed us that the wait would be about thirty minutes, a couple of giggling Americans walked up and asked for a photo and autograph from

Heath. The hostess's eyes lit up when she recognized who he was.

Heath graciously posed with the girls, who were probably no older than 19, and the hostess, now realizing he was "important," offered to seat us immediately.

He quickly eyed the other people hanging around who had arrived before us. "That's okay, we'll wait. Are you okay with that?" he asked me as he tenderly rested his hand on the small of my back. I knew he was famished, and his graciousness in waiting with everyone else made me smile inside.

"Sure," I said. We walked out to the sidewalk to wait. "That was nice of you, not to use your celebrity."

"I'm no saint, but you know already know that," he grinned as he nudged me. "I just try not to use it when I don't need to. I can wait a half hour, it's gorgeous out here anyway."

Karma must have been on our side because we were called within 20 minutes. We were seated at a small outdoor table. A cute French girl named Yvette introduced herself as our server.

"Bonjoor madem-wa-selle!" Heath said in the most pathetic, over-the-top French accent I had ever heard. I shook my head, looking down in embarrassment.

She giggled and her cheeks turned a fuchsia color. "Bonjour. Would you like to start with something to drink? An appetizer?"

"French fries?" Heath joked as he cocked his eyebrows. Again, she giggled. I watched the interaction feeling humored and embarrassed all at the same time. "I'm just kidding, Yvette. Do you know what you would like Sadie?"

"Actually, I think I need a few minutes."

Yvette nodded and gave us some time to think.

"What?" he asked innocently when he noticed the look on my face.

"You are such a flirt."

"Me?"

I almost spit out my water laughing at his 100%, pure, grade-A bullshit response. "Yes, you!" I wasn't upset, in fact I held a strange admiration for how he could just make nearly any straight (or even not straight) woman blush.

"I promise you I wasn't flirting. I just like to make people feel comfortable. Is that so wrong?"

"When you look like that," I gestured to him, "going out of your way to make women feel comfortable is automatically flirting."

"We balance each other out. You're a bit more reserved around new people."

"I guess."

"Does it bother you? That I'm friendly?"

"No...I wouldn't want to change you. As long as it's just you being friendly." *What am I saying? Is he asking for my permission?* The conversation started to enter that murky territory again that I know we would inevitably have to settle: *What is this thing? What are we doing? How can we be both employee/employer AND maintain or grow whatever this budding new thing is that we have?* I didn't feel like I was in any position to tell him to act in any way. At that point, all we were officially were colleagues fucking on vacation.

Yvette returned just in time to halt any further conversation.

"Do you have any questions?"

We hadn't even looked at the menu yet. "You know what? I am going to let my lady-friend here chose for us. Isn't she beautiful?" *That mofo could be so charming when he wanted to be.*

Yvette smirked, "*Oui*, she is very pretty." She turned to me, "You have beautiful skin."

"Thank you," I said quietly, feeling a little overwhelmed by the compliments coming from all directions. This moment was typical with Heath, when he saw me getting uncomfortable, he would often choose to lay himself on thicker. Resistance was futile.

"She's a chef. A chef to the stars." *There he goes, laying it on me.*

"That is amazing. Who have you worked with?" Yvette asked.

"I have done work for some actors and actresses, Sarah Jessica Parker, the Timberlakes, Robert DeNiro. My main client was a basketball player in New York City. Right now however, this fella over here is who I work for." *Perfect way to get the attention off of me.*

"Oh," she eyed him to see if she could recognize his face.

"He's a model. Can't you tell?" I asked playfully.

"Well..." she clearly didn't want to say anything out of line.

"I'm just messing with you! Anyway, I know it's busy in here, I don't want to keep you for long. I think we'll go with the foie gras terrine and the soft boiled egg to start. We'll each have a glass of Chateau d'Yquem." I looked over at Heath for his approval and he gestured back to remind me I was the boss here.

The appetizers arrived shortly after and we quickly both spread the foie gras onto crostini. It was dense and decadent and melted in my mouth like butter. We each let out an audible moan with the first bite.

"I've never had foie gras before."

"Really?"

"Yeah. You know I'll try anything, but usually, I stick to what I know when I eat out."

"Do you know what it's made of?"

"No..." he said fearfully as he swallowed the contents of his last bite.

"Fatty goose liver. And you don't even want to know how they make it happen. It's literally a guilty pleasure."

"You're right. I don't want to know."

We dipped into the egg, which was covered in breadcrumbs and atop a bed of ratatouille, bacon, and a parmesan cream foam. It was superb. Shortly after, the chef stopped at our table, after being told by Yvette that I was a celebrity chef. We had a pleasant conversation and he insisted in making us a special duck entree. By the time we left the restaurant, we were both as stuffed as a pre-foie gras-ed goose.

Our next stop was the Eiffel Tower, and we really needed the walking. We climbed all available staircases by foot, only taking the lift to the open air observation deck at the top. After looking out at the stunning views of Paris for a few minutes, Heath declared: "We should take a picture." He took out his phone and asked an older woman if she would snap some. He whispered in my ear as we posed, "you ask the mature people so if they try to run off with your phone you can tackle them much easier." I let out a loud laugh as she snapped the first pic.

"What a beautiful couple," the kind lady said after the first picture. "You would make beautiful children." *Awkward.*

"I think so too," Heath said, as usual, unfazed by any situation that most might find socially awkward. While my mind was still spinning about how to navigate the woman's comment, I felt my body swoop away from the ground. As I called out some random noise, I found myself in Heath's arms as the lady snapped away.

"Smile!" he said.

Onlookers watched and smiled and some other strangers began to snap pictures on their own cameras. "I'm going to kill you," I whispered in his ear.

"Looking forward to it."

CHAPTER THIRTY

Honestly, I don't think I could have planned a better day out in Paris with Heath than the one we had. Maybe this *could* work. Maybe I only made things worse by expecting the worst from Heath. And I know that a vacation is not a good time to decide on a relationship. Much like our time cooped up in his house, it was an artificial environment, but I couldn't help feeling that glimmer of hope. Heath was so much more complex than I had given him credit for. He wasn't just some crass, thoughtless jerk. He could be kind, and caring, and tender. And maybe just how he had brought out the most man-hating, conflicted version of myself I could muster when we first met, I might have caused him to be the most horn-doggy, douchebaggy version of himself.

Maybe the frog could become the prince! But in this case, instead of kissing it, you had to sit on its face. And we all know I've fulfilled that requirement multiple times over.

But now that we were relaxed, and we both could just admit that there was something between us, everything smoothed out, everything felt right. I had no idea my perfect day would get even *perfect-er* (deal with it grammar hawks!)

We entered the lobby to the hotel all smiles. We had decided to skip dinner out, having had such a large lunch, and Heath said he had dessert for us back in the room, but he wouldn't give me any more details.

When we got into the elevator, Heath grabbed my hand and pulled me close to him. *Can I just interject here and tell you how much I loved having a fully-functional Heath?* He raked his fingers through my hair and clenched it at the roots, passionately kissing me as I leaned against him, his hardness already pressing against my belly.

"Mmmm," I said, rubbing my hand over his pants.
"You smell so good."

"That's the perfume you got me. I thought you'd like it."

"I've been thinking about fucking you all day," he said as the elevator bell rang. I quickly spun around, but he kept me pressed against him to hide his raging hard-on. We both nodded at another couple as they entered the elevator and we side-shimmied out in unison.

"Come here, woman!" Heath said, throwing me over his shoulder as soon as the elevator closed behind us.

"You are such an animal," I said as he fumbled with the keycard. "I bet you're regretting this decision to throw me over your shoulder after all the food I ate today. I think I gained fifteen pounds."

"You need to promise me something."

"Oh lord. Why does that statement terrify me?"

"Promise."

"Okay."

"Cover your eyes and don't open them until I say so."

"Surprises make me nervous."

"They should when they're coming from me. Now cover your eyes."

I did, and and then felt the cadence of his steps underneath me as he walked into the suite, then he slid me over his front; from the firmness of the tiles at my feet, I knew we were in the bathroom. "Keep your eyes covered."

"Okay dammit!"

The sound of his footsteps vanished into another room and was followed the sounds of him fumbling around. "Ahhhh," I tensely called out, doing a pee-pee dance in my spot, unable to do anything else with the nervous energy.

Finally, he said: "Open your eyes."

There he was, standing in all of his butt-naked, Adonis-like glory, holding what looked like a medium-sized jar of gold paint.

"Wha-?" I instantly recalled our conversation that morning. *He doesn't waste any time.* "Is that body paint?"

"One better; edible paint. They use it on cakes and such. Now get naked."

I buried my face in my hands and laughed to myself in disbelief. "You are something else."

"I know I am," he smirked. "I pay attention to everything, so you need to watch what you say around me. Now, move it along."

"Okay," I said as I exhaled. "Could you unzip me?"

"Of course," he said, pursing his lips like he was eying a scrumptious meal. He put down the jar and helped me out of my clothes so that I was now completely naked.

"Since I am so experienced with body paint, I think I'll go first."

"I'm all yours," I said, raising my hands up.

He licked his lips and he examined my body, biting his sexy-ass bottom lip as he decided his first move. This must have been what he was talking about to the concierge. I thought he was flirting when really, he was asking her to find and deliver edible body paint to our room. *That devil.*

He took a few steps towards me, "I think you know where I'll go first." He took the brush out, and wiped it against the rim of the jar. Then he took the tip of the brush and softly painted my nipple. "Your breasts are my favorite things in the world. I just wanted to let you know that. If we were in a plane about to go down, I would say goodbye to them first."

I laughed in feigned disgust as I playfully shoved him away. As he did the same to the other nipple, his face was flush with arousal, his dick was again rigid and at attention. I wanted to jump him so badly, but watching him admire me was such a turn on too. He dropped down to one knee and made a sweeping curve across my hips. I looked up at the mirror and saw it made a huge smiley face.

"How sexy," I teased. He licked and gently bit the edge of the smile on my stomach, I instinctively grabbed at his hair, took a deep breath and stopped myself from going any further. "Where's my paint?" I asked.

"Right there," he pointed to a silver jar at the rim of the bathtub. "Thought I'd change up the color for you."

"You'd look good in any color," I scowled. I grabbed the jar, dipped my finger, and pursed my lips around the paint. "So sweet," I said seating myself on the edge of the tub. Heath was still kneeling in front of me, and now that we were eye to eye, he kissed one of my breasts and licked the tip of my nipple.

"It is."

The feeling of his lips on my breast made me squirm in my seat. *Good-god that felt amazing.* I took my brush and painted his lips and immediately kissed him. The sweet taste of the paint, mixed with the delicious taste of his kiss, made my heart speed up and my stomach swirl with arousal. I pulled away trying to figure out what to do next and felt so in tune with him, like this bathroom was our own little cocoon, and I didn't need to be so guarded. I felt safe here, and it filled me with a playful joy I hadn't felt in as long as I could remember.

I took a glob of silver paint with my fingers and slid it through his hair, laughing mischievously.

"Oh, you bitch!" he said playfully, reaching for a glob of his gold paint and smearing it on my face.

I laughed, licking the syrupy flavor from my lips, wiping my face (which only added some silver to the mix) and then wiped what I collected all over his chest. Heath's bright smile gleamed against his silver hair. He reached to grab his entire jar, and instantly I knew war had been declared. I raced for mine as quickly as I could, and then we were a mess of gold, silver, and laughter. We had both emptied our jars on each other and rubbed as much as we could on the other. He wrapped his arms around my slick body and slipped back onto the bathroom floor still holding onto me so that I landed on top of him. I laughed so hard, I couldn't even make a sound or ask him if he was okay. But he was smiling too, so I knew he was fine. He rolled over in a flash, the shock of the cold tile against my back made me finally howl aloud. I opened my eyes to see his exquisite face, his blues shone out like two beacons in a silvery moonlit ocean.

"I love to watch you laugh. I love it even more when I'm the one who makes you laugh. God, you're beautiful."

Suddenly, I felt very heavy. It was something in the way he said that, the way he looked at me. I knew he was being playful, but it was as deep and as true a thing as I had ever heard him say. My laughter faded to a wistful smile, because I knew that I was falling harder than I had ever fallen before and it was the most thrilling and frightening experience of my life.

He lowered his face down to my belly button, and using the tip of his tongue, he slowly glided up my stomach, over the crest of my breast, past my collarbone and up to my earlobe, gently biting and sucking on it. "You're the sexiest piece of cake I have ever had," he whispered into my ear. "I just want to eat you up. I want you all to myself."

"Shut up and eat then."

He cocked his eyebrow and bit his lip again and it really made me feel like a confectionary in front of a fat kid, a little scared he would literally consume me.

Again he lowered himself, sliding down my slick golden torso, this time stopping between my thighs, and he licked the inside of my upper thigh. I looked down at his glimmering silver shoulders, striped with streaks of gold, like some sort of drag-queen's vision of a sexy man-tiger, and it was surreal. *I am in Paris, on the floor of the penthouse suite at The Four Seasons, covered in silver and gold edible paint with the most popular Calvin Klein model in the world between my legs, threatening to eat me like a piece of chocolate cake. This is so fucking awesome!*

Heath delivered on his promise to eat me as he worked his way inwards, gliding his tongue over my golden labia, making me wriggle with excitement. I wrapped my shiny legs around his neck as he penetrated me with his tongue. I moaned, writhing along the cold tiles, my nipples hardening from the various sensations of touch and taste that enveloped me.

"Fuck, Heath..." I moaned under my breath. He pressed my hips closer to his face like he couldn't get enough of my taste. He only stopped to look up with that panty-terminating smirk to say "candy covered cherry, *yum*."

"Shut up!" I said, pushing his face back down, "and let them eat cake!"

His laughter muffled into my "cake" and then he artfully sucked on my clit, to which of course, my natural response was to hump his face. Just as I was about to come, he stopped and leaned over me again so we were face to face.

"I want you feel you come around me."

"I think I could arrange that, but if you tease me like that again, I'll make you pay." His thick, warm penis rested on my stomach, such a contrast to the cold floor beneath me.

"I want to see that ass of yours," he said, reaching under and grabbing a handful. "I want you from every fucking angle."

"Well then fuck me from behind with that big cock of yours." He did something to me when we were together. He was right about why I was scared to open up to him, because when I was around him I became reckless and dirty.

Without hesitation he turned me onto my stomach and again I gasped, as the cold floor hardened my nipples and awakened the entire frontside of my body. He rubbed my ass with his hands, sliding along the body paint, which was still wet, and then squeezed it firmly. I let out a moan of pain and pleasure. He kissed and nipped my cheeks what felt like twenty times, and it tickled so much that I giggled like a sixth grader. His hot body laid on top of mine, and it was so warm and close, his firm muscled physique engulfed me with his energy. Heath brushed my tiger-like hair (black with golden streaks) away from my ear and whispered in my ear "I have been thinking about sticking my cock inside that warm, tight pussy of yours all day. In the restaurant, on the fucking stairs of the Eiffel tower..." He rubbed himself just outside of my entry, but he was being a tease. He wanted to make beg him, he wanted to hear me tell him I wanted him.

"You're such a tease," I said propping my ass up.

"I just love to hear your voice when you're ready. It's smokey and sexy."

"Is it?"

"Oh yes, just then, your voice," he said, gyrating his hips against me.

"I'll say whatever you want Heath, just please put your dick inside of me and fuck me senseless."

The warmth of his breath formed a gentle breeze on my ear and he slid inside of me. I dug my forehead against the cool floor, feeling so overwhelmed by the long thickness inside of me. From that angle he was so deep, my thoughts were only of him rubbing inside of me, and that sensation might be the closest thing to heaven on earth I had ever experienced. This time he was slow and rhythmic, he wanted to savor my cake. Each time he plunged into me felt like the first time. He suckled on my neck, "you taste so sweet, Sadie. You're so wet and tight, oh god," he whispered seductively into my ear.

My moans rose with each entry, as I came closer and closer to climax. His body slid against mine like we were two well-oiled pistons, except we were lubricated with metallic food paint not WD-40, which tasted far better, (not that I've ever tasted lubricating oil, just an educated guess). I tried to stop myself from coming by clenching up and holding my breath. I didn't want this to end, but my body was betraying me. Being as in tune as we were, and every nerve ending on the muscled curves of Heath's chest and abs being in direct contact with my back, he could tell. He could feel the softness of my body harden with tension, he could feel my smooth breaths halt to short bursts as I tried to hold them in, he could see my fingertips turn white as I pressed into the limestone floor. He responded by increasing his rhythm ever so slightly.

"You didn't want me to tease you, I'm not teasing you now. I'm giving you all of me, just let go baby. I want to feel you come around me, I want to hear your moans." His voice changed too when he was hot, it got deeper and breathier, the clean scent of his breath was like a perfume for my arousal. "You feel so good, I can't hold out much longer, come with me. Let go."

I couldn't resist the fullness inside of me, sparking sensation at every point of contact, the tenor of Heath's voice, the heat of his muscles massaging against my back, the cold floor stimulating my nipples, the sweet taste of the gold liquid on my lips. He was right, I needed to let go, this would not be the last time, this was just the beginning. And my rhythm returned, my breathing flowed, my moans returned to their previous pitch and I called out his name. "Heath, come with me. I want you to come inside of me as I come," it was barely a whisper. I wanted-- needed--all of him. Every last drop.

"Yes," he said, barely able to get the word out. His hips moved faster, but still smoothly, snaking against the softness of my bottom, his fingers pressed against the floor, his chest vibrated in the way that I knew he was about to release and so, I let go. We both called out a mix of aggressive, guttural groans and moans from deep inside. His cock grew and contracted as I contracted around him, allowing us both to reach the highest peaks of our climaxes together.

***

Somehow, we found ourselves on a makeshift nest on the floor made from bath towels. Yes, we were in a penthouse in the Four-*freaking*-Seasons, but chose to remain on the bathroom floor of all places. The sun had nearly set, leaving only one dim light on in the bathroom, casting a candle-like hue throughout the space. Heath played music off of his phone and grabbed a bottle of wine I had left over from my picnic the night before.

"Turn your Lights Down Low" played in the background as I rested my head on Heath's still-bare chest. He quietly sang along to the song as I rocked my head from side to side, patting my fingers on his chest to the beat. It was another song that I discovered we both loved.

"We might want to consider getting this stuff off of us," I suggested.

"I don't know, I think we look pretty fucking incredible covered in this." I gave him the once over, he was almost entirely silver with slivers of gold, occasional patches of his skin peeking through. "Seriously, there is something incredibly hot about your naked body covered in gold."

"Well thank you, but it's starting to get sticky. I think we've far surpassed the sexy point with this stuff. Can you imagine walking through the airport like this?"

He let out a small laugh. "Something tells me we would start to gain a following of random animals and wayward children."

"I assume the hotel got this stuff for you?"

"Yeah, the concierge."

"I'm impressed that they got it so quickly."

"You get this room, you get whatever you want. Besides, this is the city of bakeries and whatnot, plenty of edible food coloring to go around."

"I don't think I can eat another sweet thing for a week."

"Bullshit, you have a major sweet tooth."

"What makes you say that?"

"I know about your secret Oreo stash in the cupboard over the fridge."

I propped up on my elbow, my mouth agape. "That was specifically designed to be non-wheelchair accessible."

"Yeah, well now I'm back to six-foot-three and I don't know where anything is in that damn kitchen, so I look through all of the cupboards and drawers just to find a goddam spatula.

Then I saw your betrayal: hiding cookies from me. It hurt, I must admit."

"Well, for one it's my job to keep you looking like this," I waved my index finger up and down at him. "Secondly, I'm hiding them from myself. If they were anywhere else, I would consume the entire bag in seconds."

"Fair enough. Want to take a shower? I realize that day I asked you to, we never made it that far."

My heart fluttered remembering that romp. "We didn't...that's because you can't keep your paws off of me."

"And you can't keep your pussy off of my knob.'"

"Jesus Christ of Nazareth," I gasped, but I have to admit, I loved the playfully arrogant side of Heath as much as I loved his tender side.

He grinned. "Shall we?" He smirked like the gorgeous devil he is.

"Let's go," I grunted out as I sat up. I gave him my hand and helped him off the floor, which immediately made me recall the circumstances of our first kiss and made me smile. "This floor is a mess. Are they going to charge for that?"

"No because you're going to clean it up. Didn't I tell you that before you made this mess?" he winked.

"This is all your fault! As usual, you dragged me into your bad behavior."

"I love turning you to the dark side, what can I say?"

I lead him by the hand to the shower.

"Sadie?"

"Yes..."

"How many calories do you think that whole thing just cost us?" he asked sincerely.

Fucking models.

242

CHAPTER THIRTY-ONE

The next morning, we found a small cafe for breakfast before heading to the airport. I was no longer able to keep up the emotional fort around me, Heath had finally disassembled the wall I thought I had so flawlessly erected. He was my one-man wrecking crew. I couldn't imagine going back to the way things were: either stopping this affair altogether or just engaging in forbidden fucks only to then pretend like nothing had happened. Heath and I were a thing and I could no longer retreat like I had before, we had moved way past mental war games. I had to concede, I had to put all of my chips in. And dammit, even though I had promised myself that I would never again expose myself to potential devastation like Kenneth had put me through, I was so effin' excited!

That being said, I'm not good at initiating that whole talking about my feelings thing, and it would be Heath, the shameless open book, who would bring up the conversation.

Over some tartine, eggs, and coffee, Heath was the one to bring our "thing" up. "So...what are we going back to? You know how I feel."

"I do?"

"We spoke about this the other night. You know, gambling, Walt Whitman, etcetera."

"Refresh my memory."

"God, you are going to make this as painful as possible, aren't you?"

"That's not the goal. I just need to know this is real because it feels like a dream. I'm in Paris for fuck's sake."

He smirked and leaned forward, placing his arms on the table in front on him. "It's not a dream. We're just really that good together. I want to be with you and that's it. I don't want to see you with anyone else. I acted like...I acted the way I do...and I almost watched you walk away with that Wall Street tool."

"He never had a chance."

"Well, I don't want to risk it. I know I am a pain in the ass, but so are you."

"How darling."

"I wouldn't want it any other way. You challenge me and you get me. And you're home for me." I looked away, feeling shy by the openness of the conversation. "So what's it gonna be, my Ice Queen?"

I looked up at him, locking my hazel eyes into his aqua blues. "You know what they say, go big, or go home." Heath smiled and it made me smile like we were mirroring each other's happiness. "I know I am ever the wet blanket, but what about our working arrangement? Are you comfortable with that?"

"You keep feeding me like that and I will pay you forever," he winked. "Seriously though, let's just keep going just as we had planned. But after September, I am firing you."

"What?" The harshness of his delivery took me by total surprise.

"No more cautiousness. You need to work for yourself. You're ready, stop working for assholes like me and Brock and get out there and use your talents."

He was right, I needed to stop waiting: waiting for the moment when I suddenly felt experienced enough to write a proposal for a book deal or sign on with Mindy so she could help me expand my career. I needed to stop telling myself I would open up a restaurant with my trust someday. I needed to stop guarding myself from possible failures in my career and my love life and just do shit now.

"That sounds like a plan, but I'll need your referral."

"Whatever you want as long as you show me those tittaays," he whispered across the table. *That's my Heath!*

***

We made it back to Heath's place in the Hamptons mid-evening. The first thing I did upon my return was run over to my phone, which was now dead, and scoop it up.

"*Muah muah muah*!" I kissed it several times.

"That's a sickness. What you just did there with your phone is sick," Heath said. I immediately turned on my professional hat, determined not to let our *thing* put me in a position to slack off on my responsibilities, and looked in the fridge. It was barren.

"I'm going to grab some stuff for tonight and tomorrow," I called out from the kitchen.

"You don't have to. We just got back, you must be tired." He was treating me like his girlfriend, which was sweet, but he was paying me and I had a job to do.

"No, I want to. It'll be quick, just so we have some basics in the fridge."

"Whatever floats your boat." When I passed him on my way through the living room he was already on his laptop, presumably catching up on emails and the like. "Aren't you forgetting something?" he asked as I headed towards the front door.

"What?" I whipped around and felt for my purse and keys.

"I want to feel your lips on mine."

"Usually that results in much more."

"I promise, I'll be good," he said, pouting. I walked over to him and he pulled me on his lap. I tucked my chin under and laughed as he showered me with kisses. "How long do you think you'll be?"

"Oh, an hour I guess maybe an hour and a half. You know I like to peruse the aisles and look for deals and such. I think I am going to stop at Walgreens. Remember? Customs made me throw out my $30 shampoo, those bastards."

245

"Alright."

The first thing I did upon entering my car was to hook my phone up to the car charger. It usually took a few minutes to turn back on when it had been drained completely like that. I blared the radio, feeling consumed with probably every happiness-inducing hormone known to man. "I Knew You Were Trouble" by Taylor Swift popped up on the radio and I jacked the volume up and sang it at the top of my lungs. I hit a red light and lost myself in the moment, pounding the steering wheel, eyes closed, belting out the words in my wobbly-pitched singing voice. A honk jolted me out of my personal concert and I looked over to see two teenage boys pantomiming me. I stepped on the gas to get out of that embarrassing situation as quickly as possible and made it to the lot of the grocery store in just a few minutes.

It wasn't until I arrived in the parking lot of the grocery store that I noticed the voicemails from a New York area code. Immediately, there was a dreadful tightness in my stomach which was confirmed by voicemails from St. Luke's Hospital.

You are listed as the emergency contact for Isabella Lucca. Please call us as soon as possible.

The voicemail didn't fully sink in, just the key sentences that informed me something was very wrong.

When I finally spoke to someone, she told me what she could on the phone: Nonna had a bad fall and fractured her hip. At her age that was very bad, but there was more. They had run some tests and found some things. I would want to come as quickly as possible. I asked to speak with her and they told me she had been sleeping a lot because of painkillers but they would try. I was lucky to find her awake.

"Nonna?"

"Bella?" Sometimes she called me that, it was my mother's name.

"How are you?"

"Eh...okay, okay." She sounded groggy.

246

"The doctors said you had a fall. What happened?"

"I don't know. I don't remember."

"I'm coming to see you, okay?"

"Did the doctors tell you I'm sick?"

"What? What are you talking about?" They said they wanted me to come to the hospital, but what she said washed me in panic. "Grandma...what are you talking about?"

"Don't worry baby, I'll be fine."

"I know, you are going to be fine. I am going to take care of you. What's this talk about being sick?"

"The doctor says I have the cancer in my lungs." She said it so frankly and so unassuming, as if she was telling me she had heartburn. My eyes welled up, it took everything I had not to lose it and cry all over the phone. I should have been there with her, I should have held her hand as they told her the news, but I was off in Paris with some guy I could barely stand a couple of months ago.

"I'm sorry I couldn't be there. I would have flown back. I forgot my phone. I am so sorry."

"No, I'm happy. I wanted you to have a good time. Is he nice? The boy?"

I laughed wistfully to myself. *I told you she was a romantic.* "Yeah, he's nice," I said, my voice wavering from the tears. And now, I knew it was even more important to her that I find someone, because she was my Alfred. And it was possible I might not have her for much longer. "I'm coming, okay? Right away."

"Don't drive fast." Typical of my grandmother, to care about the speed of my driving when she was given a potential death sentence.

"I won't. I love you and I'll see you soon." Those last words broke a seal, tears gushed out of my eyes. I knew this day would come, I always knew it, but it hurt so badly to know that I could be truly alone in this world. That I would have no one to fall back on unconditionally. That the person who was my buoy, my beacon in the lonely ocean of this world, would disappear from this earth. I covered the receiver so she wouldn't hear me.

"See you, Bella."

I cried for several minutes in the car, letting out all of the fear, emptiness, and anger I felt at myself for dropping the ball and not being around when she fell, and at the world, for taking my parents and now her. But something new stirred inside of me: I felt the urge to fall back on someone, the one person who I knew could make the ache in my chest subside. His smile, his touch, his words: they made my sadness fade. I wanted to cry into Heath's arms, I wanted him to sing me a song, I wanted him to caress my cheek like he did that morning in Paris when he thought I was asleep. I was going to go all in with him because that is what Nonna would want me to do. She wouldn't want me to live my life in fear of being hurt because she was wise enough to know that it is that fear that makes it so. I sucked back the tears and raced to the house. My plan was to tell him everything, to cry into his warm chest, to feel his kisses on my temple. Then I would go be with my Nonna and sort out what could be done with the doctors.

I wiped my eyes before opening the door to the house. I didn't want to freak him out by coming in hysterically, and I wanted to be able to explain the situation to him, which I would not be able to if I had lost it again.

I opened the front door to the house, the foyer and living room was empty.

"Heath?" I called out, but there was no answer.

"Oh, hello..." Out from behind the wall that blocked part of the kitchen from the foyer, walked Illy. All six-foot-eight, 80 pounds of her. She had on a dress that was more like a shirt in length, fuck-me heels, her makeup was done, her hair blown out. She was trying to impress.

Just as I was about to ask her what she was doing in the house, Heath walked out from the hallway, fixing his pants. His eyes expanded when he saw me.

CHAPTER THIRTY-TWO

I dropped my bags on the floor and looked at Heath with the flame of ten-thousand suns in my eyes. "What is *she* doing here?" I stabbed my finger in her direction, but didn't look at her.

"I don't need your permission to be here you basic beech," said the poor man's Giselle Bunchen.

"Shut up you desperate skank," I sneered at her. "And what's a basic beech? Is that opposed to a sandy beech? Or an exotic beech? You should speak less and do what you're paid to do: stand there and act like a human clothes hanger."

"Too bad you came, ve vere just starting to have fun. Don't you have groceries to put away, house girl?"

If it were any other time in all of time, even in an alternate universe, I would've acted like a civilized human being. I would have used my words, which as we all know can draw blood on their own. But this was not any other time, this was not some other universe, I was here in this moment. I had just found out my only living relative, the person who had been a mother figure to me most of my life would likely soon perish, and the man I had fought so tirelessly to guard my heart against betrayed it as soon as he had it in his smarmy clenches. And now he had thrown in on the floor and was river dancing on it.

I left the house for twenty fucking minutes. Twenty fucking minutes and he was coming out of the back of the house and adjusting his fucking pants like the man whore I knew he was. *Fuck me*. Fuck me for being so stupid. I had promised myself that I would rather be alone and safe, than open my heart to someone and be hurt again, and I broke that promise as soon as a pretty man told me all the things he knew I wanted to hear. I was just a challenge to him, he had said it before, he used that *exact* word to describe me. Now I had made myself easy to access. And what do people do once they have conquered something? They move on to the next challenge.

So no, I didn't act classy or like a grown up. I lost my shit. Royally.

"You stupid bitch!" I said, charging at her like I was attacking my husband-cousin on an episode of Jerry Springer. I had just about had it with her faux high-society, wannabe Linda Evangelista, snotty, cunty attitude and I was going to show her how we really handle things in New York.

"Woah! Woah! Woah!" Heath said, sprinting to intercept me; he got to me just in time to scoop me by my waist, but I got a handful of *Ill's* weave. I didn't know it was one until it easily parted with her head. Not one to take a weave removal without a fight, she clawed back at me. Heath turned me away from her, holding me firmly with one arm while stiff-arming Illy. I kicked into the air like a Rockette on meth, but Heath only tightened his arm around me.

"You are just a maid beech!" She screamed out. "You're no better than a prostitute!"

"And you're two years away from retirement!" Models don't like to be reminded they're old by 25.

"Illy stop!" Heath's voice was deep and I felt it reverberate through his chest. "Get out!"

"No, let her stay. I'll go!" I screamed out.

"For god's sake Sadie, shut up!" Heath was never serious, he rarely got angry. Everything seemed to be a joke to him. Sure he got annoyed, maybe even pissy, but never angry. Now he was fuming. "Illy. Leave. Now." She stomped her foot petulantly. I don't think she could believe he was kicking her out. "Now," he said, pointing in the direction of the door.

She sneered at him, mumbled something in whatever language she spoke, stuck her chin up and wobbled on her stilt-like legs over to where her purse was. She snatched it, and marched out of the front door, "I get vy you are acting like this, he's a good fuck, I vould know--ve have done it all over thees house!" she jabbed. I knew the witch was finally gone when the door slammed. Heath finally released me.

"You son of a bitch!" I screamed at him.

"You need to calm down."

"No, I do not need to calm down. I am not her, I am not any one of these fucking girls out here. You will not make a fool out of me. You know how I feel about her. Of all people...you fucking bastard," I pushed my fist against his chest.

"What the hell do you think happened?"

"What do you think I think happened? I saw you fixing your pants for fuck's sake. What do you take me for?"

"I went to the bathroom!"

"Of course! You just happened to have your favorite fuck buddy immediately over when I told you I would be gone for at least an hour." I clenched my fists and they shook with rage. My eyes were red, my cheeks streaked with tears of rage and fear. Everything around me was crashing, everyone was abandoning me.

"I checked my emails and I saw one from her. She said she had been trying to call me. She said she tried to visit me and you blocked her? You never told me."

Oops. I had forgotten about that.

"No, that's different. I...uh...she uses you like everyone else. She came weeks after the accident. I didn't think you needed to see her. It was late." *Oh and then I felt like fucking your brains out.*

"Her number was blocked on my phone. Did you do that?"

Shitshitshit. "So instead of talking to me about it, you had her come over? Did you even think about how that might make me feel? What it would make me think?"

"I just...she's a friend...and when she told me what she told me I felt bad that she thought I was ignoring her..."

"You call that cunty bitch a friend? Do you even notice the way she treats me? The way she has treated me since I met her? Or are you so used to women fighting over you that you don't even notice? Maybe you find it entertaining or food for your enormous ego."

"I didn't think--"

"Of course you didn't. You just do what you do and if people get hurt, so be it. Past behavior is the best predictor of future behavior. You two meet up to fuck, that's what you do. God, I am so stupid," I said burying my hands in my face. "I would be an IDIOT if I believed you didn't do anything with her."

"You're just determined to make me out to be some asshole? Aren't you? Because you are afraid. What are you so afraid of?"

"*People like you,*" I sneered.

The corners of Heath's mouth turned down, he took a step back from me like I punched him in the gut.

I should have listened to those pestering thoughts: *he's a pig, he's a player, he'll tire of you and move on. He'll fuck around behind your back and make you think you're crazy.* I needed to use to logic and rationality and ignore the pain deep in the center of my heart. I had to leave, to be with Nonna and to get out from under his spell. I was a such a fool, gallivanting around Paris, like he and I were something magical, but that's just hormones manufacturing emotions that make one temporarily insane. My judgement had been clouded. Everything between us blossomed in an artificial environment: he and I living in his house in seclusion, a vacation with just the two of us. The truth was, we would have to reenter the world, and we would go back to the people we always were.

And then I looked over his shoulder, and I saw the painting. That 20-foot-tall black and neon replica of his Times Square ad on his wall. *What the hell am I thinking?* I would never be with a guy who has a giant painting of himself hanging in his living room. What kind of mega-douche does that? That is who he is. He is *that* type of guy.

"We had a nice thing, just us two in our own little world. But that's over now, your friends will come back and you'll be the person you were when I met you."

"I'm me. I'm just me."

Then I made the final move. I was taking back my chips, or maybe I had already lost them all when I made the bet that morning. "I've been meaning to tell you this, I just found out that Brock is back and wants me to return. I'm going to take the job. I'm leaving tonight. I'll unload everything I just bought and then I'm leaving." I didn't want to tell him about Nonna, because if he showed he cared, if he tried to hug me, I feared I would melt back into his arms. I needed to get the fuck out of there as quickly as I could. We would never work, I had let him delude me, but seeing him emerge from the hallway adjusting his belt, with *Grossy* in the house holding that satisfied, shit-eating grin on her face, it all became so clear.

Hey, sweetie, will you be okay for a little while to mingle? One of my clients just called and Jules and I need to do a quick conference call upstairs.

Sadie, I'm going to be really late tonight. You can just start dinner without me. These international clients are killing me.

Oh, that was just Curtis, he had an emergency with the guys from London. I know it's late, but I need to head back into the office for a little bit.

I would not be the fool again. Never again.
"You're just gonna leave like this?"
"You don't have to pay me for last week."

253

"It's not about that." He softened his tone. "Sadie...come on. I didn't do anything with her. What about honesty? You lied to me, but I'm willing to hear you out. You're just going to walk out on me?"

"*Look at me.* Look what I just did." I laughed to myself, running my fingers through my hair motioning to the area of the house where I had just pounced Illy like a feral cat. "Look at what I am becoming. I just attacked someone like some inbred reality TV actor. I lied to you. None of that comes from a good place. We're not good for each other. You don't want me breathing down your neck. And I can't trust you."

"Sadie..." I could tell from his tone, he didn't know what to say. He knew how stubborn I was and that I had made up my mind. "Why do you have to over think everything? Why do you have to fight what feels good?"

"Because life isn't always about doing what feels good, it's about doing what feels right." I hadn't realized until that moment that we had drifted over to a wall, my back was against it and Heath hovered over me. He tried to caress my hair and I stepped off to the side and walked away.

"I'll pay you whatever you want if you'll stay."

I stopped dead in my tracks and turned to face him. We were only ten feet away from each other, but I had never felt this distant from him. *Is that what he thinks of me? That I am just another person he can buy or charm to get whatever he wants?* "You think you can buy me?"

"That's not what I meant," he said, looking immediately regretful. "I just don't know what to do."

"Let me leave and go back to your old life. That's what you do."

I headed for my room without looking back and as soon as I entered, it all erupted out of me. The disappointment and loneliness compressed my chest like a suffocating weight. I could move on, it was early, walking away now would hurt less than being made a fool of later. I needed to focus on my grandmother, I had already missed being there for her once while I was being foolish with him. He told me not to worry, that it would only be a few days without reaching her, but that's because Heath doesn't know what it's like to really care about anyone but himself. I knew logically that I couldn't blame him for missing the hospital's calls, but someone had to be the target of my anger, and he made himself the perfect one with what he had just done. There wasn't time to mope over my emotional wounds when I had to focus on getting my grandmother back to health, there was no room for Heath now that he had made himself a complication.

I took a deep breath to compose myself and shoved as much stuff into two suitcases as I could. I would ask Mindy to grab anything I had left behind during her next visit. I loaded the suitcases on the retired chairlift and put it to back to work, using it to lower my luggage. Heath was nowhere in sight. The shopping bags were on the floor where I had left them. I promised to unload, so I did it as quickly as I could hoping I could exit before encountering him again.

As much as I tried to fight it, tears streamed down my cheeks, I continued to wipe them off with my sleeve, determined for Heath not to see me like this. As soon as I was done, I grabbed my suitcases and rolled them out the front door and wrestled over the gravel with them, throwing them in the backseat of my car.

My laptop was still in the house, and that was not something I could leave behind, so I reentered as stealthily as I could, placing it in its bag. I reached for the front door.

"Sadie." My hand paused on the door knob. I took a deep inhale, and turned it. "Sadie. Wait." His footsteps moved quickly behind me. His warmth pressed against my back. I closed my eyes, scrunching my face to contain the emotional anguish. I had to be brief. Brevity was the only way I could make it out of this in one piece.

I turned around to face him. His eyes were red. *Move quickly. Tread lightly.*

"Sadie," he whispered, pressing his nose against my hair, "please, don't go," the warmth of his breath traveling down to my neck gave me chills. I wanted to hug him, to feel his arms around me, to bear some of the weight of my sadness. I took another deep inhale to stop tears from rolling out. "Please." He kissed my neck, pressing into me. "*Don't.*"

"I have to go," I choked out, grabbing the door handle behind me, sliding out the door. I had never seen him so serious, so sad. *We're not good for each other,* I reminded myself and I walked into the car without looking back.

"How can you be so fucking cold?" He yelled out. "You're a fucking coward! You act tough, but you are scared of anything that might make you feel something other than your comfortable bitterness!" This is what Heath did when he felt trapped, he lashed out, just like when he threw that plate against the wall. Hell, maybe he was right, but I'd rather be comfortable and shielded than exposed to heart-wrenching devastation.

I sped out through the bamboo-stalks of the driveway, clenching the steering wheel as if it would somehow give me strength.

I made it five minutes down the road before pulling over to stop and collect myself. There was a moment of doubt. *Could he be telling me the truth?* But I couldn't risk turning around, and I couldn't afford to put my emotional energy into being that paranoid whatever the hell I was to him. My feelings for him were too raw and it terrified me. I would never have pulled out anyone's hair extensions over Kenneth, and look how he had ruined me. I couldn't afford to feel the way I felt about Heath. It was better to sever the ties with him while I still had my sanity.

My grandmother needed me now, and she was my rock, there were no doubts about her and so I put the car back in drive and headed back home.

CHAPTER THIRTY-THREE

"Your grandmother is very ill," the doctor said to me, as kindly as he could. "She arrived with a shattered pelvis, and after doing a routine physical exam, we noticed some abnormal chest sounds. Blood work came back with some abnormalities as well. Then the chest scans revealed tumors which have metastasized."

I sighed, feeling newly resolute. I could focus my attention on making her better. "Okay, so what are our options? Chemo? Radiation?"

"Ma'am, at this point she is very far along. Stage 4. The tumors have spread to her vital organs. If we tried those treatments, they would not add much to extend her time, and would significantly reduce her quality of life. At this point, we recommend that we keep her comfortable and she spends time with family and friends." *I am all she has.*

I tried to convey strength by not reacting. "Okay, so how long are we saying here?" I expected months.

"The level to which she has progressed and the aggressiveness of the disease, we believe she has a couple of weeks."

"What? *Weeks?* How could that be? We just found out. How could we not have known?" My body went numb, and it was hard to focus on his words and keep myself on my feet at the same time. I reached out for a seat behind me and the doctor jolted forward a bit to catch me if I needed it.

"Sometimes the symptoms aren't obvious until it is this far along. It is likely she fell because she became dizzy due to lack of oxygen, which is related to the cancer. Her health aide said she had developed a cough this summer, but so do many elderly people. It doesn't raise a red flag sometimes." The nurse had mentioned it to me, but didn't seem worried. *If I had been with her, if I had paid better attention, I would have known.*

He went on for a while about how the pain and difficulty of treatments was not worth it, if she were his grandmother, he would spend time with her and let her live out her last days peacefully.

And then I was alone.

When I entered her room, she was sleeping. She looked so weak and frail. Being in bed for the past several days she had already started to lose muscle and the doctor told me her appetite had gone down. So quickly, this strong woman was withering away in front of me. The woman who stoically dealt with the murder of her daughter and the untimely death of her husband, the woman who put on a happy face for me through all of her pain, was vanishing in front of me and there was nothing I could do but be a witness to her demise. I could still touch her, hold her hand, but there would soon be a day where I would reach out for her and she wouldn't be there. No one would.

Finally she opened her eyes.

"Hi," she whispered.

"Hi Nonna," I said, kissing her on the cheek. "How are you feeling?"

"Tired, but okay." Even if she was in pain, she wouldn't say. "The food here is very bad though. I need your soup."

"You got it. I'll bring you some every day."

"What time is it?" she asked.

I looked down at my phone. Five missed calls from Heath. "It's a little after eleven."

"See if the Price is Right is on," she faintly gestured to the TV.

We watched geriatric television for a few hours. Then, I showed her the pictures of the market in Paris, which she loved. My phone buzzed and I sighed, expecting it to be Heath again, but it was Mindy. When I told her what had happened with Nonna, she promised she would come see me that evening. I told her not to bother, but she insisted. Mindy was a good friend. I know I've been hard on her because well, she's Mindy, but she might be the only person other than my grandmother who has remained a fixture. This summer had brought us closer again and I was happy to be in this place with her.

She came at around seven with Starbucks in hand. *That bitch is psychic.* My grandmother fell asleep again and she would likely be out the entire night. The pain meds for her hip made her very drowsy.

Mindy put the drink down and gave me a big warm hug. And usually I roll my eyes at her ostentatious displays of friendship and affection, but this time, I really needed it. I needed that fucking hug and I hugged her back just as hard.

"Hey sweets, it's gonna be okay," she said when she noticed my tears. Yes, she was still using *sweets*. *Sadie, be easy.* "Let's get you home. You need to shower and sleep. She'll be asleep all night. She won't even notice you're gone." I was utterly exhausted and let Mindy take me back to my place.

***

During my time away, my apartment had become somewhat foreign to me. I had become accustomed to living in an opulent house, and not some small apartment in Brooklyn, but it was far more than that. I had become used to having someone to chat with, laugh with, eat meals with, hell even argue with. But now, I was back to the fortress of solitude of my apartment. Luckily, Mindy insisted she stay the night with me during this difficult time.

"Heath called me. He asked me if I had spoken to you," she said cautiously. I hadn't told her everything that transpired in the recent weeks, after all, I kind of fibbed about ending the affair with Heath and then when it started back up, it happened so fast, I didn't have time to tell her the details. "He seemed really different. Sad."

"I'll bet," I said, rolled up in a knit throw, cupping a mug of hot tea in my hands.

"What happened between you two? I need to know because I have a feeling I am somehow going to be caught up in this."

"I don't even know. We kind of had something, or he wanted something, but then I realized he's Heath and that it was stupid of me to believe that." I tried to play it off by acting casual. Not because I wanted to lie, but because the hurt was still too raw to talk about and I was already in a fragile state. I didn't want to cry about him, he would not get any more of my tears.

"He told me everything." *Of course,* Mindy knows all. "He swears up and down to me he didn't lay a finger on Illy. He says she came over and she was bad mouthing you and he was confused because he didn't know what to believe. Then he took a piss and when he came out all hell broke loose. By the way, nice job, Brock Lesnar."

"Oh god," I buried my head in my hands, embarrassed by my Real Housewives-esque confrontation. "I had just found out about grandma...did you tell him?"

"I didn't know until after I spoke with him. So no."

"Okay, good."

"You two do what you will. After all I am his manager, not his damned therapist, though with my clients I often feel like that latter, but he seemed sincere."

I snickered. "Sincere? No he's fun and he can be charming. He knows when to tell you what you want to hear. People confuse that with sincere, but it's not the same. He's vain, he's egotistical. The man has a giant fucking neon painting of himself in his living room! I mean, really. Who the fuck does that but him?"

Mindy perked up a little in her seat. "Wait--you know the story behind that painting, don't you?"

"That it's his Times Square ad."

"No, the story behind the reason it was made?"

260

"No...I never asked. I could pretty much assume, knowing him."

"Have you heard of the artist Talulah Weston-Troy?"

"Yeah. I think so."

"She's huuuuge right now. Anyway, he was at an art show in SoHo and she was all over him. It was HER show and she was following him around all night. You know Heath, he's not one to be mean or anything and he loves attention. He was just kind of like whatever about it. And she's really weird. I mean like batshit. She wears these weird drapey shrouds even though she's like not even thirty yet and her hair is all matted in the back."

"Okay..."

"So anyway, two weeks later, he's moving into the East Hampton house and a truck shows up and drops off this enormous painting. Guess who it's from?"

"Talulah..."

"...Weston-Troy! Yes! She's fucking nuts! She went home and spent several days making him that painting. There was this rambling note attached about how she felt his soul in her and she released it onto the painting. How fucking creepy is that? Can you say restraining order? Anyway, that thing is worth like at least five hundred grand, probably closer to a mil. He didn't know what to do with it, because like you said, it's kind of douchey. So one night while I was visiting, I made a bet that if he couldn't finish five 20-ounce Kombuchas in ten minutes he would have to hang it on his wall for the entire summer." *Heath hates Kombucha, he says it tastes like piss and vinegar, but he is also not one to pass up a bet, as we all know.* Mindy howled with laughter and clapped to herself recalling that night. "He was gagging. He got down like one and a half and it was game over. He ran to the bathroom to puke. So now it's up there, but he's going to donate it to charity at the end of the summer. A place for foster kids, well because, you know...he was one."

I feel like a 5'6" asshole.

"I can't believe he never told you." But I do, because Heath doesn't care what people think of him. He doesn't feel the need to excuse himself. He probably forgot the thing was up there. And he probably thought I should have known better than to think that he would have commissioned that monstrosity. But I always expected the worst from him. I always wrote him off. "I just thought you should know. Yeah he can be an asshat, but that painting, I mean come on, he's not THAT bad."

My heart softened to him, but I couldn't show that. "Well, that's nice, but I just can't trust him."

"I get it. He's a model, all the ladies want him. It's intimidating."

I wasn't a fan of her word choice. *Intimidating.* It fits right in line with *coward* and *afraid.* I wasn't intimidated, I was being perceptive and preemptive. "He's so inappropriate. How could he have Illy over? After saying he wanted to be with me? Didn't he think about how I would feel?"

"Illy is a total nut job. She's pure evil incarnate. I never got why they hung out. In his defense...you did kind of lie a little...I get why. She's a witch, but he was a little confused when he got her email..."

"We would never work out and I'm not one of his little playthings."

"Like I said, I am going to be Switzerland here, but I know he doesn't see you that way. I don't know what you laid down on that boy, but he is *not okay* right now. Aaaand, if I may be honest here, I like you two together. You balance him out, and you are a sincere person unlike the typical LA to NYC crowd he has to deal with. Albeit you are wound a little tightly at times, but he could use that, someone who whips his ass in line."

"Heath does what he wants to do. He'll be over me soon enough. I wouldn't be surprised if he's having a threesome as we speak. Being his roomie, I know all about those."

"I understand, and you have to do what you think is best. I'm just saying, he is a good guy. I've known him for a long time,

262

and he can be silly, and shameless, and lack a filter, but when it comes the the meat and potatoes of a person, the stuff that really matters, he is solid. And he doesn't bullshit, he says what's on his mind. I have never seen him like this over anyone. Like you, I thought he would be incapable of being interested in a woman for longer than it took to bust a nut, but he seems laser-focused on you right now."

"He's just never been told no. That's why he's calling you. I won't answer his calls and it's probably baffling to him."

Mindy put her hands up in concession. "You two need to work your shit out. I have said my piece." She placed her thumbs to her index fingers like a yogi.

CHAPTER THIRTY-FOUR

The weeks after I learned of Nonna's diagnosis seemed to move painstakingly slow and too quickly all at once. There was nothing I could do but be there, talk to her when she was awake, remind her she was loved. I was the only one, I couldn't take shifts with a sibling or parent, or distract myself from my own sorrow by comforting someone else. And yet, while the days were long, it seemed like there was never enough time. She was fading, her glow was dulling. Her once thick and lush snow white hair had thinned and turned brittle. Every day she slept a little longer, the pain became a little stronger, even too strong for her to ignore. Sometimes she would wake up and moan, or say something incoherent, and the nurse would come in and do what she could to make her comfortable.

Then there were a few moments of astonishing lucidity. She might wake up in the afternoon and converse with me for a few minutes as clearly as she could a couple of months earlier. Then she would drift away again. How could someone fade so fast? It was like her battery was going out, she was expiring right before my very eyes and I could only watch her slip away.

It was two weeks and two days from the day the doctor told me the prognosis when she and I last spoke. She had withered down to just below one hundred pounds, and had slept for nearly two days straight. When she would wake up she was too tired to speak and I would have to lean in very close just to hear her. But then on the sixteenth day, she woke up, she opened her eyes, and they were the brightest I had seen in weeks. I had dozed off with my hand next to hers as I sat beside the bed. I felt her fingers brush against mine, and jumped out of my slumber.

"Nonna? How are you feeling?"

"Water," she asked, weakly motioning to the cup at the bedside table. I carefully put the straw to her mouth as she took tiny sips then stopped.

"Are you done? Do you want more?"

She shook her head. I stroked her hand, and she gripped mine. Her hold was far stronger than I thought she was capable of. Then she stared at me, looking me in my eyes, as if she knew she was taking me in for the last time.

"You're gonna be fine," she whispered.

Would I? Would I be fine? To be alone in a world so large, so full, and yet have no anchor, no home. After all, that's what Heath understood so clearly: home was not a place, it was a feeling. It was those people who made you feel safe and unconditionally loved. And I did feel like I was home when he was with me, and I know he felt the same way, he tried to tell me that so many times. But I had pushed him away in an attempt to protect myself, from what? I didn't even know anymore, and now I would be floating through this world with no tether. I was so terrified of being hurt and alone, and here I was, hurt and alone. But I knew she was in pain, and I knew I had to let her go, I couldn't greedily keep her to myself. She was a strong, pasta-eating, hearty woman for most of her life, and this is not how she would want to remain on this earth. She had lived her life, she had made her mark on this planet, and I had to let her know I would be okay, because it wasn't fair for me to make her stay. It was the hardest thing I would ever have to do. I lowered my forehead onto the wrinkly skin of her hand, the wrinkles a map of the long life she had lead. She outlived all of her friends, her husband, her only child. It was time for her to go back to them.

I wept, rubbing my cheek against her hand, knowing it would be one of the last times I would feel the warmth of her skin. It was the hand that held mine at my parents' funeral, it was the hand that wiped my tears away when I skinned my knee, it was the hand that rubbed my tummy when it ached, it took my prom photos, it pointed at me in anger when I missed my curfew, it instructed me and guided me towards my love of cooking.

When I looked up, her eyes were closed, but I could tell she was still lucid. I knew she could hear me.

"Nonna, it's okay. I'll be fine. You can go to sleep now. Say hi to grandpa and mommy and daddy for me. Tell them I'm okay and that I love them and I wished I would have had more time with them. You can let go. I love you so much, you can let go. I'm going to be okay."

She died three and a half hours later in her sleep with me by her side.

***

I sat on the floor next to Nonna's easy chair that night. It was my usual spot, since I was never a fan of her plastic covers. But I would now very much miss those epidermis-peeling furniture shields. The smell of her home comforted me, like she hadn't quite fully left. I grabbed her throw from her chair and wrapped it around my shoulders and if I closed my eyes, it was almost like she was hugging me. She was the Alfred to my Bruce Wayne. I had lost my Alfred, and how does Bruce Wayne go on without Alfred? I know she had to leave, but the grief was so fresh, and I would soon have to put on a strong face to plan her funeral. So, this was my time to just be sad, to feel the melancholy without pretending I was fine. There wouldn't be many people there, most of the important people in her life had already died, but she was traditional and I would make sure she had a traditional funeral.

Mindy told me she would help me whether I wanted it or not. She knew me well enough to know I wouldn't want to put such an emotional burden on anyone, but thankfully Mindy doesn't take no for an answer. I told her I really wanted to be alone tonight though, and even she knew when not to push it. So she said she would come by in the morning to get me and we could go to the funeral home together and finish the arrangements.

The place was so quiet: no sounds of cooking in the kitchen, no Drew Carey telling people to "come on down." It was just the sound of emptiness and, of course, my occasional crying. But there did come a point where I was out of tears; my eyes hurt, my head throbbed, and there was just silence. There I was, by myself, and it felt like the world had been wiped out and I was the only person on the planet.

And then I heard what I thought were familiar guitar chords in the distance. For a second, I thought I just really needed to get some sleep, but the strumming came closer and closer. And the song was one anyone would recognize, the one my parents had played and sang for me when I was a little girl. And only one person knew about that other than my Nonna, and she didn't know how to play the guitar, so I doubted her ghost would.

It couldn't be.

I ran over to the door, unlocking the deadbolt, but keeping the chain latched. *It was.* I unlatched the chain. Heath stood there, with the most earnest look on his face.

"How did you find me here?"

"Oh thank god. I was terrified I had the wrong address and then this would be a complete disaster." He had the slightest grin on his face, but it layered over a look of concern. He wore a pair of ripped jeans and a white t-shirt, his hair was playfully messy. God, how I missed just staring at him and his boyish grin.

"How did you know?"

"Mindy can't keep her mouth shut, she called me today and told me about your Nonna. She told me when you found out. Why didn't you tell me, Sadie? I would have been here for you." I looked down, I didn't have a real answer, not one that felt valid any longer.

"I was upset. I wasn't thinking straight. Then the way we parted ways. I thought I couldn't. I felt like it wouldn't be right to ask of you."

"You're my best friend. I wouldn't let you go through this alone."

I thought I didn't have any more tears left, but I was wrong, I had been saving them to cry into his embrace. As they streamed out of my eyes, he swept his guitar to the side, wrapped his strong arms around me, and tenderly kissed me on top of my head. God how I missed his smell, his warmth, the firm grip of his hug. He stroked my hair.

"It's okay Sadie. *I've got you.*"

"I've been such a bitch to you. I'm sorry. I believe you. I know you didn't do anything with her. You're right. I was scared. I pushed you away."

"It's okay. You're the perfect bitch and I'm the perfect asshole."

I laughed for the first time in weeks. Heath closed the door behind him and leaned back on it as he held me.

"Was this whole guitar entrance too corny? I was afraid if I said it was me, you wouldn't open the door. I even waited outside for a neighbor to let me in."

"It was perfect."

"I'm so sorry about your grandmother."

"Thank you," I said. "I already miss her so much."

"I know. Can I just tell you something I should have told you weeks ago?" he asked, holding my face in between his hands and guiding it up so that I would look into his eyes.

"I'm a mess," I said, trying to look away, not wanting him to see my puffy face.

"You're beautiful and I love you. I should have told you that before you left, but I didn't take my own advice. I held onto one chip, because I was scared that you would leave anyway. And I have never had to fear losing a woman I was in love with. I let you walk away without telling you what I have known from the moment we fell in the sand. I operated out of fear and I let you walk away."

I smiled. I wouldn't let fear dictate my decisions any longer. Nonna would have wanted me to live with an open heart. "I love you too. You're my best friend too."

He kissed the single tear that trailed down my cheek. "I want you to come back with me after all this for the rest of the summer and then I'll fire you and you'll go do the amazing things you were born to do. Can you do that?"

"Yes. I never took the job with Brock." I had already planned on taking Heath's advice and forging a new path.

"Atta girl."

"Could you play some music? It's so quiet and empty in here, and it would be nice to have some music. You know, to fill up the apartment with warmth."

"Sure, why don't you tell me what she liked and I'll do my best?"

And so Heath and I sat in the spot on the floor next to her easy chair and we sang songs late into the night. Then when we got tired, we made another makeshift nest on the floor, just like we did in Paris.

Just as I was about to doze off in his arms, Heath whispered in a serious tone, "I have a confession to make."

My heart fluttered for a moment. What could it be? The only thing I could think of was *Grossy*, but I stopped myself. I would not allow myself to expect the worst of him.

"What is it?" I asked.

"Well, you're great and all, but the real reason I came back was because I missed these puppies. I told you I would never let these go," he joked, motorboating my cleavage and tickling me as I laughed.

Heath Hillabrand, forever my Gorgeous Rotten Scoundrel.

Acknowledgements

Meg Botteon, not only did you help guide my love towards the written word when I was a hormone-riddled 16-year-old, but now you continue to selflessly help my journey as an author. I STILL learn from you every time your notes appear in my inbox.

Cassie Broadus Foote Brennan, your support and encouragement from the very first mention of my idea to write a book makes me feel a little less crazy.

Tiffany Torres, thank you for your support, energy, and laughs along the way. I am so happy that the book world has brought our highly inappropriate and snarky kindred spirits together.

Susan Garwood Cross: Seriously, you are like a blogging angel. Selfless and always willing to help without asking for anything in return. I always know I can count on you as someone to go to for advice when the crazy world of being an indie author seems overwhelming.

Shanyn Clark Doan: It's rare to meet people who champion someone the way you have done for me. I am forever grateful. Not to mention, you write some badass reviews.

My street team: You all rock and thank you for having my back and being generous with your time and energy. As an indie writer, it is hard to stick out from the crowd, and every mention or kind word of support goes further than you may realize.

Butterflies, Books, and Dreams (Jodi), A Dirty Book Affair, Book Enthusiast Promotions, Panty Dropping Book Blog (Kathy Coopmans), Wicked Women Book Blog, Two Ordinary Girls and Their Books, The Book Nuts (aka Fifty Shades of Grey and then Some), Sarah Says Read Romance (I am looking at you Erin McFarland), Eye Candy Bookstore, Submit and Devour, The Book Harlots, Red Cheeks Reads, Kafe Korner Exposed, WTRFSOG, and to all other bloggers who have extended a helping hand: THANK YOU. I am not sure people realize how much work you put into what you do, but it definitely does not go unnoticed by me.

My family, who has always supported my decisions and have always told me how proud they were, no matter what stupid crap I did. And no dad, I still won't let you read the books.

Last and most importantly, to my husband, BJ, who I have been with since the age of 19 and STILL rocks my world. You were always pushing me to find my passion, and now that I have, I have never been more grateful to have someone who cares just as much about me fulfilling my own dreams as he does his own. Trust me, I know my strong personality is not always the easiest to deal with, but at the end of the day that's why we work: you are my biggest rival and my greatest champion!

Have you read the Strapped Series, a dark erotic suspense by Nina G. Jones?

By all appearances, Shyla Ball has an enviable life: a loyal boyfriend, a great job, and family that loves her. She doesn't realize how deeply unsatisfied she is until she has an embarrassing encounter with a handsome stranger at a coffee shop. Taylor Holden, a successful businessman, takes a sudden special interest in her and offers her a job she cannot refuse. Soon after, she learns there is much more to this intensely private man than meets the eye. He is hiding many painful secrets, including why it is that he has seemingly plucked her out of obscurity for such a lucrative position. Her "perfect" world is turned upside down by her infatuation towards Taylor and in just a couple of months, her life looks nothing like it did before. While she is frightened by the changes she sees in herself, she cannot resist the lure of Taylor Holden. As Shyla slowly gains Taylor's trust, she learns of his complex history and how it has molded him into the person he has become. When elements of Taylor's secret past resurface and threaten to destroy them, Shyla finds out there may be more to Taylor's story than even he is aware of. Strapped is a story of passion, manipulation, obsession, and family secrets.

To learn more about Nina G. Jones:

Facebook: Facebook.com/Strappednovel

Twitter: Twitter.com/NinaGJones

Website: NinaGJones.com